THE BUTTERFLY TATTOO

M. D. THOMAS

ISBN 978-1-7344870-2-2 (Paperback)

For B, J, C, and G, always

ONE

JON

Moments before the car accident that would leave his son in a coma, Jon Young had a conversation about baseball. Baseball—or, to be precise, the standing of the Washington Nationals in the East Division of the National League—was the topic the Young family had been held hostage by during the holy months of April through October for the past six years, ever since Lee turned five.

"Do you think they can win the pennant this season, dad?" Lee asked from the backseat of Jon's beloved ninety-two Toyota Cressida.

Jon glanced in the rearview mirror. There wasn't much to see in the darkness, but he could just detect the ghost-white rise and fall of the baseball that always danced in his son's hands. "Who do what?"

"The Nats, dad," Lee said, oblivious to his pretended ignorance. "What about the World Series?"

"It's only mid-April," Jon said as he turned onto the Accotink Parkway, mystified as usual that he and Sarah had produced such a fanatical child.

"Not this way," Sarah said from the passenger seat. "It's slower."

"Shorter though." But the truth was that after an evening of watching Lee shine on the ball field he just felt *good*, and the parkway—wooded, winding, and yes, slow—reinforced that feeling. Sarah always wanted to get where she was going as soon as possible, never understood his perpetual desire to take the scenic route.

"You just like to remember what you did here with your girlfriends when you were a teenager," Sarah said, a hint of laughter in her voice.

"That's not true." But he was glad the darkness hid his flushed cheeks.

"What did you do here with girls?" Lee asked.

"Nothing interesting."

Sarah convulsed with suppressed laughter.

"What's wrong with mom?"

"Allergies," Jon said, and Sarah howled.

Well, I suppose it's a little funny...

"Can you believe that homer I got?" Lee asked, whatever curiosity he'd had about his parent's lives before he was born already gone. "I really *felt* like I was Arky Vaughan when I was at bat. Like he was inside me or something. Then BOOM! Smack over the right field fence!"

"I really do wish you'd idolize someone else," Sarah said, the amusement gone from her voice. "Like someone alive."

"But he was *awesome*, mom. There's nobody like him anymore."

"Arky Vaughan would've taken more walks," Jon said

with mock seriousness as he flipped on the high beams to better illuminate the bright yellow caution signs that peppered the side of the road, warning of the sharp curve ahead. For some reason Lee had become obsessed with Vaughan, a shortstop slugger who drowned not long after he retired from the Brooklyn Dodgers in 1948.

"Yeah, you're probably right," Lee said, sounding deflated.

"I was just kidding, Lee," Jon said as he started to brake for the coming turn. No sooner had his foot touched the pedal then a set of headlights slashed across his own.

"*Jon!*" Sarah's fingers dug into his arm as the oncoming car hurtled toward them, its headlights glued to the Cressida instead of sweeping past as they should have.

Better in the trees than broadsided...

It was more an image in his mind than a coherent thought, and Jon floored the accelerator, kept the car pointed straight ahead even as the road bore left.

Somehow the other driver managed to turn, but it was still too late. Their rear ends collided and Jon was slammed against the door as their car spun, as his consciousness fled, chased by the crunch of metal, by the explosion of shattering glass, by the vision of headlights spinning across the trunks of the nearby pine trees.

"JESUS CHRIST... you think we killed them?"

The woman's voice penetrated the fog that clouded Jon's mind but failed to clear it.

"They're both buckled up," a man said. "They'll be fine."

Jon's skull throbbed and he felt... wrong. *Buckled up?*

"You sure? There's no airbags in this old piece of shit and he's bleeding all over the place. Maybe we should call an ambulance?"

"We can't."

There was a pause, then, "You think that's a good idea?"

"The police show up and we're looking at a felony hit-and-run. You ready to trade bartending for jail time?"

Jon heard a low groan of pain. It took a moment to realize it came from his own throat. *Both... He said both...*

"Time to go. He's waking up."

"Goddamn, is he trying to talk?"

Jon's eyes felt heavy, but he managed to open them. Bright light was everywhere except for a shadow outside of the car door. A flashlight, moving slightly. He realized he was looking at the shape of a person, the body wreathed in a nimbus of light, the face indistinguishable. But they were upside down. His tongue felt dry as he tried to speak. "Lee... "

The shape leaned closer, blocked more light, but Jon still couldn't see the face. "What did you say, mister?"

It was the woman. He tried to speak again. "Lee... Lee okay?"

"Sounds like he's got rocks in his mouth," she said.

She leaned even closer, turned a little, and her face came into focus, surrounded by a mass of curls. He had time to notice a small butterfly, half-again the size of a quarter, tattooed high up on her cheek, not far from the eye, and then the light moved and she was yanked backwards.

"Come on. We gotta go."

"But he was trying to tell me something..."

"Forget it, okay? Come on."

"Yeah, whatever. Take your hands off me. I'm coming. Jesus, I need another hit... "

The light disappeared, their voices faded, the butterfly faded, and Jon was left in darkness.

———

JON TURNED AWAY from the door, fumbled to undo his lap belt and failed. His hands wouldn't stop shaking. With the light gone he couldn't see a thing. He raised one jittery hand to turn on the dome light and was surprised when he hit the roof sooner than expected. His fingers searched, chittered across the headliner, and a moment later the overhead light—which was now below him—came on, revealed a caved in roof.

We rolled...

The moments before the accident came back, his thoughts still sluggish but becoming more coherent by the second. His head throbbed with the steady rhythm of a marching band drum line. Sarah hung next to him in the dim light of the overhead fixture, her straight blond hair dangling, the tips brushing the ceiling. She was breathing but not bleeding, her eyes closed and her mouth open.

Her belt is on like the man said...

Lee...

Jon looked into the back of the car and noticed the rear passenger door was open and twisted on it's hinges, saw nothing else but leather and Lee's vintage Pirates hat, nestled among bits of safety glass in the middle of the roof as if he'd placed it there.

"Lee? *Lee!*" Feeling like his guts had been plunged into ice water, Jon scrabbled at the lap belt latch button until the belt finally popped free. He fell onto the roof, vertigo washing over him, and struggled out of the shoulder belt, hitting his pounding head on the steering wheel as he tried to right his body. Ignoring the pain, he peered behind his seat.

He'll be there. He'll be—

But the space behind his seat was empty of everything but more broken glass.

That was when his mind finally cleared enough to realize what had happened.

"*Lee!*" Jon roared as he tried to open his door. It moved, but no more than an inch or two, something either blocking it outside or the frame bent too much by the rollover. He pushed harder, kicked at it frantically, but it didn't budge so he wormed his way out of the window, glass tinkling onto the dead leaves below as he passed through. "*Lee!*"

A wave of pain and nausea passed through Jon, so strong that he dry-heaved once and then vomited up the remains of the ball field cheeseburger he'd eaten almost two hours ago. He swiped his mouth with the back of one forearm and then pushed himself to his hands and knees, his fingers curling into dry pine needles, his nostrils filled with the green scent of spring overlaid by the vinegary bite of puke. Panting, he reached up and grabbed hold of the car door handle and pulled himself to his feet.

"*Lee!*" he screamed again, searching the darkness.

The Cressida had come to rest upside down on the treed slope halfway between the road and the Accotink below. The headlights were still on, pointing into the trees and illuminating the dark, narrow band that was the creek, the water sliding past. The night was quiet, even the insect chorus silenced by the collision of the two cars, the surrounding city forgotten except for the low thrum of the Capital Beltway in the distance.

There was no sign of Lee in front of the car where the headlights still shone. His eyes beginning to adjust to the moonlit darkness, Jon stumbled toward the back of the Cressida, his left hand on the car to steady himself. His legs felt okay, but his head still swam and he thought if he let go he might fall over.

"*Lee!*"

Panic started to fill him, the urge to scramble around the car until he found Lee overwhelming.

Be calm, Jun-Young... The thought was his, but the voice and image was of his father tending to the orchids in the back room of their Koreatown home. *Before everything else you must be calm, Jun-Young. Be calm, think of what you need to do next, and then do it...*

Jon paused at the rear of the Cressida, his eyes still searching the ground around the car as his breathing deepened and slowed, as he tried to ignore the fear that filled him. *What next?*

He had to get help. He dug into his pocket to find his cell, but there was only some change left over from buying Lee popcorn after the game ended.

I took the phone out and left it on the console...

Jon lurched back to the driver's side door and looked through the busted window, the dome light still illuminating the inside, hoped he would spot the phone lying on the roof. But the rollover had thrown it somewhere out of sight, if not out of the car. *Just like Lee...*

Calm...

Jon looked around again and spotted Sarah's purse below her. He pushed inside once more, and grabbed it, then turned the purse upside down. It was like breaking a dam open, as a pile of stuff fell out—mints, a hairbrush, a small notebook, loose change, enough pens and pencils to stock a classroom, lipstick, chapstick, fingernail clippers, a fingernail file and more.

And right on top her cell phone.

"Jon?" Sarah's voice croaked as her head rolled toward him, her eyes fluttering. A rivulet of blood had crept down the side of her face.

Jon ignored her and thumbed awake the cell as he pulled back out of the car into the darkness. On his knees, he selected the emergency icon when the pin pad came up and dialed 911.

"911 emergency," the operator said a moment later.

"My family and I were in a car accident on the Accotink Parkway," Jon said, voice wavering, "just a few miles south of the Franconia-Springfield Bridge."

"Is anyone hurt?"

"My son was thrown out of the car. I... I haven't been able to find him yet."

"Okay. Are you or anyone else injured?"

"My wife was unconscious, but she's waking up now. I don't know how badly she's hurt."

"Were any other vehicles involved?"

"One other," Jon said.

"Any injuries to the people in that vehicle?"

"I don't know. They left."

"Okay. I need you to stay on the line until EMS and the police arrive."

Jon took the phone away from his ear, pulled up the function screen and tapped the small flashlight at the bottom. The camera flash LED lit up the ground.

"Lee?" Sarah moaned again and Jon glanced up in time to see her eyes roll toward the empty back seat. They widened and she screamed, a guttural cry ripped out of her.

Calm...

Jon got to his feet and trotted around the car, moved the phone to illuminate the ground before and around him. It didn't light up anything farther than a few feet away. When he passed Sarah's door she was trying to get her lap belt off, screaming Lee's name over and over. Jon ignored her and jogged past the front of the car, the light bouncing ahead of him. When he still hadn't seen anything after a full circuit, he went ten feet farther out and circled around once more.

JON WAS on the third trip around the car when he spotted Lee, his dim form crumpled near the base of a pine tree close to the Accotink.

So far... if the tree hadn't stopped him, he would've gone in the creek...

The absurd thought came to him that if they'd been the home team he would've seen Lee right away. The home uniform was bright white, away was gray.

Calm...

"Lee?" Jon ran over, his fear spiking when Lee didn't respond. He pointed the phone at Lee's face and recoiled. The right side of Lee's head was a bloody mess, his cheek covered in abrasions, and his limbs were splayed around his body like a rag doll. His glove was still on his hand.

Jon fell to his knees beside Lee. Hand shaking, Jon reached out and placed his index and middle finger below the swell of Lee's jaw, pressed his fingertips against the soft flesh there and felt for a pulse. At first there was nothing and his stomach started to roil again, but he shifted his fingers and detected the tiny flutter of Lee's heart. It wasn't strong, but it was there and constant.

Calm...

Every shred of his being urged him to pick Lee up and take him back to the road, to run toward the ambulances wailing in the distance. But it would be a mistake to move him. If his neck or back were injured, moving him could result in paralysis.

Jon kept the small light trained on Lee's face and grabbed hold of Lee's right hand, needing to feel his son. The thought of Lee, who loved to run, to hit, and to throw baseballs, trapped in a chair, his legs useless, maybe his arms as well, chilled him to the bone. *No, that won't happen. He'll be fine...*

The stillness of Lee's small body argued otherwise. Jon smoothed the dull black hair on the side of Lee's head that wasn't injured, tears running down his cheeks. If there was a chance that his son was dying Jon didn't want him to be alone, even if he was unconscious.

"The ambulance is almost here, Lee. Hold on, buddy. Just another minute. Hold on... "

SARAH'S SCREAMS had never really stopped as she tried to get free of her seatbelt, but they changed pitch as she fell to the ceiling just as Jon had and then struggled out of the car.

"Over here!" Jon called out, and she lurched upright and stumbled toward them.

Her screams changed to a wail as she fell to her knees on the other side of Lee and moved to pick him up.

"No," Jon said, reaching out to stop her. "If his neck or back are hurt you could make it worse."

Sarah brushed him aside, scooped Lee up and rocked him into her arms, still wailing. She had one arm under his neck, but his head flopped.

She made it to her feet despite Lee's weight, stumbled

up toward the road and the sound of approaching sirens. She passed the car, struggled to make it up the slope until Jon fell in beside her and kept her from falling, from dropping Lee, pushing her up the hill as much as he dared. They were almost to the top when Jon felt a puff of cool air brush past him in the darkness. Sarah's hair fluttered in the moonlight.

Calm, Jon. Be calm...

They cleared the shoulder of the road just as flashing lights came into view in the distance, the wail of the sirens piercing the night.

TWO

SARAH

She couldn't remember the last time Lee's face had been so calm, so placid. Her Lee was always so animated, always smiling or frowning or scowling at whatever in the world had gathered in his attention for that moment of the day. Usually baseball. But in the back of the speeding ambulance he looked so—

—*no. Not dead. He's not dead and he's not going to be...*

The ambulance had stopped before them on the road, blinding her with its lights, the sirens deafening. Less than two minutes later they were in the back, Lee strapped to the gurney, his spine immobilized by a strap across his forehead. The right side of his head was a bloody confusion of hair, torn skin, and dirt. She couldn't look at the injury for long, afraid she would lose her mind.

Her head throbbed and she felt woozy, but she gripped his hand, held on as if letting go would be the end of him.

...he won't die... he won't, he can't...

"You can't let him die, do you hear me?" she shrieked at the paramedics who hovered over him, poking and prodding, inserting needles and fluids, measuring pulses and pressures, monitoring his breathing. One of them bumped into her arm but didn't ask her to let go of Lee's hand. She wouldn't have anyway. Nothing would take her from him or him from her. Not her Lee. Nothing.

THE AMBULANCE DROVE to INOVA Fairfax in Falls Church, a run of less than ten minutes from where they'd been hit on the Accotink Parkway.

If only Jon hadn't turned. If he'd stayed on the main road we wouldn't be here right now. My son wouldn't be unconscious, his head a bloody mess...

The paramedics threw open the rear doors as soon as they halted in the ambulance bay, pulled the gurney out, then hurried toward the entrance. Sarah followed alongside, holding onto Lee's hand. The medic in front waved a security card over a sensor and the sliding doors parted to reveal a wide hallway, occupied by a few people who started moving as soon as they entered. One of them—a tall, wiry woman with her long red hair in a ponytail—intercepted Sarah as the medics steered the gurney through another set of double doors.

"Ma'am, you need to come with me, okay?" the woman said as she put a freckled hand on Sarah's arm.

"I have to stay with my son," Sarah said without stopping.

"I understand, Ma'am," the woman said, gripping Sarah's arm harder and peeling her away from the gurney, "but if you want your son to get the care he needs, the staff has to be able to focus on him and they can't do that if you're in the room."

"I'll be quiet, I promise," Sarah said as she tried to pull away. The inside of the room was full of people and equipment, all centered around a large, overhead light that shone down on an empty hospital bed. The ambulance gurney was wheeled next to the hospital bed and Lee was quickly transferred, people already cutting away his clothes and shouting orders. "Just please don't take him away from me."

The woman grabbed Sarah's upper arm with her other hand and started dragging her away. "I'm sorry, Ma'am, you can't. Besides, you're injured too, so you have to be checked out as well."

"I'm fine," Sarah said as she tried to break free. But the woman had an iron grip and she pulled Sarah out of the trauma bay and back into the hallway. "*I love you, Lee!*" she screamed as the doors closed away the sight of her son.

Sarah fell to her knees, sobs wracking her body. *My baby... how did this happen to my baby?*

"HOW LONG UNTIL I CAN LEAVE?"

The short Latina nurse sighed. "It all depends on how quickly we can get your CT scan done, Mrs. Young. Maybe an hour if everything goes well. We haven't been too busy tonight, but that can change in a heartbeat."

"Have you heard anything else about my son?"

"No, Mrs. Young. As I told you before, he could be in surgery for hours. I'll try to find out more when I'm done checking you in. Assuming you're fine, I'm sure we can get you over to the surgery wing before the doctors are done operating."

Doctors. It's so bad he needed more than one of them. He could be dead already. My son, dead on some cold operating table...

No! He's not dead! He's not. They would've told me...

The nurse looked up from what she was doing, a slight smile on her lips. "I almost forgot. Your husband is just down the hall getting the laceration on his head sewn up. He'll probably need a CT scan as well, but for now he seems to be fine."

She couldn't think about Jon. Not when Lee was alone somewhere in the hospital with a bunch of people trying to put him back together. Just thinking of her Lee on a surgery table under bright lights made Sarah feel like she might faint.

So she tried again to piece together what had happened. What confused her the most was how Lee had come free of his seatbelt.

Did he take it off and I didn't notice?

Surely he'd begun the trip with it on. Had he come free somehow anyway? She tried to remember if the seatbelt had still been buckled after the accident, but in her memories they were driving along the Accotink Parkway one moment and the next she was walking down the roadway with her son's limp body cradled in her arms, the ambulance and police lights flashing as they approached. The emergency physician had told her their car was hit and then rolled over, but she had no recollection of it.

Maybe Jon knows. Maybe he saw whether the seat belt was still buckled or not. But did he even check Lee's seat belt? That was his side of the car. He should've checked...

AN HOUR and a half later her CT scan came back negative for any internal bleeding and they cleared her. She ran through the hospital to the surgery wing, was panting and dizzy by the time she reached the family waiting area. The reception desk was staffed by a young man.

He looked up when she approached and cocked his curly head to the side, lips parting to reveal teeth that were too white. "May I help you?"

"My name is Sarah Young. My son Lee is in surgery and I'm trying to find out how he's doing?"

"Hi, Mrs. Young," he said. "My name is Benton." He stood and offered his hand and after they shook he remained on his feet. "I've been expecting you. Your son is still in surgery right now, but I'll let the staff know you've arrived and see if someone can update you on his condition. In the meantime, it would help me tremendously if you could fill out some paperwork. Is that ok?"

He's been in surgery a long time... that can't be good...

"Paperwork?" she said, trying to ignore her thoughts, trying to decide if he'd actually told her anything that mattered.

"Just basic stuff, Ma'am. Insurance coverage, your son's medical history, drug allergies. Nothing unusual. I know it's the last thing you want to deal with, but better we get it done now before the surgery is over. You won't want to leave your son's side to do paperwork later."

She wanted to reach across the desk and shake the man. "Can you tell me anything about how he's doing?" She couldn't bring herself to ask if he would live.

Benton held up empty hands, his face apologetic. "I'm sorry, Mrs. Young. I know the uncertainty is hard to deal with, but I really don't know any more than you do at this point. We just have to wait I'm afraid."

He's just too scared to tell you what's happened...

Benton picked up a clipboard as he walked out from behind the desk and then escorted Sarah down the hallway to a small waiting room. He opened the door and held it for her, handed her the clipboard which held a thick sheaf of papers to be filled out. "Make sure you sign everywhere that's highlighted in yellow."

———

WAS THERE a click from the back seat before we left the ball field?

She couldn't remember. Nothing to do with the accident, she just hadn't been paying attention because Lee was on Jon's side of the car.

Jon's side.

Maybe he put the seat belt on and then took it off. Maybe he dropped his ball and couldn't stretch far enough to reach it...

Except that Lee never dropped the ball.

You've got to let it go... it doesn't matter...

But was there a click?

"Mrs. Young?"

Sarah twitched and looked at the door. The man wore navy scrubs above brown clogs. He was a little older than Sarah and handsome, his hair jet black and wavy, his eyes dark.

"I'm Dr. Takeda, your son's surgeon," he said as he entered the room and took a seat caddy-corner to hers before she could stand.

He held out a hand and she took it, his flesh warm and

strong. He oozed that air of confidence every surgeon possessed. If the doctor expected her to speak, he didn't let on, no doubt used to such a situation. He let go of her hand but remained close, leaning toward her, his eyes never leaving hers. "The most important news I have for you is that your son has been stabilized. He didn't lose much blood, he never had any cardiac or respiration issues, and his spinal column wasn't injured. However, he did sustain severe trauma to the right side of his head. His brain is swelling due to the injury, which can be dangerous. Because of that we had to perform a decompressive craniectomy, which just means we removed a piece of his skull so that his brain could expand without causing more damage. We placed the skull fragment in a pouch in his abdomen, between the muscle and fat. The bone cells will be kept alive that way, will stay sterile, and will make for a better cosmetic result when it's reimplanted later."

"A piece of his skull?" Sarah felt as if she'd been kicked in the stomach. "What does that even mean? Is he awake?"

Dr. Takeda shook his head, his hair momentarily catching the overhead lights. "He isn't awake right now. The best treatment in a case like this is to place the patient in a drug-induced coma to increase the chances for a full recovery. He seems to be breathing okay on his own, but while he's on the drugs he might not be able to swallow safely or protect his airway, so we put an endotracheal tube in his mouth that will be attached to a ventilator just in case he needs help breathing. We also put in a nasogastric tube to keep him fed and hydrated. When the worst of the swelling is gone, we can stop giving him the drugs, try to get him off the ventilator, and hopefully he'll wake on his own. However, he may not. You can never tell with injuries like these."

Sarah could only find one word to latch onto. "Hopefully?"

Dr. Takeda nodded, his lips pursed. "It's possible he could be in a coma for some period of time."

"How long?"

Dr. Takeda had the grace to look contrite. "There's no way to know, Mrs. Young. He might wake up right away. He might be in a coma for a week. Possibly a month. All I can tell you is that most patients with these kinds of injuries wake up within three months."

"Three months?"

"Yes, Ma'am," Dr. Takeda said. His gaze never wavered.

Three months.

Most patients.

She tried to wrap her mind around that and failed.

Dr. Takeda's voice was compassionate. "I know it's a lot to take in, Mrs. Young. For now what you need to focus on is that your son is stable. That's the most important thing. If everything goes well, he'll begin to improve soon. Regardless of what happens, he'll need your support. All of it. Is that something you think you can do?"

Dr. Takeda looked expectant, but Sarah struggled to answer. She was still trying to digest what he'd said. "Yes. Yes, I can do that."

"Good," Dr. Takeda said. He reached out, put a hand on her shoulder that she assumed was supposed to be reassuring. "I know this is hard, Mrs. Young. Just take it day to day. Moment to moment. Okay?"

Sarah couldn't speak, so she only nodded.

THREE

JON

Jon stood in the middle of the Accotink Parkway and watched the ambulance doors close on Sarah and Lee, the darkness around him disrupted by the blinding lights of the emergency vehicles. They disappeared from sight and the terrible feeling spread through him that his existence had reached its zenith, that everything from that moment forward would happen to a lesser man, to a lesser life.

She didn't even ask if I could come with them...

...she's focused on Lee. That's how it should be.

Calm...

"Let's get you on the gurney, sir," a voice said beside him. In the dark he hadn't even noticed the approach of one of the paramedics. "Your head got pretty banged up and we need to get you to the hospital to make sure you're okay."

Calm...

Jon nodded and let the man steer him toward the

remaining ambulance, whose doors stood open. The stark, cluttered interior was a bright square of light shining out into the darkness. As Jon and the paramedic approached, a police officer angled out of the shadows to intercept them.

The policeman was tall and muscular, with a thick, impressive mustache. Jon, whose own facial hair came in as thin and scraggly as the hairs on a rat's tail, stared at the dark slash that hid the man's upper lip and tried to convince himself that he would see his son alive again.

"How's he doing?" The officer addressed the paramedic, but his eyes returned to Jon, considering what he saw.

"Hard to tell yet," the paramedic said as he helped Jon sit on the rear of the ambulance. "Concussion probably. But with that much blood on his head he'll need a scan to make sure he doesn't have any internal bleeding. No choice but to take him in."

"Sir," the officer said, "can I get your name before they take you to the hospital?"

"Lee Jun-Young."

The officer sighed. "I could guess, but I won't. Can you spell that for me, sir?"

Jon opened his mouth then stopped. He hadn't made that mistake in a long time. He raised a hand to his head, but the paramedic intercepted it and returned it firmly to his lap.

Calm... "I'm sorry. My name is Jon Young."

The officer exchanged a glance with the paramedic, who'd taken out a small flashlight and was shining it in Jon's eyes. "Which is it, sir?"

"Jon Young. My father Americanized his name when he immigrated. We only spoke English at home, but he always called me Jun-Young."

"You live in Koreatown?" the officer asked.

Jon started to shake his head then stopped as the throbbing in his skull redoubled. "No. Grew up there."

The officer nodded. "Can I please get your home address and your phone number, Mr. Young? We'll need to talk to you about what happened, but it'll have to wait until you've been cleared at the hospital. An officer will be in touch with you as soon as possible. "

Jon recited the information as his mind replayed the sight of Lee on the ground, his head a mess of matted blood and hair. *His seatbelt was on when we left the baseball field. I'm sure of it...*

...are you though?

His thoughts were still muddled, but he remembered getting in the car because Lee had been babbling about that hit he'd gotten, that three-run homer over the right field fence. Lee couldn't stop talking about it, had been bouncing around the back seat until Sarah had told him to quiet down and get his seat belt on so that they could get home before it was too far past his normal bedtime.

Sarah told him to get his seat belt on. He grabbed it and I closed the door...

He hadn't waited to see if Lee buckled it. Had Lee, so excited by the home run, let go of the seat belt and never buckled it? Or had Lee put it on and then taken it off again later? Jon tried to recall if he'd heard the telltale *click*, but there was a gap in his memory—the next thing he remembered was hearing the woman's voice outside the shattered window.

"Let's get you on the gurney, Mr. Young," the paramedic said as the officer walked away. "You're still bleeding and we need to get you to the hospital."

Another paramedic appeared out of the flashing darkness, a young woman with her hair cut short and shaved on the sides, with tattoos on her neck that made him think of the woman surrounded by light. The paramedics helped him into the back of the ambulance, each with a hand under one of his armpits, made him lie down on the gurney.

"We done here?" the female paramedic asked, one hand on one rear door.

"Yeah," the male paramedic said, who'd sat on Jon's left and was searching the drawers built into the walls of the ambulance. "The other two are already en route."

The female paramedic closed the doors, shouted that all was clear, and sat across from her coworker as the ambulance started moving.

There was more talking and more questions. Jon answered but didn't pay them close attention. He stared at the ambulance ceiling, replaying over and over the moment he'd closed Lee's door.

CALM...

"When can I go?" Jon asked for what must have been at least the tenth time. He was desperate for information about Lee, but all they'd say was that he was in surgery.

"Very soon, Mr. Young," said the social worker who'd been assigned to him shortly after he'd arrived in the emergency department. She was a plump, docile looking woman who had the kind, patient air of a grandmother even though she looked a bit too young for that milestone. The frequency of the question didn't rattle her and she'd given nearly the same response every time. "We just need to get the results of your CT scan back. Assuming everything looks fine, you'll be given the okay to leave and we'll get you up to your wife and son."

Calm, Jon...

More than two achingly slow hours had passed since his arrival, most of that time spent staring at the ceiling. After a physician assistant had cleaned and sutured the laceration on his head, he'd decided to get out of bed and leave. But one of the nurses—a giant of a man whose hairy arms were as thick as Jon's lower legs—had persuaded him that it was in his best interest not to leave until they said he could. Sometime later a tech had taken him to get the scan.

Very soon turned out to be almost an hour later, when the scan results came back negative. When they discharged him, he threw on his filthy clothes and sprinted through the hospital corridors, the cut on his head throbbing in time to the fall of his feet. He didn't bother with the elevator, instead taking three flights of stairs up to the surgery floor.

A quick conversation at the reception desk resulted in an escort to the waiting room where Sarah sat alone inside, unaware of his presence behind a plate glass window.

He stood outside the waiting room breathing hard, resisted the urge to rush inside and find out what had happened to Lee. It was important to be calm. Sarah would need him to be calm.

Jon breathed deep, heart still racing, and examined his wife. He wasn't surprised that she was alone. His parents were dead, his brother and sister on the west coast, while Sarah's family was two states away and two states too close. Both of them had acquaintances but no close friends. Work, school, and travel baseball ruled out free time for socializing.

Sarah stared ahead, eyes fixed and hollow, and her face appeared more gaunt than it had earlier that day, as if some of her vigor had already been sucked out by the accident. Jon wondered how his own face looked.

Calm...

Jon took one last deep breath and pushed through the door. Sarah rose, but when she saw who entered the room the fear and hope on her face faded and she sat, dashing the expectation that she'd jump up and embrace him, perhaps cry on his shoulder. She stared at him for a moment, her expression unreadable, then looked away. Jon let the door close behind him, took one hesitant step toward her, then stopped.

A sense of awkwardness toward her filled him for the first time. Their marriage had been solid before Lee, built on mutual trust and admiration and a deep love for each other, and had become even stronger when their family went from two to three. But now Jon sensed a gulf between them, an emotional gap as real as the physical space between their bodies. Fear that the survival of their marriage depended absolutely on Lee's recovery crept into him. For years Lee had been at the center of their relationship, and if he died, there would be a void. Jon didn't know if they were capable of filling such an emptiness.

Lee won't die... but Jon knew the thought was as much an admission of the possibility as it was a denial, and it filled him with terror.

Calm...

Jon walked slowly across the room and sat next to Sarah. He was afraid to ask and he waited, hoping she would speak, but she remained silent until the need to know outweighed his fear. "How is he?"

"Stable," she said without looking at him. "They said that's important." Her voice didn't tremble, didn't waver or halt, lacked any emotion at all. "His brain is swelling from the injury and they had to remove a piece of his skull to give it room to expand. They'll keep him in a drug-induced coma until the worst of the swelling has gone down. And then, hopefully he'll wake up when they stop administering the drugs. He might not though. Maybe not for months."

JON MIGHT HAVE ADMITTED to himself that Lee could die, but that speculation, that nightmare possibility, didn't compare to the reality of what Sarah told him. A piece of his skull removed and placed in his abdomen. A coma that might last for days or months. His body wasting away. Jon had trouble speaking. "When will they know?"

"They won't," Sarah replied, her voice still flat, still... dead. "Whatever needs to be corrected is beyond their ability to fix. He's on his own. It's up to him if he comes back to us."

"There isn't anything they can do?"

Sarah didn't respond which was answer enough.

A piece of his skull... months...

Calm...

Jon rested his head against the wall and closed his eyes. The bite of pain from the injury on his head—forgotten since his arrival in the waiting room—returned, though without the teeth it had earlier.

Months... no. Not months. He's strong. He'll wake up when they take him off the meds and he'll get better.

He wanted to believe that but wasn't sure if he could.

"He got three hits tonight," Jon said, eyes still closed. "One of them a three-run homer. He stole two bases. Slid into home. How is this possible?"

"Because you took the parkway."

Jon picked his head up and looked at Sarah. Her head was down, staring at the floor. "Because *you* took the goddamn Accotink parkway," she said and her voice was not so dead as it had been.

Sarah never cursed—*never*—and a baseball bat to the temple couldn't have stunned him more. He had no idea what to say. Out of that blankness surfaced the memory of blinding light. "There were two of them. The people who hit us. A man and a woman. They were talking."

Sarah's head shot up, the look on her face one he'd never seen before. "What does it matter if there were two of them or ten? We wouldn't have been there if you hadn't decided to take the scenic route."

"They ran us off the road, Sarah. That wasn't my fault."

"No? Well then whose fault was it that Lee didn't have his seat belt on?"

Jon flinched as if she'd slapped him.

"He was on your side of the car, Jon," Sarah said. "You were supposed to make sure he had his seat belt on."

Jon started to tell her that Lee had his seat belt in his hand, but then snapped his jaws shut. He hadn't waited to see it on. Lee had been so excited. Excited enough to forget his seat belt. He should've waited.

Three more seconds and everything might have been different...

FOUR

ELLE

The coke made it hard to be quiet.

That's what he wants too... quiet quiet quiet. She'd known him for less than forty-eight hours but she damn sure knew that much. Drinking had made him even more quiet. But she had as much chance of keeping her mouth shut as the guy with the bloody face had of strolling away from his car without a headache.

"That guy looked pretty fucked up," she said. "And who knows what was wrong with the chick. She was stone cold out. Or dead."

Harvey kept his eyes on the road. "She was breathing."

"She looked dead to me." That was a lie though, because she couldn't even remember what the woman looked like. The man either for that matter, except that his face had been covered in blood. A lot of it. Like a mask. "You should call 911."

Harvey shook his head. "I haven't changed my mind."

"Why not? What difference does it make to you, Mr. Keitel? We're not there anymore. No one would ever know it was us. Unless they can trace the call. You think they can do that?"

"I told you not to call me that."

Quiet Keitel said no gonna go to hell... the made up tune danced through her head. "That man was fucked up. And who knows about that chick. You don't want to feel guilty tomorrow."

"They'll be fine."

"You sure about that, Mr. Keitel? How do you know? What if they had internal injuries or something?"

"Christ, would you let it go? They'll call an ambulance and they'll be fine."

"If you say so," Elle mumbled as Harvey brought the car to a stop at an intersection.

Quiet Keitel said no wants to ring my bell... well, he was probably right. They'd spend a few hours in the emergency room and that would be the end of it. "Where in the hell are we anyway? You'd think we were like fifty miles out in the country or something. Bum fuck Egypt, right?"

"Nowhere," Harvey said as he took a right. "Better for you to forget about it anyway."

"You can be a real downer, Harvey. You know that?" Elle turned on the overhead lights and searched the console and floor. "I need another hit after that. Where's the coke?"

"You snorted it all."

"Really? Jesus. Let's get drunk then."

Harvey shook his head. "Fun's over for tonight."

Elle shook her head, her curls dancing. "Hell no. It's early still. Crazy early. Let's go back to your place and get a drink. I could make it worth your time, Harvey." She reached over and ran her hand over his thigh and onto his crotch.

Harvey glanced at her. "Forgot about those two in the car already, huh?"

"I come down without something else in my system and I'm gonna feel like shit the rest of the night. Come on." She squeezed and felt him respond as he sighed.

"We'll see," he said. "But we go to your place, not mine."

Quiet Keitel said yes who coulda guessed...

———

THEY PARKED in front of her apartment building twenty minutes later. Harvey shut off the engine, got out, then stood eyeing the damage to his car, a grimace on his face. Everything past the rear tire was a crumpled mess, the end of the bumper swept outwards, although it looked like it was still solidly attached to the car. Somehow none of the windows had broken, although the rear glass was spider-webbed.

Elle stepped up beside him, was quiet for the two seconds she could tolerate, then said, "I hope you know a good body guy."

Harvey only grunted.

"You're getting me down, Mr. Keitel. Worry about it tomorrow."

Harvey turned away from the car and looked at her, his Italian features blank, hard, unreadable. She was dying to know what he was thinking, but damned if she'd ask. Normally she could tell—shit, with most men it didn't take a mind-reader to know what was going through their one-track brains—but Harvey was a mystery. That attracted her and made her nervous at the same time. She put on her best smile.

"Is that how it works for you?" Harvey asked. "You just put everything off?"

She stepped forward and kissed him before he could react, bit his lower lip, then pulled away. Ending the kiss was harder than she'd expected. He was damn good-looking and close up he smelled like a mixture of shaving cream and cinnamon, a scent that made her want to lick his naked body from neck to knees and back again with some lingering pauses in-between. "Life's a bitch and then you die, Harvey. So might as well live today like it's all going to hell tomorrow."

She wanted him to smile, was disappointed when his face remained blank. "You really believe that?"

"I said it, didn't I? Now stop worrying about your goddamn car and let's go inside."

"IT'S NOT the Ritz but I can afford it on my own," Elle said as she entered and flipped on the living room light. She tossed her keys and money clip into the ceramic bowl on top of the rickety table by the door and kicked her shoes off. "No roommate."

Harvey didn't say anything as he followed her inside, only looked around the small one-bedroom apartment. He was always looking at everything and she wondered what the hell he was trying to find.

He wouldn't notice anything interesting in the apartment. It was neat, but only because she owned so little. The worn and stained carpet was straddled by a few pieces of furniture that were all second- or third-hand. The scuffed beige walls were bare. The television in front of the saggy black couch was small and cheap, only displayed what the bent antenna next to it passed along. There was a microwave, a toaster, and a fifth of Jim Beam White on the six feet of laminated kitchen counter. That was it.

"Nice place," Harvey said as he closed the apartment door, his voice as flat as paper.

Elle reached past him and flipped the deadbolt, grabbed him by the arm and led him to the kitchen. "Don't bullshit a bullshitter, Harvey."

She pulled a couple of mismatched glasses from one kitchen cabinet and set them down on the counter, filled them halfway with bourbon. She picked up one glass for herself and pushed the other toward Harvey, who raised it and said, "Salute."

"Bottom's up," she replied, drained the glass, and returned it to the counter with a clink.

Harvey took a sip and set the glass down gently.

Elle poured herself a second and took him by the arm again. "Come on."

The inside of the bedroom was a little more personal, the room dominated by a large psychedelic tapestry hung on the wall behind the full-sized bed. She'd gotten the bed and the tapestry at the thrift store, along with a nightstand, a lamp, and a dresser. A stereo—also used—sat on the dresser along with stack after stack of jewel-cased albums. The only other thing in the room was a framed picture on the wall opposite the bed.

Harvey glanced at the bed and the dresser, then went to the picture, which hung askew. He straightened it and examined the image, a snapshot of Elle standing behind her mom—who was sitting in the grass and glancing over her shoulder at her toddler—both of them smiling.

Elle turned on the bedside lamp, then went back to the door and turned off the overhead light, leaving the room dim. She went to the dresser, drank a third of the bourbon before setting down the glass, and rifled through the CD's.

"That hair came straight from your mother," Harvey said.

"I didn't get it from the family dog," Elle said as she discarded yet another disc. She'd know what she was looking for when she found it.

"She's beautiful, just like you."

Elle felt her face flush, was glad her back was toward him. The picture was taken when Elle's mother was twenty-three, probably during one of the few times she'd been around for more than a day or two before flitting off on another adventure. Elle had taken the photo with her when she left home at sixteen and it'd been the only constant in her life for the past ten years. "I already invited you into my bedroom, Mr. Keitel. You don't have to work your way into my pants."

Harvey sat on the end of the bed. "How long have you been here?"

She found the album she wanted—turned out it was an early Zeppelin—and put it in the stereo. "Since I started working at the Hill."

He didn't respond and she wondered if he was waiting on more. Well, he'd keep on waiting. She hit play and turned the volume up to the level that was just below what would make the neighbors call the super.

She stood in front of Harvey, the picture behind her, and undressed down to her underwear. He watched, his eyes expressionless and unflinching, taking her in the same way he'd examined the apartment and the picture. She could feel the coke starting to wear off, but the warm bourbon in her belly and the thumping music in her ears were almost enough to ignore it. One more distraction and she wouldn't even notice as she came down.

"You sure this is a good idea?" Harvey asked.

"Good ideas are overrated," she said as she straddled him and wrapped her arms around his neck. She inhaled, caught a whiff of cinnamon. "I want to. You want to. What else matters?"

His only answer was to pull her closer.

THEY LAY in the bed later, the stereo on a second disc and her glass empty, their naked limbs tangled together beneath the sheets. Normally she didn't linger in bed with a man—it gave the wrong impression—but she couldn't make herself move. Even the thought of the bourbon in the kitchen wasn't enough to rouse her.

She spoke first. "You think we did the right thing?"

Harvey, who'd been staring at the ceiling, turned his head and examined her. "We did what we had to do."

"You sure?"

"Yes. A few stitches, a headache, and they'll be fine."

Elle contemplated that, then said, "I wish I had a cigarette. Do you smoke?"

"Yeah. You need one?"

"No. I smoked for a while but then the goddamn things got too expensive. Quitting wasn't really a choice. I think about starting up again pretty often though."

She was rambling and knew it, but couldn't stop herself. Harvey got out of the bed and gathered his clothes. His body was lean and fit.

Like a greyhound, she thought as she watched him dress.

Lithe. Fast. He hadn't been tender during sex, but not rough either, had given as good as he'd gotten. She realized with surprise that she wanted to fuck him again.

"I've gotta go," he said, as he pulled on the boxer briefs she'd barely noticed earlier. "Hope you don't mind."

She rolled onto her side to get a better view, hated herself for what she said next. "I'll see you again?"

"You won't," he said, as he pulled his shirt over his head. Pants followed and a moment later he sat on the edge of the bed and started pulling on shoes and socks, his back to her. "It's best if we don't ever see each other again."

Quiet Keitel said no gotta go go go... and the bourbon called out to her.

Harvey glanced over his shoulder and it was hard to keep her face blank. "There's really only one way we get into trouble for what happened tonight. You know what it is?"

Elle didn't try to figure it out. "You grow a conscience?"

Harvey stood and looked down at her as he pulled on his coat. She felt a small sense of satisfaction when she shifted positions and his eyes roamed her body for a moment before returning to her face. "The only way we get in trouble is if you blab to someone about it."

"I won't," she said. Guilt or not—and she would never admit there was any—she wasn't going to risk her job bartending at the Hill, not after so many years of shit work hostessing and waiting tables.

"Good," Harvey said.

Quiet Keitel said hush hush hush no gush gush gush...

He turned to leave, but stopped in the bedroom door to look back, his eyes on hers. "Keep away from the coke, okay? That shit'll ruin you."

He left without waiting for a response and a moment

later she heard the apartment door open and close. Still naked, she got out of bed and padded after him. Harvey had turned the doorknob's button lock, unaware it was broken. The deadbeat super had been putting off fixing it ever since she'd moved in. She threw the deadbolt and peaked through the blinds at the landing outside the apartment, but Harvey was already gone.

Hollow and confused, Elle went to the kitchen and grabbed the bourbon.

FIVE

HARVEY

He needed to sober up.

Driving wasn't the issue—he wasn't that drunk anymore, and if he got pulled over all he'd have to do was flash his badge—but he needed to clear his head and get his thoughts in order.

She could ruin everything...

Elle Rey didn't know much about him, none of them ever did, but she knew enough. Maybe she wouldn't remember what happened—coke did funny things to people's memories sometimes—but he wouldn't bet a nickel on the chance.

He turned into a 7-Eleven about a mile from Elle's apartment, parked in the lefthand corner so that the smashed rear fender wouldn't be as obvious to anyone on a late-night beer run. He was miles from the accident scene, but if a detective had been assigned to the case there'd be a

BOLO out for damaged cars. The guy in the ditch shouldn't have been able to see them, but still. Some of the detectives were damn smart.

You feel that sucking at your soul, Harvey? That's what the bottom feels like...

Harvey went inside the 7-Eleven and the clerk looked him over, dismissed him as a harmless, thirty-something white guy. He went to the restroom, a dismal cave that was little more than a glorified broom closet, and peed as he read the missives scrawled on the wall above the urinal.

Bebe luvs Trayvon...

Jazz D Sucks Big Cock...

Julianna is a tranny hore...

That last gem was inked beneath a cartoonish picture of the presumed man-lady, the head crowned by a nimbus of hair that made him think of Elle. After sex he'd enjoyed feeling her sweaty skin against his, but he couldn't stop thinking about the accident, about how much power she had over him, and that the only way he could make sure she never got him in trouble was if he killed her. But he'd already crossed one moral divide in his profession and had no desire to cross another. Besides, she'd probably go coke crazy in the next month or two and wind up in the gutter anyway.

Harvey zipped up, flushed the toilet with his foot, and went to the sink. He looked drunk, but not memorably so. He splashed his face with cold water and discovered there were no paper towels, used his coat sleeves to dry off.

Harvey left the restroom, skirted a couple arguing about pizza versus chicken wings, and walked to the coffee station where he filled a large paper cup with Colombian and half a packet of Splenda. He didn't drink coffee often, but when he did, he liked it strong and bitter.

He sipped the coffee on his way to the register. It was hot, but not scalding, and would go a long way toward sobering him up. Even more important, it would help keep him awake during the long drive ahead.

BEFORE HE LEFT THE 7-ELEVEN, Harvey turned off his phone so there wouldn't be a record of the trip. His car—a Jeep Cherokee that'd seen better days—didn't have a GPS.

He drove to the Beltway and took the northbound entrance ramp, got onto I-66 a few minutes later, and headed west. There were a number of body shops Harvey could take the jeep to, especially in Baltimore, but he wanted to avoid the obvious. The detective working the hit and run would look for repairs done a day or two after the accident, and probably wouldn't look any farther than the local chop shops. But if they were diligent they might look at Baltimore or Richmond, and when they did they'd check with the detectives there and they'd hear all about the dirtiest places in town.

So he settled on Morgantown, West Virginia. He could've gone north into Pennsylvania, maybe to Harrisburg, but the idea of driving west across the Appalachians in the dark brought back pleasant childhood memories of a fishing trip with his grandfather. Besides, if he went somewhere too close he'd end up having to kill a lot of time waiting for the body shops to open.

HARVEY DROVE into Morgantown just after six. He'd taken his time, driving just under the speed limit and stopping every hour or so to stretch his legs. It was a good trip. The miles had ticked by and the more he thought about Elle the more certain he was she'd never say a word—she was too invested in her own skin.

She won't squeal and the couple will be fine after a short stay in the hospital. All you have to do is take care of the Jeep and it'll be like this night never happened...

The biggest thing Morgantown had going for it was West Virginia University, so it wasn't hard to find a diner. Harvey took a booth in the back of the first one he found—where he could see everyone coming and going—ordered a big breakfast, and then unfolded the paper he'd bought outside the entrance.

An hour and a half later the waitress, an older white lady with more gray in her hair than black, and the weathered face and gravelly voice of a lifetime smoker, topped off his coffee cup for the third time. "Anything else I can get for you, honey?"

Harvey nodded as he finished the last bite of his western omelette, dialed up the alter-ego he thought of as Harv. "You know any good body shops around here? I swiped a tree going home last night and need to get some work done, but I haven't lived here long enough to know where I should go."

The waitress put her free hand on her hip and gave him a knowing smirk. "Few too many beers, huh?"

Harvey gave her his best aw-shucks grin and shrugged. "Wasn't me. The tree just jumped out of nowhere."

The waitress chuckled at the expected joke. "Whitmore's over on Cary street is a good one. I've had some work done there before. Priced fair and they're quick."

"Sounds perfect. Thanks."

"No problem, hon. You need anything else before I bring the check?"

"Just some directions."

WHITMORE'S HAD JUST OPENED when he arrived, and a few of the employees were still loitering outside of the building drinking coffee and smoking cigarettes. They ignored him as he entered the office, a small square of a room with a scuffed linoleum floor and brown walls decorated with old pictures of race cars and girls in swimsuits. The receptionist was a beefy girl who looked like she should be in class at the local high school instead of stationed behind the cluttered desk.

"Good morning, sir," she said with only a quick glance up from her computer. "How can I help you today?"

Harvey leaned his elbows on the counter. "I've got a Jeep Cherokee with a damaged rear-end I need fixed and I need it done this morning."

The receptionist looked away from the computer, one thick, caterpillar-like eyebrow raised. "You realize this isn't a fast-food restaurant, right? It takes time to get parts around here. Time to paint 'em."

"I know it," Harvey said, still channeling Harv. "You see, the problem is my wife. If she finds out I dented up her car, she's gonna rain fire down on my head. It's a pretty common make, so I think you can get whatever parts you need quick. And I'll pay for it in cash, no insurance claim."

The girl rolled her eyes and sighed. "Well, let me go talk to Daddy and see what he has to say."

HARVEY AND DADDY stood looking at the smashed rear panel of the Cherokee a few minutes later. Daddy was at least six and a half feet and looked like he weighed three hundred pounds, the faded blue coveralls he wore large enough to make a good-sized tarp. His hair was thin, his eyebrows almost non-existent, and Harvey wondered what Mommy might look like.

"Got in a bit of trouble last night, huh?" Daddy asked, his hands in his coverall pockets.

The damage wasn't that bad considering what'd happened. "It's only trouble if I can't get it fixed right away."

Daddy examined him and sucked at his teeth. "Well, it happens to the best of us I suppose."

"Can you fix it this morning or not?"

Daddy pursed his lips and rocked back on his heels. "Janise said you mentioned cash?"

"That's right."

"Well... I suppose in that case we can get it done. It's gonna cost you though."

Harvey thought about all the bills he'd have to pay late because of the repair. "It'll cost a lot more if my wife sees what happened."

Daddy chuckled.

SIX

SARAH

In the beginning each day was filled with contradiction. Every time she looked at her Lee, every time she left the hospital room and came back, she was filled with hope that he would wake, that in the next moment his eyes would flutter open, would fill with life. Hope in every heartbeat, every breath. At the same time she was sure he would never come back to her, that she'd be left with nothing but the husk of his body for the rest of her life.

Days passed, Lee's condition didn't change when the coma-inducing drugs were stopped, and contradiction faded. The endotracheal tube remained in Lee's mouth, still connected to the ventilator, but the temporary nasogastric tube was removed and a permanent gastrostomy tube inserted directly into Lee's stomach. Dr. Takeda assured her Lee could still regain consciousness, that he wasn't brain dead, but it was a struggle to make herself believe when all she had to go by was the quiet boy that lay before her day in and day out, his only movements involuntary muscle spasms that had at first fooled her into believing he was regaining consciousness.

So she did what she could. She kept Lee clean. She moved him constantly so he wouldn't get bed sores. She flexed his arms and legs, even his fingers, to prevent permanent shortening of his muscles and joints. And, of course, she read him the daily baseball stats. But mostly she sat in a chair next to the bed and knit socks, sweaters, and scarves, the working of the smooth bamboo needles enough to pass the time, but not enough to suppress the bad thoughts that were overtaking the good. She felt the way she had in the pond when she was a kid, when she was desperate for a way out, for an escape, when any option, no matter how terrible, was better than doing nothing at all...

THE BIT of summer vacation before the family's annual Fourth of July picnic was wonderful, capped by Sarah's ninth birthday the day before—a quiet celebration led by her father that nevertheless pleased her. Every day had been sunny and warm, a blur of running through the grass in the fields with her brother Adam, of picking flowers, of climbing trees, of catching fireflies. Time outside was time away from her mother, and that had been fine, too.

The day of the picnic started out well enough. She and Adam hid in the bushes at the end of the long driveway and surprised their arriving aunts, uncles, cousins and grandparents by jumping onto the side of the road and waving American flags they'd saved from last year's picnic. They ran alongside the slow-rolling cars, shouting back and forth through the open windows, escorted them to the house where everybody spilled out of the cars and hugged them before they lugged the food they'd brought inside. Once everyone had arrived, they'd run off with their cousins to play.

Sarah's mood started to sour when her father yelled at the kids that it was time to eat. Adam and their cousins sprinted toward the house, shouting and yelling about how many hotdogs and hamburgers and ears of corn they'd eat, but Sarah took her time, all too aware that the hours she'd spent playing were hours her mother had been drinking. Sarah walked behind the house to the patch of flat lawn overlooking the pond down the hill, where three picnic tables had been set in a long line. Her mother sat at one end, and as soon as Sarah saw her mother's glassy green eyes, she knew the rest of the day would go badly. She wished she could just avoid the meal, but of course that wasn't allowed —everyone ate together.

Her mother—sun dark, thin and ropy, her thick blond hair long and straight and gathered at the nape of her neck by a leather band—led the gathering with the raucous air of a gleeful drunk. She'd joked and jeered, gesticulated, brought smiles to faces young and old, like an ancient queen presiding over a feast.

Sarah got her plate together, took just enough food that she could eat quickly but avoid getting called out for skimping, and then sat as far from her mother as possible, picking a seat next to her paternal Grandma Tate. Her mother noticed—Adam couldn't do wrong, but when it came to Sarah, she noticed everything—but she said nothing, only finished off her beer and grabbed another from the huge cooler that her father had stocked that morning with Busch and bags of ice from the Giant over in Chambersburg. The trashcan next to the cooler was already filled with empty cans—when it came to beer on the Fourth, the whole Tate family partook with enthusiasm.

Sarah kept her head down while she ate, only talked when someone spoke to her first. Still, when she tried to slip away from the table, she didn't make it two feet before her mother's voice filled the air.

"Go get in your swimsuit, Sissy. Your brother and cousins will be wanting a dip in the pond to cool off after eating out here in the sun."

Adam and her cousins whooped in excitement, a couple of them already sprinting from the table to get into their suits.

Don't look at her, don't say anything. It'll just make it worse...

So she nodded, tossed her empty plate in the nearest trashcan, and walked into the house with her back straight and stiff. She took as long as she dared to get changed, then left the house and walked past the table where most of the adults still sat—not her mother of course—on down the hill toward the pond.

A dip in the pond was always part of the picnic. The kids went in first—giving the adults some alone time with their food and conversation until they were ready to change and amble down the hill themselves—but her mother always accompanied the kids to make sure none of the younger ones got in trouble.

The pond—well over five acres according to her father—was oval-shaped, with a T-shaped pier on one narrow side that went far enough out into the water that an adult could jump in and not worry about touching the sludgy bottom. The end of the pier had enough space for a few lawn chairs and when Sarah got there, her mother was planted in one of them watching the kids already in the water. Anchored about two hundred feet from the end of the pier was a floating dock shaped like a square—the Tate kids always favored it, reveling in the little bit of freedom it gave them from the adults, who tended to stay close to the pier.

When Sarah stopped a few feet from the end of the pier her mother looked up, a Busch in one hand and a Pall Mall cigarette in the other. Beads of condensation slid down the outside of the aluminum can.

She furrowed her brow. "What took you so long?"

"I had trouble finding my suit," Sarah said as she looked at the worn, gray boards that were hot against the soles of her feet.

"Sure you did," her mother said as she took a gulp of beer. "You going to make it to the dock this year?"

"I'll try."

"Just like you tried last year, no doubt. And the year before that." Her mother gestured with her beer. "Look at Caitlyn. She's only six and she made it out there without any floats."

Sarah's cheeks grew hot. Being shamed by her mother was nothing new, but the comparison to her youngest cousin was embarrassing. Wanting only to be done with the inevitable, Sarah took a deep breath and walked to the ladder that hung off the end of the pier. *Get in, make it as far as you can, and she'll let it go...*

Sarah turned and—avoiding her mother's gaze—started down the ladder.

"Hey! Come on, Sarah!" Adam shouted, his voice carrying over the water. "Swim out here with us!"

Sarah's feet slipped into the dark, still water and despite its warmth, a chill passed through her. She wasn't sure where her fear of the water originated—it'd just always been there. Adam understood, even though he was a natural swimmer. *Don't worry, Sarah,* he'd said more than once, as he'd effortlessly tread water next to the pier, *when you're ready it'll be easy peasy lemon squeezy.*

Easy for him to say, she thought as she continued down the ladder until the water covered her legs to mid-thigh, her face just above the decking. She tried not to shudder as she reached the end of the ladder—it was the point where she always started to get nervous.

"Go on, Sissy. Stop screwing around and get in the goddamn water."

Sarah took one foot off the bottom rung of the ladder, then let it hang free. She knew how deep it was there, knew that the bottom was still far beyond reach. She lowered her torso and took her remaining foot off the ladder, but her breaths came faster and the water sliding over the bottom of her swimsuit made her stomach flutter with nausea.

Just do it, stupid. Just go the rest of the way in, go out as far as you can and make her happy...

Behind her, her brother and cousins shouted and laughed, some of them just playing, some of them encouraging her.

"Don't get back on the ladder, Sissy," her mother said, the Pall Mall dangling from the corner of her mouth. "Your brother and your cousins are waiting on you out there."

Sarah closed her eyes and took a deep breath before she pushed away from the ladder toward the dock. Her head went under and she flailed until she rose up enough in the water to tilt her head and get her chin clear. She started to swim, her movements awkward but adequate enough to propel her forward.

"Relax, Sarah!" Adam called out from the side of the dock closest to her. "You can do it!"

Encouraged, Sarah struggled a little less, and soon her movements smoothed out enough that she moved a bit faster toward the dock.

"That's it!" Adam said. "Keep it up!"

I'm going to make it. I'm finally going to make it...

She was probably three-quarters of the way there when something slick brushed against her leg.

Fish...

She knew the pond was full of them. Her father fished for them almost every evening during the summer, catching largemouth bass and catfish, some of the latter upwards of ten pounds. The bass never bothered her, their flesh covered by pretty green and silver scales, but the catfish with their gray skin and soft, pallid bellies revolted her.

Just move faster.... almost there...

The touch came again—this time curling briefly around the bottom of her thigh—and Sarah's mind filled with the image of a catfish wrapping around her leg.

The vision was so powerful that she suddenly wanted nothing more than to be out of the pond. And not just on the dock, because that meant she'd have to go back in the water. She wanted out for good.

Sarah spun in the water, her breath coming faster, her heart racing more than it already had been as she struggled back toward the pier.

Where is it? Oh god please don't let it touch me again...

Just the thought of another brush of that slick, gray skin was enough to send her over the edge into panic. She churned her arms and legs harder, forgot the bit of pattern she'd used to make it out, and she went under.

Her mouth filled with warm water and she coughed it out, struggled back to the surface, no longer moving toward the pier but just fighting for air.

"Kick your damn legs, Sarah!" Her mother yelled, but Sarah barely heard as she imagined the catfish whiskers

thick as a pencil lead

brushing against her skin, and used her hands to beat at the water around her legs even though it made her sink—she *had* to scare the fish away, *had* to stop it from touching her again. She held her breath and flailed blindly at the huge, disgusting fish she saw in her mind but not in the brown water, and she sank until she touched the bottom.

Her feet went into the pudding-soft muck up to her ankles, and her fear of the catfish was replaced by utter revulsion at the feel of the mud around her feet. She pushed off the bottom—as well as she could when it was so soft— and clawed toward the surface, her lungs starting to burn, until she got her mouth clear of the water. She sucked at the air as her arms churned through the water.

"Sarah!"

The voice came from behind her, and when Sarah turned in the water she saw Adam swimming toward her. He moved through the water fast, his hands and arms dipping in and out of the water with ease. "Hold on!"

She tried to answer but got another mouthful of water instead, her muscles starting to fatigue as she struggled to get her head farther out of the water. She sputtered and spit until her mouth was empty, and when Adam made it to her a moment later she grabbed onto him with both arms. He sank immediately, but freed one of his arms and used it and his legs to get his head out of the water again while Sarah clung to his other arm.

"Relax... let me pull you," he said between gulps of air.

But she couldn't. All she could think about was the fish and the muck and she wanted to be as far from them as possible—she pulled her brother closer.

"Adam! Let go of her!" Her mother's distant scream was accompanied by the pounding of feet down the pier, followed by splashes.

Whether he heard their mother or just sensed what was happening, Adam tried to move away from Sarah, but she just pulled him closer, her body strong with panic.

Gotta get out...

She dragged herself farther onto him, wrapped her arms around his neck, and he went under, sputtering but still kicking, his arms pinned uselessly between their bodies.

Gotta get...

Adam broke the surface again but only enough to get his nose clear of the water. His eyes were wide and wild as Sarah pushed him down again, as she tried to climb his body like a ladder to get as far out of the pond as she could.

Gotta...

Her mother's screams still seemed far away as Adam tried to make it up one last time. But Sarah pushed against his shoulders and he didn't even break the surface of the water...

"SARAH?"

I'd go back into the pond right this minute if it meant Lee would wake up. I'd drown Adam all over again, do whatever it takes to get Lee—

"Sarah? Are you okay?"

Sarah blinked, realized Jon was kneeling next to her chair, his hand on her arm, his face tight with concern. "What?"

"Are you okay?" Jon asked, emphasizing each word.

Sarah stared at him, but in her mind she saw Adam's

terrified expression as he sank into the water for the final time, his eyes locked on hers. She pushed the image away as she spoke. "I just drifted off. Why are you here?"

Jon's lips pursed and he stood, his hand sliding off her arm with reluctance. "I left work early because we're supposed to meet Dr. Takeda at four. Remember?"

"Oh."

Jon tilted his head. "Are you sure everything's okay?"

Anger filled her yet again, the feeling too hot and poisonous to hold inside. "Of course I'm not okay, Jon. Do you see our son there behind you? He's been in a coma for more than two weeks and hasn't shown any signs of improvement. None. So yes, of course I'm okay. I'm great. How are you?"

Jon's face went blank as usual. She almost wished he'd scream back at her, but no, he was too much like his father. He opened his mouth to answer—another quiet apology no doubt—but was interrupted by a knock at the door.

A moment later Dr. Takeda stuck his head into the room. "Okay if I come in?"

"Of course," Jon said, no doubt relieved.

"You're fine where you're at, Mrs. Young. Why don't you have a seat as well, Mr. Young?"

Jon nodded and took the chair next to Sarah. Dr. Takeda dragged a chair from the other side of Lee's bed and sat. "I apologize for asking to meet on such short notice, but if there's one thing I've learned over the years, it's that if a time slot opens you take advantage of it." Dr. Takeda paused as if waiting for a response, but when neither Sarah nor Jon said a word he continued. "I'm not able to put myself in your shoes, and I can't even imagine how hard this is for you. There's been precious little good news since Lee was injured. But I have a small bit of good news for Lee today. He's no longer in any immediate danger from his injuries."

"What does that mean?" Sarah asked.

"It means that he can finally leave the hospital," Dr. Takeda said. Sarah opened her mouth to respond, but Dr. Takeda raised his hands in a shushing motion. "I know, it seems ridiculous. He's clearly still in a coma, and you can't take care of him at home. Nobody expects you to do that. But hospital policy is that once a patient is not in imminent danger, they shouldn't be in the hospital. This is not in the interest of the hospital, but in the interest of the patient. Lee doesn't need the level of care we provide here. What he needs is rehabilitation and basic care, so what's best for him at this point is to be transferred to a long-term care facility."

"Are you sure?" Jon asked.

Dr. Takeda nodded right away. "Yes. It's what's best for him."

"What about the ventilator?" Jon asked. "The feeding tube?"

"The ventilator has only been aiding his breathing and is probably no longer necessary. After another round of tests, we'll know for sure, and if everything checks out we'll be able to take out the endotracheal tube and let Lee breathe on his own. As for the feeding tube, the care facility is equipped to handle that."

"Where?" Sarah asked, trying not to latch onto the bit of hope that arose when Dr. Takeda said Lee could stop using the ventilator.

"There's a wonderful facility near here named Rainbow Pines. I know the physician in charge of the neuro patients —Dr. Kamarti—and he's excellent. He and the staff there can provide the kind of environment that will give Lee the best chance of recovering."

"You're sure of that?" Sarah asked.

"Yes," Dr. Takeda said with a nod. "Absolutely."

There was a silence then, as heavy as Sarah had ever felt in her life.

Jon broke it.

"Okay," Jon said, and Sarah thought he was making an effort to sound upbeat. "So what do we need to do to get him transferred? And after that, what do we need to do to make sure he has the absolute best chance of recovering?"

Sarah listened to the two of them talk but found she couldn't invest in the conversation. It was too unreal. Her Lee had been fine, had been running and sliding and hitting and catching and then he was trapped in a hospital bed and he was gone and she only had Jon, and Jon had turned onto the parkway and then everything had changed and life was no longer what it was supposed to be. Nothing was what it was supposed to be.

Why did he have to turn? Why? Why did he have to turn and ruin everything?

SEVEN

JON

Lee looked smaller than he had before the accident.

That was what struck Jon more than anything else when he looked at his son lying on the bed. In the three weeks since the accident, Lee had lost some weight—the staff at Rainbow Pines assured them that was due to muscle atrophy, not because there weren't enough calories and nutrients pumped through the feeding tube that went into his stomach—but Jon didn't think that was what made him look smaller.

Maybe it's the shape of his skull...

That was possible. The bandage that had wrapped around Lee's head was gone, leaving a flat swath of skin directly over the tough, membranous dura where the bone had been removed. That out of place plane reframed his face, redefined how he looked compared to the rest of his body. The removed bone—still secure in a pouch in Lee's abdomen—wouldn't be replaced until the surgeons thought his brain was ready.

"The Nats had a good game last night," Jon said. Lee's doctor, the therapists, the nurses, and Sarah all said talking to Lee was crucial, but Jon hadn't noticed any reaction from his son. Lee's occasional muscle twitches—usually his arms —never even coincided with when Jon was talking. "They were down by one run in the bottom of the ninth when Edelstein hit a two-run homer over the left field wall."

Nothing.

Lee had been off the coma meds and ventilator since before leaving the hospital, but his eyes were still closed. That was apparently one of the major differences between being in a coma and being in what they called a vegetative state—the latter's eyes would often open, although they still didn't respond to stimuli, still couldn't follow any commands.

If he's not even a vegetable, then what is he?

Dr. Kamarti—a middle-aged man with a too big nose and too small eyes—assured them there was an excellent chance Lee would wake up, although he cautioned that Lee would likely have some brain damage and would need years of therapy to recover. If pressed, Dr. Kamarti admitted a full recovery might not be possible.

Calm...

Jon took a deep breath and forced his eyes away from his son. Rainbow Pines was nice enough, but not even the dozens of get well cards that covered the walls—sent by teammates, coaches, classmates, teachers, some of them handmade kaleidoscopes of colored construction paper, others straight from the store shelf—could disguise where they were. There was more furniture, more artwork, more normal color schemes, but throw in an adjustable bed, monitoring equipment, and an IV stand and a room at a long-term care facility didn't look much different than one in a hospital. That, and the inescapable antiseptic smell.

The room looked lived in. Sarah's spare clothes occupied a small shelf in the corner, while an end table by Lee's bed was covered with drinks and bags of snacks. A chunky chair in the corner and the table next to it were littered with Sarah's knitting stuff—it had only been an occasional hobby before the accident, but now she spent most of her waking hours sitting there, rambling to Lee, the needles click-clacking away as she churned out an endless stream of clothing that she gave to the staff, who all loved the gifts as much as they loved her.

At the rate Lee is progressing every person in the building will have enough clothes for next winter...

The thought filled Jon with guilt—there'd been a never ending supply of guilt since the accident—so he stood up and walked to the head of the bed where he leaned over and kissed his son on the forehead. Lee's skin was cool and dry. *Like a mummy,* he thought, the comparison rising unbidden from the depths of his mind. *Except he doesn't even get the peace of moving on to an afterlife...*

"I'll be back in the morning, Lee. I'll be sure to watch the game tonight so we can talk about what happens."

Sarah would turn on the television when the game started. It was one of the few things that was easy for them to talk about, thinking that surely the sound of the game must reach into Lee's brain, that he must hear Bob Carpenter calling the action even if he wasn't conscious of it.

If baseball can't bring him back, Jon wondered, *what can?*

LEE HAD BEEN in star-eyed love with baseball ever since he'd started T-ball at age four. They signed him up because he loved to play catch. He started barehanded, the two of them tossing a ball back and forth underhanded while Sarah watched—cringing—and reminded Jon not to throw too hard. Lee would toss the ball for hours, and when Jon couldn't take any more, Lee would toss it up and down by himself. Soon Lee was throwing too hard for bare hands. He'd been reluctant to try a glove, but once he learned what he could do with one he was inseparable from the thing. He wore the brown Spalding everywhere and would've slept and showered with the glove if Sarah allowed it. Once he was on a team, Lee had never looked back. By the time he was eight he'd outpaced his peers and joined a traveling team.

It was after that first season of T-ball that Lee became interested in the Nationals. Or the Nats, as he always called them, even asking once why they were named after such an annoying bug. Jon's father—who was only months away from the stroke that would kill him—had taken Lee to a baseball game one summer afternoon and that had been that. Lee had gotten his Nats hat and he became as inseparable from the hat as he was from the glove. Worse, since he insisted on sleeping with it on. Eventually Sarah had bought two more hats so that one was always clean enough to wear to bed. Only after he'd discovered Arky Vaughan had Lee sported another team's logo, occasionally shedding his red and white Nats cap for the Pirates 1930's era blue cap with red P.

It was the Pirates cap he'd been wearing the night of the accident, the cap that had miraculously ended up in the middle of the seat when Lee had been thrown from their car. That cap had been collecting dust on a hook next to Lee's bed ever since his first day in Rainbow Pines. On really good days—which came less and less often as the days since the accident stretched into one week, then two, then three—Jon could imagine Lee setting the cap back on his head and striding out of the room. On the bad days, Jon stared at the cap and could only envision the past, couldn't imagine a future where his son ever played baseball again.

———

JON CLOSED the door softly behind him and walked down the hall to where Sarah sat on a couch in the small visitor waiting area. There was free coffee and a couple of vending machines, as well as a television and a bunch of magazines to choose from, but as usual Sarah only sat on the couch, her eyes ahead, staring at the hallway wall. She stood when she saw him and asked the same thing she always asked. "Anything?"

Jon shook his head. "No. I told him about last night's game."

Sarah's face fell. He didn't understand how she could get her hopes up every time she was away from Lee only to have them dashed.

She started to walk past him, but he stopped her with a gentle hand on her arm. "Sarah, we need to talk."

Sarah pulled away from him but at least she stopped. "About what?"

Calm...

"You need to come home." Sarah—who'd quit her job as a reading specialist at the neighborhood elementary school two days after the accident—hadn't spent a night at home since Lee went to the hospital, only going there to shower and get new clothes before she left again. First to the hospital, then to Rainbow Pines. She wasn't sleeping or eating enough either. She'd always been thin, but since the accident her face had become almost gaunt. He'd tried to tell her the way she was leading her life wasn't healthy, but she listened to him no more than she did to her work acquaintances who were too scared to come around much anymore.

Sarah shook her head. "No, Jon. I can't. I belong here with him. Lee is my responsibility. Everything else—the house, the bills—those are your responsibilities. You do whatever you have to do to take care of them. But leave me out of it."

"It's not that. I can manage that stuff. But I think it would be better for you—for us—if you spent a little more time at home." What he couldn't bring himself to say was that he just wanted to *talk* to her. Just talk. Like a husband and wife. Like people that loved each other. "We—"

Sarah started shaking her head before he was even done speaking. "I can't. Lee needs me here."

Jon had a sudden urge to tell her that just for once he'd like to talk about something—anything—other than Lee. But he knew how that would play out. "I know. Listen, Sarah. I'm sorry. I know I've said it before and I know you don't want to hear it, but I'm sorry."

"I've got to put Lee through his stretching exercises," Sarah said, refusing to meet his gaze as she walked away.

EIGHT

SARAH

"Do you have a moment, Mrs. Young?" The head poking through the cracked door belonged to Lee's doctor.

"Of course," Sarah said as she put aside her knitting and got to her feet, her heartbeat rising.

"No, no, you're fine," Dr. Kamarti said, gesturing her back down as he entered the room. "No need to get up." He grabbed a plastic chair from the corner, moved it in front of her, and sat.

Sarah's stomach began to churn. Sitting meant bad news. They didn't sit if it was good. If they had something good to share, they told you as soon as they walked in the room.

As usual Dr. Kamarti didn't bother with small talk. "The results of the culture came back and it turns out Lee does have a urinary tract infection."

The nurses had warned her that was the likely result,

but it still sent a bolt of fear through her. "But he's already getting antibiotics, right?"

"Yes, since we found out yesterday that he had a fever. The problem is that the culture came back positive for an antibiotic resistant bacteria called MRSA. Methicillin resistant staphylococcus aureus. It isn't susceptible to a lot of common antibiotics so sometimes it can be harder to get rid of."

"But there are drugs that will kill it?"

"Yes," Dr. Kamarti said, his porcine eyes squinting. "Sometimes they take a little longer, or we have to use a couple of drugs in combination, but we'll be able to clear it."

"How much longer?"

"It varies. Unfortunately, there isn't a clear-cut answer. But I promise you, we'll be able to get rid of it."

She asked the question she'd learned had to be asked. "What's the worse case scenario?"

Dr. Kamarti didn't hesitate. "Kidney damage or a blood infection. Neither likely though. Infections like this are common when patients use a catheter and rarely are they ever a serious problem."

Dr. Kamarti continued, told her the same thing over again in a different way. She nodded her head and pretended to pay attention, but she barely listened because a voice she hadn't heard in years, a voice she'd hoped was buried for good, blossomed inside her head like a poisonous flower.

If you'd made sure he was taken better care of, this wouldn't have happened, Sissy...

SHE HAD to leave the room.

There was a garden behind Rainbow Pines for visitors or patients seeking a little natural serenity. The garden was rectangular and large, covered almost two acres, and was filled to bursting with ornamental plants, all bisected by winding paths that led to secluded benches that gave views of flowers, or bird feeders, or fountains. It was called the Peace Garden and Sarah had gone there on Lee's first day at Rainbow Pines and never again.

Instead she went to the loading dock that was a short walk down the hall from Lee's room. Rather than green leaves and flowers, she stared at cracked asphalt and trash that had blown into corners where it was left untouched, where the view was of the stark walls of a nearby warehouse and a swath of weed-filled grass that stretched toward the back of the Rainbow Pines parking lot. A concrete platform overlooked the asphalt, accessed by a blank metal door whose emergency exit siren was broken. Disabled according to Sarah's favorite nurse—it was where most of the facility employees went for smoke breaks.

She pushed through the door, eyes already full of tears, sagged against the short section of railing next to the stairs that led down to the asphalt and sobbed, thankful there were no delivery trucks unloading.

Every time she thought Lee's condition couldn't get worse, she was proved wrong.

Cry cry cry, Sissy, cry cry cry, that's all you ever do. Go and feel sorry for yourself, that'll make my grandson better...

Dr. Kamarti and the nurses all said Lee would get better. Every day they told her he would get better. Every day.

Every day they lie, Sissy. You know he'll be in that bed the rest of his life...

She sobbed harder, wished she couldn't hear her mother's voice, great gasps driving her to her knees, her hands rigid around the upper section of railing while her forehead rolled against the lower. Snot dripped from her nose and she bit her tongue so hard that a metallic burst of blood filled her mouth.

Cry cry cry, Sissy, cry cry cry...

The tears fell as dark clouds scuttled by overhead, didn't ease until the damp air filled her wet nostrils with the smell of stale cigarettes and brought back the memory of sipping the last bit of soda from a can next to her mother's bed and getting a bitter mouthful of wet ashes.

Sarah felt drained as she pried her fingers off the railing and settled onto the concrete, used the underside of her shirt to clean her face. A wind gusted through and tumbled her hair around her head, blew away the lingering smell of burnt nicotine.

Sarah pulled herself to her feet and saw Lee standing in the long stretch of weedy grass next to the parking lot, his glove on, his free hand moving a ball. She could almost hear the ball smacking against the worn leather, that pop that came each time it went home in the pocket.

Lee?

He looked so real, so... *there*, that she almost started toward him. But no, Lee was back in his bed, his urinary tract teeming with bacteria. He had to be a hallucination, a creation of her own distressed mind, just like her mother's voice. She missed her Lee so much the realization didn't even bother her.

What am I supposed to do, Lee? I don't know anymore...

As if in answer, Lee tossed the ball straight into the air, spun in a circle, and caught the ball as it came down. He did it again and again, and as always she wondered how he never got dizzy.

"It's easy, mom," he'd said once when she'd asked. *"I figured it out watching ice skating during the winter Olympics last year. Whenever the skater twirls, they pick one thing to focus on and they look at it every time around, watching it as long as they can. It stops the dizziness."*

"Only you could take something from ice skating and use it for baseball," Sarah murmured, repeating what it felt like she'd said years before and a moment ago.

The door opened behind her and she turned to see an orderly emerge from the building. He was tall and thin, green scrubs hanging off his shoulders like too-big overalls on a scarecrow, his features angular and harsh, as if his moon-pale skin was pulled too tight. His arms were so outlandishly long she could almost envision him flapping them and taking off from the back of the loading dock, flying off into the sky like a frigate bird, all wings. "Sorry, Ma'am. Didn't know anyone was out here."

"You're fine," she said.

He nodded in thanks, his bony shoulders looking like they could just keep going forever and swallow his entire head. He moved a short ways down the loading dock and lit a cigarette, took a puff, and then let it dangle from his left hand, held close to the palm by long fingers as he stared across the asphalt. He couldn't see Lee standing in the grass of course.

Lee no longer spun, the ball popping in and out of his glove again.

What do you want, Lee? she asked. *What do you need me to do?*

Lee didn't answer, but her mother did, and while Sarah didn't want to listen, she couldn't help herself. *He wants you to find the people that did this to him, Sissy...*

"Won't be able to come out here this evening," the orderly said, his eyes on the sky. "Rain's coming."

Sarah glanced at the orderly, surprised by the comment because she'd already forgotten he was there. When she looked back at the grass, Lee was nowhere in sight. She closed her eyes, willed him to reappear to her, but when she looked again he was still gone.

My Lee. Mine...

Again her mother's voice filled her head. *He wants you to find them, Sissy. Find them and punish them for what they did...*

NINE

JON

"The police will never find them," Sarah said. She sat in the big chair, wringing her hands as she spoke. Instead of leaving the room when he arrived that evening, she'd bit her lip and started talking. "After what they did to Lee, they just get to walk away. It's not right."

"No, it's not. But the detectives—"

"The detectives didn't believe you," Sarah interrupted.

That was probably true. His memories of the accident were incomplete. Some were terrifying in their clarity—like circling around the car looking for Lee—but others were blurry and indistinct or gone altogether. He couldn't remember finding Lee. He remembered seeing Sarah in the car, but no longer had any memory of when she picked Lee up and carried him to the road. But one memory was as clear as fine glass—the man had said the woman was a bartender. Jon couldn't remember what she looked like—the glaring light in his face was all that came back to him—but he knew she had a tattoo on her face and she was a bartender. What the tattoo was had been lost, the memory a victim of the concussion he'd suffered during the rollover, but there couldn't be that many female bartenders with a tattoo on their cheek in the city. When the detectives had come to interview them the day after the accident—Jon and Sarah still under the naive assumption Lee would wake up when he was weaned off the coma drugs—Sarah had little to tell since she'd been unconscious until right before the police arrived, but Jon told them everything he could remember, from trying to get out of the way of the other car, to the man and the woman, to looking for Lee. He had no physical description other than an unknown tattoo to give them, but he told them what he'd heard. They'd been skeptical.

Sarah continued. "But if you could find them, we could turn them in."

"It's not much to go on."

"No," Sarah agreed, "but it's enough."

Jon didn't understand why Sarah had brought up the subject, but the idea and how to execute it spun through his mind, and after a moment, he realized Sarah could be right. "But they might not even live around here. Just because they were on the Accotink Parkway doesn't mean anything. It's an assumption."

"It is. But... we can't do anything about that. Isn't it worth a chance, though? For Lee?"

"Of course it is," Jon said. He realized the best way to find the woman was to start at the bars closest to the parkway and circle out from there. Just the way he'd found Lee after the accident.

JON WAS astounded at how many bars there were. Google and a radius ten miles from the parkway gave him a list of fifty-three. If he could visit two a night that still meant nearly a month to check every one. But the woman with the tattoo wouldn't work every day, so to be safe he really needed to visit every bar at least twice, preferably on different nights of the week. And that was only ten miles out. When he expanded the radius to twenty the number of bars went into the hundreds. Assuming it was even possible, it could take months to find her.

But Sarah is right. They shouldn't get to just walk away...

So a month to the day after the accident he went to the first bar on the list. Terry's was a disintegrating hovel on the Little River Turnpike right off the beltway, the small, poorly illuminated parking lot littered with trash and the exterior of the building covered with faded, crooked beer posters that had to be older than Lee.

Jon got out of the boring Volvo he'd bought to replace the Cressida totaled in the accident and closed the door with reluctance, more than a little concerned he was setting himself up for a mugging. Guilt drove him onwards.

The inside of Terry's might have been worse than the outside, but Jon couldn't tell because it was even darker, lit only by a few neon signs—the largest of them a Pabst Blue Ribbon monster that had less than half its letters still glowing—and a green, half-burned out fixture that hung askew above a crooked pool table in the center of the room. There were no televisions, but Merle Haggard's voice filled the room, a tune that Jon—whose father had an inexplicable obsession with classic country music, listened to while he snacked on rice cakes—recognized instantly as *The Bottle*

Let Me Down. It was the kind of establishment where the regulars started drinking in the morning, and the few patrons inside faded and blended into the decor as if they'd been there for years.

Jon walked to the bar—no women on either side of it that he could see—and sat on a rickety stool. The bartender appeared from a back room a moment later, a black apron covering his bulging stomach, his head bald and shiny even in the dim light. He put meaty hands on the bar in front of Jon and spoke with a deep voice. "What'll it be?"

"What do you have?" Jon asked. As much as he'd imagined the moment since making the list he'd never really considered that he'd have to order a drink.

One of the bartender's thick eyebrow's rose a fraction of an inch as he stared at Jon. "We have alcohol," he said, no hint of a smile on his face.

"Good one, Carl," said one of the permanent fixtures a few stools down.

"Budweiser, I guess," Jon said, deciding that asking for more details would be a mistake. He hated beer, but he didn't want any liquor, and asking for water might get him thrown out.

Carl walked away without expression and returned a moment later with a full glass. "Three-fifty," he said as he placed the beer in front of Jon.

Jon dug out his wallet and gave Carl a five-dollar bill. "Keep the change."

If Carl was impressed by the tip, he didn't show it. He tucked the money into an apron pocket and disappeared into the back room again.

Jon took a few sips of the beer and left a couple of minutes later without having spoken another word to Carl or anyone else there, convinced no woman in her right mind would work at such a place.

Back inside his car, the doors locked, Jon picked up the small spiral-bound green notebook that lay on the passenger seat. He could have used his phone to store the names and addresses of the bars, but he found the notebook easier. Jon flipped it open and put an x next to Terry's, as well as the day and time he'd visited, and then looked at the address of the second bar.

Finding the woman he'd seen shrouded in light was probably impossible, but he would try anyway. He owed Lee and Sarah that much and more for what he'd done.

TEN

ELLE

The first thing she became aware of was the pounding in her head. She tried to ignore it, to dive deeper back into sleep, but the throb was steady even when she lay still.

Did it again...

She slit her eyes and looked for the clock on the nightstand. Instead she saw the cord running down to the floor. To see the time would require moving, which she knew with absolute certainty would set off an even bigger throb in her head.

She noticed the stereo was on, the volume low. She listened for a moment and realized it was playing country music.

What in the goddamn hell?

Then she remembered.

I brought a cowboy home to fuck...

BRACING HERSELF, Elle rolled over, the movement driving a knife of pain through her right temple that quickly took over her entire head.

The bed was empty thank god.

She stared at the ceiling, an army on the march through her skull, tried and failed to remember what had gone on the night before.

I hope it was worth this headache...

Elle wasn't sure what she wanted more—painkillers or a cigarette. Painkillers were the smart choice, but she wasn't smart, and she was pretty sure she didn't have any, so a cigarette won the day. Unfortunately, they were in the kitchen.

She levered herself up to a sitting position on the side of the bed and her head exploded. After the worst of the pain had subsided, she noticed a couple of empty condom wrappers on the floor close to the still unreadable clock, its face turned away. She looked down and saw that she was wearing an old t-shirt and underwear. That meant she'd kicked the cowboy out at the end of the night, whenever that'd been. When she woke up naked that meant they'd left her passed out in bed.

Elle struggled to her feet and stumbled toward the bathroom.

Might still be drunk...

She couldn't remember how much she'd had, but there was a vague memory of a tipping bottle in her hand. That and the feel of a cowboy hat on her head.

Elle was a few steps from the bathroom when her stomach began to roil. "Oh shit—"

She sped up, sure she wasn't going to make it to the

toilet and she'd have to puke in the sink or, worse, on the threadbare rug that lay before the vanity. But she fell to her knees and managed to get the toilet lid out of the way in time to retch into a bowl full of stale brown piss. She heaved once, twice, and—the smell assaulting her—a third time so violently that it felt like her stomach turned inside out.

Panting, her long curls threatening to fall in the filth in the toilet, she groped for the handle. She found it a second later, flushed the vile mix of vomit and old urine. The whoosh of foul air that pushed up when the water went down engulfed her head and threatened to turn her stomach yet again. As the water gurgled and swirled away beneath her, Elle wondered—not for the first time—if she was better off dead.

———

WHEN HER STOMACH settled enough to risk movement, Elle got slowly to her feet, fighting the sway of her body. Once steady she took the two steps to the vanity and leaned her hips against it, her head beating bass in a steady rhythm. She avoided looking in the mirror as she held her hair back and rinsed the bile from her mouth.

Gotta stop doing this shit...

A quick rifle through the vanity confirmed the absence of any painkillers. The shower held some appeal, but not as much as a smoke, so she shuffled out of the bathroom and into the kitchen. The counter was a mess of Chinese takeout cartons, empty beer bottles—that'd been the cowboy, she avoided the swill at all costs—and two fifths of bourbon, one bone dry, the other with no more than an inch of liquor riding the bottom.

Jesus, I tied it on last night...

She spotted the cellophane wrapper of the smokes under a paper plate, extricated it, and found the pack empty.

Sighing, she picked up the bottle of bourbon and finished it off. Hopefully it wouldn't make her throw up again.

ELLE WENT to the bedroom and dressed in ripped jeans and a black tank top. Hair of the dog or no, the headache wouldn't give until she had a smoke.

She plucked her keys and money clip from the ceramic bowl by the front door, tucked the money clip in the back pocket of her pants. She stomped on black boots, and stepped outside into a warm bright day that made her want to go back inside, close the blinds, and watch shitty game shows.

Except its gotta be after noon already, she thought after squinting at the bright sky. *Nothing but shitty talk shows on now...*

Elle took the stairs to the ground floor slowly and walked to her car, where she opened the door long enough to lean in and grab a pair of sunglasses. Then she followed the sidewalk out to the street and turned left. The convenience store wasn't far and gas wasn't cheap.

Not far from the entrance to her apartment complex, she crossed the bridge that spanned one of the small creeks that were all over the hilly area so close to the Potomac. She glanced at the water below, saw instead the Accotink sliding by in the moonlight on the other side of that goddamn car, and looked away.

After smokes, I'll have to go by the liquor store...

Head still throbbing, she walked faster, passing a rundown community park on the other side of the creek. A group of boys were playing a game of baseball in the overgrown grass that bordered the road.

Is it the weekend already?

She supposed they might be out of school for the year, but she didn't know. She knew she worked that night and compared to that knowledge what did it matter what day it was?

A breeze came down the street and swept across her, chilling her despite the temperature, her stomach still nauseous. She was cursing herself for deciding to walk when a baseball rolled across the sidewalk in front of her and caused her to stumble and nearly fall.

She found her balance and turned in time to see a dark-eyed boy wearing a blue baseball hat run across the sidewalk after the ball, which he scooped up with his glove before it could get to the street. He glanced at her as he ran back toward the ball field but said nothing as he crossed the sidewalk once more, flipping the ball from his glove up over his head and down into the waiting palm of his free hand as he ran.

"*Goddamn* kid, you could fucking apologize!" Her heart wasn't in it though, and when he ignored her, she turned back toward the convenience store, the smoke still calling her.

She glanced back once but couldn't pick the boy out of the crowd of brats on the ball field. That bothered her, but she wasn't sure why. Shaking her head, she walked faster.

ELEVEN

HARVEY

Fast Freddie Franklin sweated like a pig when he was nervous. "I can't do this, man."

"You can," Harvey said as he taped the wire in place on Freddie's chest. "You've got no leverage to cop a plea, Freddie. Blow this and you go to jail."

They were in Freddie's house, a dump sandwiched between the I-395 HOV corridor and Crystal City. Harvey sat on an ashtray-littered coffee table in front of Freddie, who was sunk into an old couch, his legs splayed, his shirt off. He was tall and thin and pale, his hair buzzed short, his face clean-shaven. Slick was the word that came to mind, and it was a good description for Freddie's appearance and personality.

"You sure this shitbox ain't gonna start buzzin' or cracklin' while I'm wearing it?" Freddie asked as he eyed the wire on his chest.

"Not unless your sweat short circuits it," Harvey said, checking the tape one final time.

The shitbox was the simple audio transmitter Harvey always used on informants. The Narcotics department had nicer equipment—even a specialized version of Google Glass the search giant made specifically for undercover governmental agencies—but Harvey used the basic transmitter because it was less prone to glitches. More than that though, Harvey had noticed informants were more nervous when they were wearing a camera. For some reason they couldn't forget the camera like they could an audio transmitter, always certain it stuck out like a fifty-dollar hooker at a black-tie dinner.

Harvey leaned back, satisfied. "Go over it again."

Freddie used the t-shirt in his hands to wipe sweat off his forehead. "I drive to Mack's place but stop a block away and turn on the wire. At Mack's—"

"How do you know it's on?" Harvey interrupted.

Freddie rolled his head. "Shit, man. Come on... "

"How do you know?" Harvey pressed. He had a knack for running informants, but he hated using them. They were about as reliable as a ten-day weather forecast. But Mack was too skittish to risk using an undercover agent so there'd been no choice. Costillo had volunteered to try going undercover anyway, but he was crazy, one of those guys who got off on risking his balls.

"The fuckin' green light flashes twice."

"Good. Go on."

"I park in the same spot I always do, then go up to the house. When I get to Mack, I tell him I need more than last time because I'm sellin' the shit so fast."

"How much more?"

"Double."

Harvey nodded. It was the right amount. Enough to put Mack in jail for a while, but not so much he'd get nervous about it. Mack was dumb enough to trust people like Freddie but he had good instincts.

"And if he balks?"

"If he *what*?"

"If he doesn't want to give you that much."

"Tell him fine, but I'll be back in a couple days. Show him the money. If he won't do it, I take the regular and leave."

Harvey stood. "Good, Freddie. You might get that plea deal yet."

"I better," Freddie said. "No way I'm doin' two fuckin' years for slingin' buds." He picked up the bag and rifled through the cash. "This don't look like five grand. You sure there's five in here?"

"There is. And you know what'll happen if that money doesn't go to Mack."

"Yeah, fuck, I know," Freddie said as he dropped the bag on the table. He peered at his phone, slid it in one baggy pants pocket, then went and checked his appearance in the cracked mirror by the front door. "Now get the hell outta my house."

Harvey headed for the back door without another word. Freddie had his mojo back, which meant there was a chance he might actually pull off the buy.

He'll do it. And if Mack is sitting on the kind of cash Freddie claims, I might be able to skim enough to hold the bank off another month...

HARVEY SPEED-DIALED the second number on his favorites list before he was a block from Freddie's.

Dave picked up after the first ring. "How'd it go? Our boy ready?"

"Ready as he'll ever be."

"He leave yet?"

"Soon. I left him wound pretty tight."

"Good," Dave said. "It's hot as hell in this house and Costillo is starting to chap my ass. Plus, I think there's a goddamn raccoon sleeping in one of the closets. It smells funny in here."

Dave and Costillo were in a vacant house three lots from Mack's that probably hadn't been lived in for five years. They didn't need to be that close, but the nearer they were the better the audio quality would be.

"Everything set?" Harvey asked.

"Yep."

"Good. Let me know when you confirm everything's working."

"You know it."

THE WEATHER GUY on the radio was barking about the low-pressure system that would collide with a dome of high-pressure from Canada over the next couple of days when Harvey parked at the rendezvous point.

The call from Dave came a couple of minutes later. "He's here and hot, Harvey. We're a go."

Dave hung up, leaving Harvey to wait. He sat in the idling car and tried to plan the bust-out on Mack's house but he couldn't focus.

He pulled the clipping from the Fairfax Times out of

his coat pocket, unfolded it and smoothed the soft white creases as he read yet again about Lee Young and his parents, about the coma. The first time he'd read the article, he didn't believe it. No one else had been in the car. But when he'd closed his eyes and relived the scene—the man, strapped in and bleeding; the woman, strapped in and unconscious—the back of the car had been unoccupied but not empty. There'd been a baseball cap on the seat.

So he'd known and blocked it out, either because he was drunk or because he would've had to search for the boy and that would've been the end of his career. And after that? Well, things would've been bad. So he'd ignored the hat and fled the scene.

He'd had no other option. He knew that, and he knew if it happened again, he'd make the same decision. That didn't make it any easier.

The phone buzzed in his hand and Harvey swiped to answer. "Well?"

"We got it. Your boy came through like a champ."

AFTER HE FOLLOWED up with Freddie, Dave, and Costillo, Harvey went to the station and completed the paperwork necessary to request a search warrant for Mack's house. Once that was done, he drove to the small green house on Haywood Street.

The neighborhood was mostly blue-collar and the houses reflected that demographic, most of them one-story, older, faded, a bit worn around the edges. But the sidewalks were free of weeds and litter, the yards neatly mowed, the houses maintained as well as the owners could afford. Most of the inhabitants didn't have much, but they were proud of what they had.

Harvey knocked and waited. When the door opened a moment later, the wrinkled face on the other side of the screen broke into a wide, beautiful smile that took off twenty years.

Harvey's grandmother pushed open the screen door and said, "You were worrying me! Come here."

"Hi, Nonna," Harvey said as he stepped inside. She kissed him on each cheek, the worn skin of her face cool and dry. "How are you?"

"Right as a rainbow," she said, the smile never leaving her face.

"Where's Nonno?"

"Your grandfather's taking a nap," she said as she took his coat without asking. "Come sit down and I'll get you something to eat."

HARVEY HADN'T LIVED with his grandparents in the house on Haywood Street for fifteen years, but going inside always felt like coming home. The interior of the house was a time capsule from Nonna and Nonno's younger days. The same faded pictures from Harvey's youth occupied the same spots on the walls, the same Madonna and child figurines were on display in the same places throughout the living room, the same pieces of furniture rested where they'd sat for decades. The only thing that'd really changed was how clean the house was—since Nonno got sick, the dust had taken hold.

Nonna walked swiftly down the hallway, her gray hair held in place by the green and gold barrette Nonno gave her on their twenty-fifth wedding anniversary. She'd be seventy-six in a couple of months, but you wouldn't know it from the way she moved, her body slim, straight, and strong beneath her plain floral dress.

"Sit and I'll fix you a plate," she said as she led him into the small kitchen.

Harvey took his usual spot at the table next to the window and watched as Nonna bustled about the stove. She didn't have to cook anything of course—the meal was already made. The woman only had two or three people to feed every day, but there was always a meal on the stove or in the oven.

"How was your day?" she asked.

"Good," Harvey said, running a hand over the worn wood of the table. His fingernail snagged in a long scratch he remembered making with a butter knife when he was a teenager, the result of an argument during one of the infrequent visits from his mother. She'd left him with his grandparents when he was four, not long after his father died in a construction accident. "How's Nonno? He say anything today?"

"No," Nonna said, her shoulders slumping a bit. She brought his plate to the table, then went and got him a glass of water. She sat across from him, her forearms resting on the table.

"What did the two of you do?" Harvey asked to distract her.

"Eat and I'll tell you," Nonna said, and the smile returned to her lips.

"I KNEW he'd stop talking eventually, but—" Nonna's

voice broke and she reached out, grabbed hold of his hand and squeezed hard as tears began to well up in her eyes. "I'm sorry, Harvey. I don't mean to cry. I knew losing your grandfather this way would be hard, especially once he started to forget. But, to not even hear his voice anymore... it's like watching the life leak out of him one slow day at a time and now he's finally almost gone."

Harvey squeezed back. "It's okay, Nonna."

Nonna gave his hand a final squeeze and let go, dried her cheeks.

A year after Nonno's diagnosis with Alzheimer's, Harvey suggested they look for a care facility that might take him. Nonna's response had been immediate and sharp, sharper than she'd ever spoken to him before. *No, Harvey. Even if we had the money I wouldn't send him to one of those places to die. I took a vow. Forever. For better or worse. I was there for him in the good times and I won't abandon him just because it's getting hard. Do you understand me? If you love me don't you ever,* ever *suggest that to me again, do you understand?* He'd understood. Mary, a home help aid, was the one concession Nonna had made, and not until just a couple of months ago. "So Mary is over her cold?"

"She is," Nonna said after a deep breath. "You know she'd never risk getting Nonno sick." She shook her head. "Are you sure she isn't too much money, Harvey? I'd be okay if she didn't come."

"It's fine, Nonna. I got a nice bonus at the end of the year so it's not a problem." He hated lying to her, but there was no way he could tell her she was nearly broke because Nonno had been secretly sending their deadbeat daughter money for years. Those checks and an earlier bout with cancer had left them nearly bankrupt, their savings gone and the house mortgaged to the hilt.

"Are you sure?" Nonna asked. "You shouldn't have to work like a slave just so that I have some help."

"It's not a problem, Nonna. I'm not working any more than I was before." He pushed back his chair and stood, took his dirty dishes to the sink and rinsed them. "Can I say hi to Nonno before I go?"

TEN MINUTES LATER, Harvey left Nonna holding Nonno's hand and let himself out.

He went around to the street side of the Cherokee and leaned against it while he lit a cigarette. Nonna hated the habit, but she'd be in the bedroom for a few more minutes and wouldn't see. He needed the calm that followed the nicotine.

This thing with Mack has got to work out...

There were only a few people visible in the neighborhood, either sitting on their porches or taking a walk, but when the wind gusted out of the south a kid ran down the street toward him in hot pursuit of a baseball. He wore a blue hat with a red P on it.

The kid caught up to the ball a few feet away from Harvey and pinned it to the ground with his right foot. Instead of picking it up, he pulled back on his foot then kicked underneath the ball, flipped it into the air and caught it in his glove.

"Nice trick, kid," Harvey said, impressed. Harvey didn't follow many sports, but baseball held a special place in his heart that went all the way back to watching minor league games with Nonno when he was a kid, the two of them parked in left field with hot dogs, popcorn, and gloves to catch any homers. "The Nats gonna win the pennant this season?"

The kid looked at him but said nothing as he tossed the ball between the glove and his bare hand, back and forth, back and forth. He had dark hair and dark eyes and as the silence stretched thin Harvey began to feel uneasy.

"Go on then if you don't wanna talk, kid. Get out of here."

The kid gazed at him for a moment longer, then tossed the ball backwards over his head in a high arc that went dead center down the street. The kid spun on his heels and fled, held out his glove without even looking up or breaking stride and the ball fell right into it as he ran away. He turned at the next intersection and disappeared.

"Damn," Harvey said, squinting through the smoke that puddled around his head, the air abruptly still. He'd played ball growing up and knew how hard it was to do what the kid had just pulled off so casually. But his amazement was tempered, dulled by the sensation that he knew the kid.

Not from the neighborhood...

Harvey dropped the cigarette and stamped it out. There was no use worrying the familiarity—his subconscious would figure it out eventually.

It didn't take long—he was pulling away from the curb when it came to him. He'd never seen the kid before. But he'd seen that hat.

TWELVE

JON

The dark clouds moving across the sky were lit by the setting sun and a stiff breeze ruffled the greening June leaves on the trees when Jon walked out of Rainbow Pines.

Leaving the facility was the worst part of the day. As much as he hated her decision, he understood why Sarah chose not to do it. But staying wasn't an option. He had to work and to do that, he had to sleep. So he left and she stayed. But leaving his family behind wasn't what made it the worst part of the day. No, what made it so terrible was that he couldn't wait to leave, that walking away filled him with a sense of relief.

Jon found the Volvo, opened the door and slid into the driver's seat. He started the engine but just sat, stared through the window at a minivan in front of him as the meteorologist on the radio warned listeners about the rain that was coming.

Jon was tired. The trips to Rainbow Pines bookended his day at the architectural firm where he worked as a structural engineer, the hours between spent first recovering from the morning visit then gradually shifting to steeling himself for the evening one. He talked to Lee about nothing and everything, mostly baseball of course, holding Lee's hand and spewing words into the silence, because that's what Dr. Kamarti said to do and because Sarah got upset if he didn't follow orders. She said Lee needed to hear and feel them constantly since he couldn't see them. She said it would help Lee come out of the coma sooner. *She said, she said, she said.* His hour up, Jon would go home and prepare his meal alone in the too silent kitchen that Lee's voice used to fill, the ticking of the old clock over the fridge unbelievably loud. He'd cook rice and a bit of chicken or fish, make fresh kimchi from his mother's recipe—the way Lee had loved it. He'd set the table and eat as he stared at the chairs where Lee and Sarah used to sit, as he replayed conversations they'd shared and wondered if they'd ever have more. He'd clean up, which didn't take long since the house was barely lived in, then he'd go out to the next bar or two on the list, cap off the day with more *x*'s in the little green notebook. He tried to make it back home to watch at least some of the Nats game if they were playing. If they weren't playing, he'd put on anything that would distract him. Most nights he fell asleep with the television on, wishing Sarah were there to chide him for it.

JON STARTED at the beginning of the notebook, scanned the names on each page until he found where he'd left off.

Xavier's Bar and Grill, just outside of Koreatown. Number thirty-nine on the list.

Gallows Road would take him straight to Xavier's from Rainbow Pines, but—and if Sarah knew she would marvel that he hadn't learned his lesson—Jon decided to take the scenic route that wound through the neighborhoods that melded one into the other, some nicer, some not so nice, as you moved from West Falls Church into Annandale.

Jon enjoyed riding through the neighborhoods, enjoyed avoiding the kids out on their bikes after dinner, enjoyed having to stop at every intersection. It all reminded him of before the accident. But that wasn't really why he'd picked the route. He chose that way because it took him past the ball fields where Lee grew up.

The Annandale Recreation Association complex—four ball fields in all, in a number of sizes, with a clubhouse and a playground—was where Lee had spent the majority of his free time for the past five years. Even after joining a travel team his practices were still at the ARA complex, and whenever Lee wanted to play around with Jon, that was where they'd gone. It was like a second home to the entire family.

Since the accident, Jon went out of his way to drive by the ball fields. Most nights there were kids practicing on some or all of the fields, and most nights Jon just cruised by, slowing to a crawl and scanning the fields, remembering times he'd been there with Lee and Sarah. But on his way to Xavier's the complex was deserted and quiet in the evening light, the green of the turf and the orange of the clay blending together in the sunlight that angled across the ground.

Not sure why, Jon slowed and turned into the parking lot by field number three, the one Lee's team had been using for practice that spring. Since no one else was there he pulled the Volvo right up to the chain link fence by left field and shut off the engine.

Maybe it's not a practice night...

The thought startled him because it made him realize that for the first time in years he didn't know the schedule of Lee's team. He'd fallen outside of the insiders.

Filled by a strange reluctance, Jon got out of the car and surveyed the field, the parts of so many games he'd watched over the years melding into one long, disordered scene. Lee getting his first hit in kid-pitch, a low drive to center field that went just inches above the shortstop's outstretched glove. Lee hitting the ball off the tee and running to first base, his short legs churning as fast as they would go. Lee diving to grab a line-drive at shortstop, his preferred position, then leaping up to hum the ball across the infield to first base and getting out the runner who'd started for second, his first double play. The scenes went on and on, a hundred different memories plucked from a hundred different games. Tears began to slip down his face, the grief of Lee's injuries mixed with the joy those games had given their family.

Jon walked over to the fence and leaned against it. He let the tears come, did his best to accept the pain. He might not feel any better on the other side of those tears, but they were important, reinforced what it meant to be alive. To love. So he leaned against the fence and cried, the tears and sobs lessening and then fading, leaving him feeling spent and depressed. That was okay too.

Life was perfect until I turned onto the parkway. It didn't feel that way at the time, but it was...

The sun was just starting to touch the tree tops behind first base and the breeze had built into a gust when he noticed a kid climb the short fence that paralleled the first base line, close to where it transitioned into the higher, homerun fence that girded the field.

He probably lives in one of those houses on the other side of the complex. Lee had always wanted to live close enough to walk there, perpetually dissatisfied with the ten minutes it took to drive. *Must want a little bit of play before the sun goes down, before the day's over and homework or baths have to be done...*

The setting sun was bright in Jon's eyes so he couldn't see the kid very well. The kid didn't seem to notice him, but he didn't come any nearer either. He was in his own world, tossing a ball high up in the air and then catching it again. If the boy was trying to throw the ball straight up, he was failing miserably. Every toss went wildly left or right and he would have to sprint one direction or the other to catch it before it hit the ground. It was likely on purpose, because the ball never went over the fence and never came any closer to where Jon watched in left field.

Funny how they all do that, Jon thought, all those kids who loved the game more than they loved anything else. Most of the ones who didn't—the ones whose mothers and fathers wanted them to be good at sports or just wanted them to have the experience of playing for a team—had already been weeded out by Lee's age, tired of the heavier practice loads or the harder games. Once the kids started pitching the games got pretty boring—the kids didn't get many hits, there were a lot of walks, a lot of steals. Many kids quit at that point, leaving only the ones who drove themselves or those whose parents forced them to play on even when they no longer cared for the game.

Jon watched the kid run around the outfield for a few more minutes. At first the sight had been a bitter reminder of happier days—bitterness for the lost present, for Lee's lost future. But the longer he watched the kid play, the more content he felt. Not happy—not that—but content in the moment. It was the first time he'd felt that way since the accident.

Jon decided to watch one last toss and then leave, suddenly anxious to get to the next bar on the list. The kid threw a wild one, the ball moving toward the center field fence, and he had to sprint to get it, not looking at the ground in front of him at all. Jon was certain the kid would come up short, the ball thrown too far. But then the kid did something amazing. At the last possible moment he dove forward, stretched out above the ground, his glove extended, his eyes still glued on the ball. An instant later the kid came down hard enough that his hat fell off. But he caught the ball.

Not many kids that dedicated, Jon thought, and he smiled as the kid ran around in circles thrusting his arms into the air. *That boy and Lee would have gotten along fine...*

XAVIER'S BAR and Grill was located on the Columbia Pike near the edge of Koreatown, close to the heart of Annandale, sandwiched between a decades-old dry-cleaners shop named Hwang-Cho's and a Verizon store that had a grand opening banner strung across the facade.

Jon drove past the place frequently but had never noticed Xavier's in the middle of the bland strip mall. That had become a common theme on his trip through the list. Apparently he wasn't very observant when it came to restaurants and bars, a realization which shouldn't have been a surprise given that he and Sarah had never been big on eating out or drinking.

He parked the Volvo a few storefronts down and walked inside at half-past eight to find the long bar stretching down the left side of the restaurant nearly full and the tables on the right only slightly less crowded. Three large flat-screens mounted above the liquor bottles and beer taps were tuned to sports channels and the space was filled with music and conversation as wait staff moved among the tables and the two bartenders—one a woman—served the stool-riders arrayed before them.

The woman tended the far end of the bar but there was nowhere to sit there, so Jon walked to the near corner and claimed an empty stool between a young couple whose faces were only inches apart as they talked and an older man who stared glumly ahead, his hands wrapped around a half-full glass of beer that was nearly the same dark color as his wrinkled skin. All three ignored him. The male bartender—his black hair high and tight above a jaw that was obscured by a luxuriant black beard—approached a moment later and asked, "What can I get for you?"

"Budweiser."

"Bottle or tap?"

"Whatever's cheaper."

The man left without giving any indication as to his opinion of the order and Jon turned his attention to the other end of the bar where the woman hustled back and forth. Her skin was powder white, her hair dyed an unnatural shade of red. She was thin bordering on bony and wore a black t-shirt above tight black pants. She could've changed her hair color since the accident, and he wasn't close enough to see if she had a tattoo on her face, but he would've remembered that skin. Not even headlights in the background could've made skin that white appear the caramel shade he saw in his dreams, both waking and asleep.

"You want to start a tab?" the bartender asked as he placed a glass of amber beer before Jon on a cocktail napkin.

"No, thanks," Jon said as he pulled a ten-dollar bill out of his wallet and handed it to the man, who took it and returned a moment later with change. Jon stuffed a few dollar bills back in his wallet, left the rest for the bartender, then picked up the glass and took a gulp of the beer. It was cold and bitter as he swallowed.

Certain it wasn't her, Jon drank half the beer, went out to the car and flipped open the little green notebook to the page with Xavier's Bar and Grill where he added the date, the time, and yet another little x.

THIRTEEN

HARVEY

"Your warrant for Mack came through," Dan Robertson said. He loomed behind his desk, every inch the defensive lineman he'd been back in his college days, his neck still as thick as his head, his jaw big enough to stop a runaway train. "How soon can you execute it?"

"If I can get the men I need, then probably in a day or two, no more," Harvey said as he rocked back in his chair. There was no channeling Harv around Robertson—his boss would see right through the act.

Harvey respected Robertson. Lately he'd come to fear him. Robertson—who passed up a chance at professional football because he didn't think it was intellectual enough—had an uncanny ability to sniff out problems.

"Make it a day," Robertson said as he ran his hand through his short, thick hair. "This scumbag Mack has been running too long and I don't like giving him any extra time to get a whiff of what's coming. You know how they are. Like goddamn wild animals, all instinct."

Harvey knew. If Mack got wind that something might be going down he'd clean house within hours and lay low for a while. "Tomorrow then."

"Good," Robertson said. "Get your plan to me for approval as soon as you've got it ready."

"Will do," Harvey said. He started to rise but Robertson gestured him back into his chair. Harvey sat again, tried to ignore the sudden tightening of guts that had barely loosened since seeing the kid the day before.

"Can you believe that sky?" Robertson said, jutting his massive jaw toward the office window and the dark clouds that were flowing by. "Weather guys are saying it's a bad one coming. Storm of the century bad or some shit like that."

Harvey didn't answer. He knew Robertson well enough to know that his boss didn't really want a response.

Robertson leaned back in his chair. His office walls had the usual framed degrees and commendations, but the desk was bare except for a phone, a computer, and a cup of coffee. Most of the higher-ups had papers everywhere, some of them even had files stacked across their desks like mountain ranges. But everything Robertson heard or read went in and stayed in. Whenever Harvey worried about getting caught skimming, it was Robertson that made him nervous. Not Dave or Costillo. Not Internal Affairs. Robertson.

"How's everything been going, Harvey?"

"Well enough," said Harvey as his guts tightened farther. "It's been slow lately, but maybe this operation with Mack will turn things around."

Robertson shook his head, his voice as amiable as his face. "It's all wrong. The shit is out there. People are using

as much as ever. But it's harder and harder to nail the dealers. I don't know if they're getting smarter or we're getting
dumber. It sucks for you guys. I know you prefer it when
there's more busts going on."

"Costillo certainly does," Harvey said, wondering if
Robertson knew something. If he did, would he tip Harvey
off about it? Maybe. Robertson was different than everyone
else he knew in the department.

"I can understand it. It's easy to get your rocks off
busting down scumbag's front doors and then taking all the
drugs and cash they've worked so hard to get. Compared to
that, who would want to sit around this dump all day with
their thumb up their ass? There are times I wish I could
take down a few doors again."

"You could ask for a demotion. Get back on the front
lines."

"Shit. My wife would let me get a mistress before she
agreed to that."

"Just a thought, boss."

"A daydream. Ah, well. Get the hell out of here and get
this thing set up, Harvey. I want this problem wrapped up
as soon as possible."

Harvey nodded as he got up and left the office. He
couldn't help but wonder if Robertson was talking about
Mack or about him.

"TOMORROW, HUH?" Dave said an hour later as they
sat across from each other at the Macho Burrito where the
salsa was divine and the fajita's big and cheap.

"Robertson's worried Mack is going to get wind of the
operation."

"No way. I heard him on the tape," Dave said around a mouthful of peppers and beef. He always ate too much, too fast. His waistline was proof of that. "Fast Freddie was good. That douchebag Mack doesn't have a clue."

"We'll know soon enough," Harvey said. He hesitated, then added, "Robertson acting weird to you lately?"

"Dan Robertson is always weird. Nothing new about that. Why?"

"He seems wound up."

"Probably cause the chief has been up his ass about how few busts we've made," Dave said as he set his fork on his empty plate with a clang. "This is the slowest I've been through in years. If it doesn't pick up soon, the shit is gonna start rolling downhill and you and I are gonna get creamed by it."

Harvey shook his head. "Nah. We're just not getting much information."

Dave belched and wiped his chin with a napkin. "Then maybe we need to hustle a bit more, Harvey. I can't afford a demotion, I tell you that. You've met my wife, right? Short little Polish thing that likes shoes and clothes? If I take a pay cut, she's gonna get cranky, and when she gets cranky you know what happens?"

"What, Dave?"

"Kaboom!" Dave said as he threw his hands up in the air, a tortilla chip flying across the table. "The lid blows off, Harvey. She goes ape and I get the sharp side of her tongue. Do you know what that's like for me, Harvey?"

"Like any other day?"

"Ha. Funny guy." He shook his head and took a swig of his Pacifico. "Nah. Whatever's up with Robertson doesn't matter. *We* gotta turn things around, Harvey. Us. Soon."

THEY WENT dutch on the meal and Harvey headed outside into the cloud-dim afternoon while Dave went to the head. The man never could leave a restaurant without taking a piss.

When Harvey pushed through the tinted glass door, bell jingling and miniature sombrero swinging, the kid was sitting on the hood of the Cherokee, his feet on the front bumper. It was a solid fifty feet away, but Harvey knew right away it was him, would've known even if the kid wasn't tossing that damn baseball up in the air over and over.

He almost yelled at the kid to scram, but something held him back. He glanced around the strip mall parking lot, but the only other people visible were the ones driving past on the street. Hackles up, he started toward the Jeep.

The kid had on the same blue cap with a red P and was wearing a white Pirates jersey above his blue jeans, the team name in red. Had he been wearing a jersey the day before? Harvey couldn't remember, which was weird—he could always remember stuff like that. And how far was Macho Burrito from Nonna's house? At least fifteen miles. But there the kid was, sitting on the damn Jeep like he owned it.

When Harvey was about ten feet away, the kid slid off the Cherokee's hood. Harvey stopped, worried the kid would run, but he only stood staring at Harvey, his eyes shaded beneath the brim of his cap. A Pirates cap apparently.

Harvey glanced back at the entrance to Macho Burrito, but there was no sign yet of Dave. He was probably copping a squat in the damn john. When he turned back the kid was still staring at him, tossing around that ball.

"What do you want, kid?" Harvey asked as he fished out a cigarette. How had he found him twice? And how'd he get around town? The bus? Coincidences happened, but the kid in front of him was no damn coincidence.

The kid didn't say anything, but he yanked the ball out of the air and walked it across the back of his right hand as if it were nothing, the ball too big to dance on his fingers that way but dancing all the same.

"I don't like you following me, kid," Harvey said as he stared at the ball. He'd almost asked the kid his name, but... "Keep it up and I'm gonna find your parents. You got that?"

The kid was silent, moved the dancing ball to the back of his left hand where it kept right on going. The kid was a creep, but he was a whiz with a baseball. Maybe he was one of those savants, but instead of being able to tell you the day of the week on a date four hundred years ago he could make a baseball do things that shouldn't be physically possible.

Harvey heard the door jingle and he turned around to see Dave emerge from Macho Burrito, still tugging on his belt as if he'd just clasped the damn thing. Relief that he wasn't alone filled Harvey—which both surprised and ashamed him—and he turned back to the kid.

But the kid was gone.

———

"WHAT'S WRONG WITH YOU?" Dave asked as he ambled up. "You got indigestion? I hope the salsa wasn't going bad or something. Last thing I need is the trots."

Harvey didn't answer, not trusting his voice. He swung his eyes around the parking lot but saw nothing. He wondered if the kid was hiding behind one of the cars. There weren't many though. He fought down the urge to run to the nearest one and peer behind it. *How in the hell did he disappear like that?*

"No," he said as he turned toward Dave. "Did you see the kid I was talking to?"

"Nah," Dave said as he opened the passenger door. "He hit you up for some money or something?"

Dave didn't miss much. The skin on his neck crawling, Harvey scanned the lot one last time.

Nothing.

"Yeah," Harvey said as he got in the Cherokee and closed the door. "Something about Boy Scouts. I told him to scram."

Dave shook his head. "Too bad it wasn't the girls. A box of Thin Mints would hit the spot right about now. Or those coconut ones. I can't ever remember what those damn things are called, but they sure are good."

"You think about food too much," Harvey said as he pulled out of the spot. He glanced in his rear view mirror, unsure if he wanted to see the kid back there or not. But there was only asphalt. "Let's get back to the station so we can get this plan wrapped up."

"Robertson really lit a fire under your ass, huh?"

Harvey shook his head. "Not that. You remember the Hill?"

Dave chuckled. "I don't think I could ever forget that crazy chick dancing behind the bar. My wife was some kind of pissed when I came home shit-faced that day. Have you seen her since then?"

"No. But I think I'll check on her tonight."

FOURTEEN

ELLE

The Hill was busy that night and Elle lost herself in the rhythm of the music, the chatter of the crowd, the dance of the drink.

She'd been born to be a bartender. She reveled in talking to the customers, distracting them if they were bothered, fueling their enthusiasm if they were just out for a good time. She played into whatever role they needed from her, all the while connecting to them but never committing. It was a job of a million small attachments and none of them mattered. She drank when a customer offered to buy her a round—someone always did—and fuck her boss's complaints and threats because she brought in more money than all her coworkers. She had a talent for inspiration, encouraged abandon in her patrons, and they reciprocated. She danced behind the bar, buzzed but not drunk, sweating from the heat of so many rocking bodies, from the constant shuffle at one end of the long bar to the other, tossing bottles to Angela, her fellow tender that night, fetching beers, getting rid of the head, making mixed drinks, shake shake shake, no wine at the Hill, it wasn't that kind of a bar and they didn't get that kind of customer.

She loved every damn minute of it.

———

A COLLEGE BOY was flirting with her, trying too hard and drinking too fast, when Harvey edged his way up to the crowded bar.

"You were telling me more about yourself," the boy said over the din of the band. They liked coming out here from Georgetown. Slumming it.

"No, I wasn't," she said, unable to take her eyes off Harvey. "Go find yourself an easy freshman, honey. I'm mean and I'll just hurt you."

He gaped as she walked away.

Elle fetched a bottle of bourbon and two shot glasses then walked over to Harvey. He had on a suit as usual and damn if he wasn't better-looking than she'd remembered. Despite the press of bodies around the bar he seemed to float inside a bubble—he was the kind of man people gave space. She set the shot glasses on the bar in front of him and filled both, pushed one toward him while she tossed the other down. "Thanks for the drink."

He looked at her for a moment before he picked up the bourbon and downed it. "I wasn't sure you'd still be here."

"Where the hell else would I be?"

"After lighting out early last time I thought you might get canned."

Elle shrugged. "The boss says he's gonna fire me all the

time. Said it tonight when I came in late. But I make him a lot of money so it hasn't happened yet." She parted her lips and sucked at the back of her teeth. "It's busy tonight though. No way I'm getting out of here before closing."

Harvey looked around as if to confirm what she'd said. "We need to talk."

"What do you think we're doing?"

"Don't play stupid."

She resisted the urge to tell him to go fuck himself and walked down the bar. Angela was lining up a row of shots for a group of squealing girls who looked like they belonged in a sorority. Old enough to be Elle's mother, Angela had smoked away her younger days traveling across the country on the back of her boyfriend's motorcycle following first the Grateful Dead and then Phish. Whether it was the years of dope or just her personality, Angela was always laid back and agreeable. Elle shouted over the din. "Okay if I take five?"

Angela nodded without hesitation. "Sure. Don't take long though. Boss man has his eye on you. Hey—can you spell me when you get back? I'm dying for a smoke."

Elle nodded and left Angela with the hooting college girls, went back to Harvey, grabbed the bourbon and the ten he'd put on the bar, replaced the bottle and drawered the cash. She walked out from behind the bar and Harvey followed.

SHE COULD'VE TAKEN the side door where they'd be alone, but she didn't know what the hell Harvey wanted so she chose the front, nodding at the circling bulk that was

Earl as they exited. He took his job of managing the drunks seriously, but not as seriously as he did protecting her and the other bartenders.

The night was warm and breezy outside, the air heavy with moisture. She took a right, walked from beneath the large black awning that protected the entrance and stopped a few feet from the corner of the building. Overhead the city's lights illuminated thick clouds that hurried across the sky.

Harvey followed and when she came to a halt he pulled out a pack of cigarettes, put one between his lips. He held the pack out to her and she took one, which made the edges of his mouth curl upwards. She flipped him off as he held out a lighter, then leaned in to puff the cigarette alive. He lit his own and for a moment the two of them smoked in silence as people passed through the Hill's entrance, a fair amount entering, a lot exiting, most of them to smoke, only a few to leave, the music cresting and falling every time the door opened. A number of those coming out stumbled despite the early hour.

She squinted at Harvey, who stared ahead as if he were seeing something other than what was in front of him. Either he'd missed her—*not fucking likely*—or something about that night was bothering him. Or what'd happened since then.

Damned if I'm asking...

Halfway through the smokes Harvey's eyes refocused and he turned to her. "You know about the kid?"

"What the fuck are you even talking about?"

"The kid in the back seat of the car."

She shook her head, didn't have to ask what car. "There wasn't anybody in there. I looked." She'd remember if there was someone in the backseat of that goddamn car. Even full of coke she couldn't have forgotten a detail like that.

"He was thrown out the door when the car rolled."

"You're shitting me." She spoke casually, as if she knew he was trying pull one over on her. But she knew he wasn't. Not him.

Not serious-as-hell Harvey Keitel...

All of a sudden she wanted nothing more than to go back to the bar, fetch the bourbon, and drink herself piss-blind.

Harvey only shook his head.

Elle took a hard drag on her cigarette, amazed her hand wasn't shaking. "He die?"

"No. But he had a disagreement with a tree and was in a coma."

"Was?"

"He's out of it."

I'm not asking. I'm not... goddammit... "How do you know?"

"Because I've seen him. Twice."

The coward inside her wanted to run. Just go, leave the whole damn city behind her flat ass. The state for that matter. It was the same feeling that made her leave home two years before graduation, that made her flee from count-less other problems.

No. I'm not my mother. I'm not running again...

Running would mean losing her job at the bar, the only thing she'd ever done that made her feel worth a damn, like she actually had a place in this shit-ass world. "You sure it was him?"

He nodded. "It's him."

"So you saw him. Twice." She tossed the spent cigarette

onto the asphalt, didn't bother to toe it out. "You come here just to tell me that?"

A new expression appeared on Harvey's face and it took her a moment to recognize it as discomfort, or perhaps uncertainty. He hesitated, then said, "He's ten or eleven probably. Dark hair, dark eyes. A little bit Asian looking, but it's subtle. Wears a Pirates cap. Any chance you've seen him?"

Elle thought about the guy with the blood mask, thought about the little shit who had run past her at the park. "No," she said, shaking her head. "Never seen a kid like that before."

Harvey didn't take his eyes off her. "Sure about that?"

She resisted the urge to ask him for another cigarette. "I said it didn't I?"

Harvey's mouth turned up at the corners again. That smile was dangerous—it made her want to wipe that shit-eating, know-it-all grin off his face then take him home and fuck his brains out.

"Today I saw him at least fifteen miles from where I saw him yesterday," Harvey said. "You realize what that means?"

"You've got a new fan?"

Harvey stepped closer and Elle resisted the instinct to back away. His voice was quiet when he spoke, his face inches from hers. "It means he knows. I don't know how, but the kid knows. You can see that, right?"

That last wasn't quite a question, but almost. She noticed Earl by the entrance and waved him away. "That's bullshit. How could he know?"

"It's not bullshit. But that's not even the issue. He's following me."

She shook her head. "You're paranoid, Harvey."

He stepped back a little. "No. No, if I'd just seen him yesterday, I'd agree with you. But not after today. This is too big a city, with too many people, for that kind of coincidence. The kid's following me, and he has no reason to do that unless he knows. Which means he knows you were there too."

She'd never heard him talk so long. It was practically a goddamn speech. "I told you I haven't seen him."

"You're a shitty liar, Elle. Give it up."

She shook her head. "No. The only person I've seen that I don't want to is you." No smile that time. "So if he's following you, what do you think he wants?"

"I don't know. He didn't say a word. But he hasn't told anyone or the police would've found me already."

"How could he tell? He doesn't know who you are."

"The kid knows something. He couldn't have found me if he didn't. You must have said something that night."

"I didn't say shit, Harvey. Besides, he hit a *tree* for christ's sake. He didn't hear a damn thing."

"That doesn't mean he was unconscious."

"Believe whatever the hell you want, Harvey. I didn't say anything."

"How well do you even remember that night? Because I don't remember it too well. You were high and I was drunk. Who knows what either of us said?"

"I know you said there was no way we'd get caught." That didn't get so much as a raised eyebrow out of him. "So what now?"

"Avoid the kid if you see him. You understand? There's a lot at stake here. So don't go anywhere near him."

"What if that pisses him off?"

"Hopefully it won't."

"So that's it? Avoid him?"

"Yes."

"What are you gonna do?"

Harvey answered without hesitation. "I'm going to figure out what the hell he wants."

FIFTEEN

HARVEY

A light, misty rain had just begun to fall early the next morning when Harvey saw the kid again.

He'd spent most of the night awake, his mind flitting between Robertson and the kid, trying to understand what was happening and figuring out nothing. He had to go to a court hearing that morning and testify about an operation from a few months before, so when dawn finally came he got out of bed, had the day's first dose of nicotine on the back porch, then dressed and ate a plain bagel smeared with a bit of cream cheese. He needed to get out of his own head and that wouldn't happen as long as he was at home.

He looked over his shoulder through the rain-spattered rear glass as he reversed down the drive, braked to make sure no one was coming before he pulled into the street. When he faced forward again the kid was twenty feet away on the sidewalk.

Harvey gaped, the car forgotten, the street and any approaching traffic forgotten. Then he threw the shifter into drive and screeched tires toward the kid. He slammed on the brakes next to the sidewalk, put the Cherokee back in neutral and jumped out of the car, left the door open in the rain.

"We gotta talk, kid," he said as he stepped onto the sidewalk and stopped, the rain leaving a few dark spots on his coat. He felt on edge, recognized the hunted feeling he'd experienced every time he'd gone undercover. Unlike Costillo, it wasn't a feeling he enjoyed.

The kid didn't answer. He was wearing the same Pirates cap he'd had on outside of Macho Burrito. Same Pirates jersey, same faded leather glove. There was something wrong about his clothes, maybe something different. After a moment Harvey realized what—the kid was wearing cleats. He'd been wearing sneakers when he was perched on the Cherokee's hood.

The kid was rolling the baseball around his hand, the movement slow and hypnotic. Harvey stared at the ball, sure the kid would drop it at any moment, but it flowed like mercury. He tried to take his eyes off it and couldn't.

Look at his face... his face, not the ball...

Harvey tore his eyes away from the ball and back up to the kid's face, his breathing heavy.

"You get around, huh kid?" Harvey said, an edge of fear beneath his words. The certainty filled him that at any moment the kid's face would morph into something horrible, something so utterly frightening that it would bend his mind until it broke.

He's just a damn kid, Harvey...

Harvey closed his eyes, swallowed hard, then opened them again. Relief filled him when he saw only dark eyes, a small nose, and an unremarkable mouth instead of the gaping bloody hole he'd imagined. "I know you're not supposed to talk to strangers, kid, and that's good. But you want something from me and there's no way I'll figure out what unless you tell me. So out with it."

The kid said nothing as he continued to roll the baseball in his hand. It was so slow, so hypnotic

no. don't look at it

and Harvey forced his eyes upward again. "I've had enough of you following me around, kid. Got that?"

Nod kid. Back away. For Christ's sake do something...

Nothing.

Again the terrible feeling came over Harvey and he was sure that at any moment the placid mouth and eyes would change into some kind of satan's maw of raw, angry red flesh.

No. No, that won't happen...

...enough. That's...

"Enough. Get the hell out of here, kid," Harvey said as he walked toward the kid. "If I ever see you again you'll regret it."

But instead of running the kid wound up and threw the baseball straight at Harvey's head. The ball moved as if in slow-motion, yet Harvey knew it was traveling at immense speed. To Harvey's eyes the approaching ball grew and grew until it was as big as a horizon moon.

Harvey threw himself to the ground as he cried out in shock and surprise, certain he wouldn't move fast enough, certain the ball would take the top of his head clean off like a buzz saw.

He rolled around on the damp grass, his feet dangling past the curb, filled with the sickening vision of his wrinkly white brain exposed to the rain as blood drained down the sides of his head. It took a full five seconds, his hands clutching at his skull, before he realized the ball hadn't hit him.

When he looked back at the sidewalk the kid was gone.

———

HARVEY STOOD, spun in a circle searching for the kid.

You're going fucking nuts, Harvey...it's this shit with Robertson. Its gotta be...

But there was nothing. No kid. No witnesses to confirm he wasn't losing his mind. Nothing.

Harvey's clothes were coated in grassy mud and he knew he'd have to go back in the house and change, but for the moment he didn't care. He looked at where the kid had been standing, looked at where he'd been, then followed the line across the street. He wanted to find the ball.

He stared at the houses across from his, remembered how incredibly fast the ball had been moving. *No. That was just an illusion because he was close. Anything thrown at your face from ten feet away would look that fast...*

Harvey decided where the ball should be and crossed the street, avoided a lone car that almost stopped as it passed. "Nothing to see here fucker," Harvey said as he gave them the finger with a hysterical laugh. "Move along!"

Harvey walked into a yard that was a barren wasteland of weeds and half-dead shrubs. He pushed through the vegetation for a couple of minutes but found nothing, the rain finally making it through his coat to his shirt.

He stopped and looked back across the street to where the two of them had been standing.

It has to be this yard...

There was nothing though. And nothing in the yards to

either side. He looked until his clothes were sopping wet and then gave up. The ball was as gone as the kid.

Fear filled him again as he walked back to the Cherokee and returned the car to the driveway. He went inside the house and changed, his movements mechanical as he remembered the face he'd seen and the ball racing toward his head.

It happened... it did...

But had it?

It scared him that he wasn't sure, but not nearly so much as the certainty that he'd see the kid again soon. He ran a hand across the top of his head, remembered what he'd felt after the ball had been thrown at him.

Soon.

HARVEY HAD TROUBLE FOCUSING.

The hearing was rolling at the courthouse and it wasn't long after he arrived that he took the stand. He gave his cut and dry testimony, the whole time expecting the kid to show up with that goddamn magic baseball. *Big as the moon,* he thought as he pictured the flying toward him on the witness stand.

He made it to the station in time for the daily operation meeting, where there wasn't much to discuss other than the upcoming bust-out. It was his operation, so he did most of the talking, which was good since it limited the amount of time his mind could wander—with Robertson acting funny he couldn't afford to fuck things up. All of the narcs had participated in dozens of operations, so the plan was finalized by lunchtime. They'd gear up that evening before heading out.

MOST NARCS HAD operation day rituals—you never knew when your ticket might get punched so you'd best spend some time with family, let the people that mattered know how you felt. Harvey's ritual was a sharing some fresh cannoli with Nonna and Nonno.

He picked up the cannoli at Fiducci's Market and made it to Haywood Street shortly after two. He stepped out of the car, white paper bag in hand, shoulders hunched against the rain, and half-expected the kid to appear. He wasn't afraid anymore, but there was an edge to his nerves that he'd only felt a couple of times in his entire life.

The closer he got to the house the more certain he was that if he looked behind him the kid would be at the end of the sidewalk, his arm winding up into another throw that would put the baseball right through his entrails. He walked faster.

"It's Harvey, Nonna," he called out as he knocked. "You there?"

The door opened up a moment later, concern on Nonna's face. "Good grief, Harvey, is something wrong?"

"No, I'm fine," Harvey said, the itch between his shoulder blades stronger than ever. *He's not behind you. Don't you think Nonna would have noticed?*

"Fiducci's?" Nonna said as he hurried inside, her voice anxious. "You've got an operation?"

"Nothing dangerous," Harvey said, his heart finally slowing as Nonna closed the front door.

"They're all dangerous. Well, you're in luck. Nonno's already at the table. But let's get you out of that wet coat first."

NONNO SAT in his usual seat, his once tall, strong body hunched and withered, his remaining hair wispy and thin, his gaze unfocused as he stared at the wall, mouth open. The man that'd intimidated Harvey as a child, the man who'd skipped around construction sites tossing bricks and cinder blocks like they were feathers, was nearly gone. Even as an older man he'd been strong, immutable and immovable. But his mind had left him and his strength had gone along for the ride.

"Hi, Nonno," Harvey said as he kissed his grandfather's papery scalp. "I brought your favorite—cannoli from Fiducci's."

Nonno only stared ahead.

"Sit, Harvey," Nonna said as she brought plates and forks to the table.

Harvey obeyed, placed the Fiducci's bag in the center of the table. Nonna doled out the cannoli then sat between the two of them. She scooted her chair closer to Nonno and began to spoon feed him, prompting and encouraging him like she would an infant. Harvey stared at them, his thoughts running between the kid and his grandparents.

Everything is falling apart...

Nonna glanced at him. "Eat, Harvey."

Harvey nodded and forced himself to it. "He's had a bad day?"

"No. Not really. He's actually given me a run for my money." She sounded happy, but she looked tired as she wiped ricotta off her husband's chin. "He decided to take a walk on his own this morning. I found him at the end of the sidewalk. He even remembered an umbrella."

Harvey sighed. It was the third time that month Nonno

had gotten out of the house without Nonna realizing it. How long before he made it far enough to get lost? Or he wandered into traffic and got hit by a car? Harvey thought of bringing up a care facility again but it would be useless. Nonna was one of the sweetest women he'd ever known, but she had a stubborn streak a mile deep. "I think we need to go ahead and get those safety locks."

Nonna pursed her lips as she placed another bit of food in her husband's mouth. "I know. We should have done it weeks ago. I think I just wasn't ready to admit to myself that he needed them. He loved walking so much." Nonno had taken two walks a day as long as Harvey could remember. One at dawn most days, and a second right after dinner. *Keeps your guts moving, Harvey,* he'd said almost every time as they set out. *Keeps you from eating too much because you know how uncomfortable it'll be to walk if you do.*

"I'll get them this week, okay?"

"Okay. I hope they're not too expensive."

Harvey grimaced, thinking about the bust-out. "Don't worry about that, Nonna." He hesitated, then asked, "You haven't noticed a kid hanging around the house have you? Always has a baseball and glove?"

"No. Why?"

"No reason." He put his fork down, the cannoli only half-eaten. *Big as a goddamn moon...* He had to find the kid's parents. It was stupid and risky, and he didn't know how he'd play it, but he had to get that kid off his back. He needed to worry about Nonna and Robertson, not Lee Young. "Tell me what other trouble Nonno got into today."

SIXTEEN

JON

That night Jon didn't make it to the care facility until almost eight because of a deadline on the specs for a new high-rise out in Herndon. He opened the door to Lee's room, the minuscule bit of hope he had every visit dying as soon as he saw his son still immobile in his bed, turned on his side to avoid bed sores.

Sarah sat in her big chunky seat, knitting forgotten in her lap, staring at the bed, her face blank. It was an expression he'd grown to expect. It told him nothing about her day, but what needed to be told? Lee was still gone, still missing in action, still AWOL.

Jon stood in the doorway, stared at his not-even-a-vegetable son, and emotion passed through him like light through water, bent and distorted. Sadness. Despair. Anger. Confusion. Everything negative. The only thing near pleasurable since the accident had been the boy at the ball field the night before, wildly tossing the ball, reminding him of Lee. But even that memory became darker the more it aged.

"Do you think he's dreaming?" Sarah asked, startling Jon. He hadn't been sure she'd even noticed his arrival.

"Dr. Kamarti says maybe." There'd been discussions of what some coma patients remembered upon awakening, discussions of dreams, of time passing. None of it mattered.

"I didn't ask what Dr. Kamarti thought. I asked what you thought."

Calm...

"Sorry." He tried to consider the question, tried to pretend it mattered, thought of what she wanted to hear. "I hope so. I like to think he's dreaming about playing baseball."

No reaction.

He hesitated, then, "What do you think?"

Sarah was silent for a long time before she answered. "I hope he's not. Not all dreams are good and the thought of him being trapped in there, dreaming about something like the accident scares me beyond comprehension. I hope wherever he's at, it's deep and dreamless and when he wakes up, it'll be like no time at all has passed for him."

Jon stared, uncomprehending. "But isn't it better if he's dreaming? Doesn't that mean his brain is more active?"

Sarah's mouth thinned. "They say that. The truth is, they don't have a clue. Haven't you realized that by now? They don't know what they're doing or what they're talking about. They know how to keep his body alive, but they don't even know what's broken in his mind, much less how to fix it. His brain is as much a mystery to them as it is to you and I."

Jon supposed she was right, but he didn't want to think about it. "Maybe when Lee wakes up, he'll be able to tell us if he was dreaming." He was careful to say *when*, not the *if* that first came to mind.

Sarah stared at Lee for a moment before she turned her gaze on Jon. "How is the search going?"

Jon was surprised by the subject change, but not by the question. Sarah had asked more and more often lately, seemed almost obsessed with the quest she'd sent him on. "Nothing still."

"It's been almost a month since you started looking."

"There are a lot of bars around here, Sarah. A lot. I've been to forty already. You knew it was a long shot from the beginning."

"Forty," Sarah said, and something about her expression disturbed him—she looked harder than she ever had before. "You should be going faster."

"I'm going as fast as I can."

"You need to go faster, Jon. If you don't find her, he might not—" She snapped her mouth shut and the hardness on her face was replaced by wariness.

"Might not what?" Jon asked. "And who are you talking about? The guy that was with the bartender?"

"Nothing," Sarah said with a shake of her head. "I'm just tired, that's all. Go faster, Jon. We've got to find her. For Lee."

AFTER JON TOLD Lee goodnight and walked away from Sarah in silence, he went straight to the next bar on the list.

Some joint in Falls Church full of modern furniture and reflective surfaces, the kind of place that served more wine and mixed drinks than beer, the kind of place where the majority of the patrons wore suits and ties or fitted dresses after a day at the corporate office slash courthouse slash financial firm, where the talk was a mix of business and coital fencing, mostly the latter. The single male bartender wore a burgundy vest. Jon took one sip of an over-priced foreign beer, contemplated and then rejected the food, and hurried out.

x.

Rain falling, he sat in the Volvo outside the bar, engine running, his head on the steering wheel, his eyes closed, tried to figure out what in the hell he was doing. What did it matter if he found the people who'd hit them? Justice down the road wouldn't wake Lee up. And why did Sarah care so much all of a sudden? Was that the only reason he continued to search, because that's what Sarah wanted him to do? Or was he still searching because he wanted revenge? Because he didn't know what else to do?

Calm...

He raised his head off the wheel and looked at the clock on the dash. Half-past nine. There was the next bar on the list but he had no desire to go there. It was nothing but a waste of time. He was hungry and tired and done. He needed to reevaluate, to try and reconnect with Sarah somehow and that meant he belonged at her side with Lee, not wandering to yet another bar searching for what might never be found.

He leaned into the wheel again. Tears came, silent and hard, went on until there was nothing left but the hitches in his throat. Spent, he sat up, ready to head back to Rainbow Pines, and saw that Lee was in the passenger seat.

JON DIDN'T CARE that it wasn't real, didn't care what it said about his state of mind.

Lee had his ball and glove, the same worn-in brown Wilson that lay perfectly flat when a hand didn't hold it open. The glove had been so stiff when they'd first brought it home, had rested wide open. Lee had oiled it, stomped on it, left it rolled up with rubber bands, had Jon run over it again and again with the Cressida. Only time had loosened it. Time and a thousand games of catch, a thousand tricks Lee taught himself, game after game until it had become perfect.

On Lee's head was the same old dirt-stained blue Pirates hat, shrouding his torso a Pirates jersey. Below the jersey were a pair of scuffed jeans and cleats.

Lee started smacking the ball into his glove. Over over over, his eyes staring through the rain-streaked windshield at the pretentious bar.

Jon tried to talk and realized he couldn't, his throat as tight as a tensioned steel cable, and he swallowed against the restriction. After a moment a croak emerged, and after that a word, garbled and harsh. "Lee... "

Lee didn't respond of course.

Again. "Lee. I miss you. I don't know what to do. Ever since the accident nothing has been the same and I don't know what to do."

Lee looked at him, his hands never ceasing in their movement. Smack. Smack. Smack. That look said *why are we sitting here? Let's go...*

Jon nodded and shifted the car into reverse, left the lot and pulled into the stream of traffic headed south. "It's all my fault, Lee. We never should've been there. I'm sorry. We never should've been there."

Smack. Smack. Smack.

"I understand if you're ready to move on, Lee. I don't want you to keep suffering."

Smack. Smack. Smack.

Calm...

Jon breathed deep, did everything he could to stifle another apology. It burned to come out again, and even as he held back part of him wanted to repeat the words.

"The Nats have been on a tear the last few weeks," Jon said after swallowing hard. "Thirteen and two, and one of those wins against the Red Sox. They're second in the division right now, but only two games back from the Mets."

Jon rambled as he drove, and it wasn't until he'd made two successive left turns that he realized he hadn't been driving toward Rainbow Pines at all, but had made his way out of Falls Church and into Arlington. A moment later the next bar on the list came into sight. The Hill. He thought of driving by, of turning toward Sarah, but Lee was there and that meant something. He coasted the Volvo into the parking lot, looped for a spot, his eyes off Lee, and when he looked back at the passenger seat his son was gone.

THE DULL THUMP of a band washed through the swinging doors ahead of him when a couple pushed out, hanging on each other, drunk, their faces slack. Jon slid past unnoticed and let the doors carry him inside the Hill.

The roar of the band matched the cacophony of shouting laughing talking voices, the press of bodies a swarm that obscured the floor and tables. A wall hugged the bar and small stage in the corner, where a long-haired rocker with sunglasses and a cowboy hat belted out a song that was part rockabilly part pop that was familiar but unplaceable. A cover no doubt, Jon just couldn't remember who.

A behemoth of a man stood just inside the doors, eyed him, dismissed him, bouncer instinct sure there was nothing to worry over. Wondering if entering had been a mistake, Jon struggled toward the bar, tried to see over the people before it and failed. He dodged a scantily-dressed college-aged girl—spinning and dancing with a beer raised above her head, her hair arcing, her eyes closed, two guys attempting to close on her and failing because of the whirl-wind—and squeezed through a chink in the wall of people.

"Just need a beer," he apologized to annoyed glances as he shoved his way through. Two girls wearing cowboy hats at jaunty angles pushed aside, bestowed the dismissive glances of the young for the old, Jon so ancient they felt sorry enough for him to move out of the way.

He got one elbow up on the bar—sitting wasn't even an option, there were no stools that he could see—and spotted a bartender pulling bottles from the wall of liquor that ran for at least twenty more feet to either direction. Her hair ran in unruly curls down her back, a turbulent waterfall the color of dark chocolate. She wore a denim shirt that the sleeves had been ripped off of at the shoulder—it was hard to tell if the shirt was made that way or altered—above a loose black skirt that swirled above bare knees. She was thin, her brown skin spotted by a handful of dark moles. On her shoulder was a Celtic tattoo, the ink faded, the lines dull, the overlaps of the knots indistinguishable.

The bartender finished prepping the drink, returned the last bottle to the wall, and turned around as she shook the mixing glass in her hand. She stepped up to the bar near him and poured the drink into a serving glass, set it down in front of a woman to Jon's right. She moved squarely in front of him and said something and he saw lights through the shattered car window, saw that billow of curls and thought he must be dreaming.

She frowned, leaned closer. "What can I get for you?"

It was dim inside the Hill, just as it had been dim that night, and with the lights from behind the bar outlining her face, Jon felt suspended between the past and the present. Her face was attractive but a bit harsh, her nose sharp and slightly hooked, her lips curled into a natural sneer, one corner higher than the other, a faint scar running across her left cheek. Opposite the scar a small tattoo sat high up on her cheek, not far from the corner of her eye on the thin skin above a prominent cheekbone.

"That tattoo on your cheek. What is it?" he asked. Like the knot on her shoulder, it had the look of cheap ink applied by someone without much talent.

Her eyes—a piercing green that gave her a bird of prey appearance—narrowed and the sneer grew. "It's a butterfly. Why in the hell do you want to know?"

SEVENTEEN

HARVEY

"What in the hell are we waiting for, Harvey?" Dave asked. "The rain's only gonna get worse and SWAT's been in place for five minutes."

The three of them were in one of the narc vans, parked in the darkness a house away from Mack's, the view from the windshield obscured by the rain. Harvey sat in the driver's seat, Dave next to him and Costillo in the back. "Just waiting for the right time."

It was as big as the moon... it was...

"You worried something's off?" Dave asked, his voice serious, and Harvey heard Costillo perk up in the back seat.

Harvey shook his head. "No. Maybe it's just the rain."

"SWAT is gonna leave if you don't move 'em soon and then the three of us will have to clear the house by ourselves," Dave said. "You and I could handle that, but I think it might be a little much for Costillo."

Costillo snorted. "Stop pretending your dick is bigger than it is."

"Fuck off, Costillo," Dave said, but there was no anger in his voice.

Focus on what you need to do for Nonna, Harvey. Focus...

He picked up the small the handheld radio that connected him to the head of the SWAT unit and clicked it on, tried to push the kid and his baseball to the background. "Let's do this."

———

I'LL HAVE to clean my gun tonight, Harvey thought absently as he trotted through the rain, his pistol pointed at the ground before him as the six SWAT guys approached Mack's front door. Dave and Costillo were arrayed around the house with the rest of the team to make sure no one tried to duck out the back or take a shortcut through a window.

The judge had granted Harvey's request for a no-knock warrant, and as soon as they were in place one of the SWAT guys ran forward with the master key. He swung the battering ram in a long arc by his hip and crashed it into the door, which popped open like a tank had plowed through it instead of thirty pounds of hardened steel.

"POLICE!"

Harvey went in last as SWAT swarmed into the house, continuing to identify themselves as they moved farther inside, guns raised before them. They'd already disappeared down the hall by the time Harvey walked into a living room occupied by a couple of leather couches and a big flat screen tuned to ESPN. Open beer bottles and half-empty glasses littered the coffee table. Shouts came from down the hall.

"Get the *fuck* outta my house!"

"Hands where we can see them!"

"On your knees!"

"Fuckin' pigs!"

"Get your hands off of him!"

"All clear!" came a moment later and the shout was repeated throughout the house.

Harvey stepped into the hall at the same time as Dave and Costillo.

"No shots fired," Dave said, nodding with approval.

"Goddamn miracle," Costillo said as he holstered his gun. "How are you always so fucking lucky, Harvey?"

"Because he's not an idiot like you, Costillo," Dave said.

MACK and two others were face down on one of the bedroom floors. Harvey always kept double-cuff zip ties in his coat, but SWAT had already restrained them, the plastic bands dark against the lily white skin of their wrists. All three wore wife-beaters, their bare arms covered in tattoos, but Mack had more than the other two combined, the ink climbing up his neck like a parasitic vine.

"I'm suing the shit outta you motherfuckers," Mack said as he was Mirandized. His buddies weren't so vocal, and even Mack fell silent as SWAT dragged them to their feet and herded the three of them out of the house.

Harvey followed a few feet behind, confirmed the patrolmen were stationed outside. They'd keep an eye on the house and make sure the gawkers didn't get too close, though the rain might keep the neighborhood busybodies away. Once Mack and his cronies were in one of the SWAT vans, Harvey went back inside. Dave and Costillo were staring at the television and bickering about the game.

"Dave, you start here in the living room," Harvey said as he pulled a pair of gloves from his back pocket and put them on. "Costillo, you take the bedrooms. I'll start in the kitchen."

THE KITCHEN TABLE was covered by drugs and paraphernalia, but Harvey ignored it. He needed cash, had to find it before Dave and Costillo. They'd give him whatever they found so he could turn it into the officer in charge of asset forfeiture back at the station, but he couldn't skim from what they might have counted already.

He went to the left side of the kitchen and started pulling open cabinets. Paranoid drug dealers hid money in crazy places—he'd found stashes inside mattresses, light fixtures, in zip locks inside toilets, even buried in a tub of dog food. That'd been a decent haul, nearly twenty grand in large bills stowed in the Alpo.

"Nothing in the living room," Dave called out before Harvey was halfway through the lower cabinets. "I'll get the bathroom next."

Harvey moved faster.

There's got to be some, Harvey. You need it. Nonna needs it...

Harvey moved on to the upper cabinets and found nothing.

"Both bedrooms clear," Costillo called out.

"Bathroom clear, too," Dave said.

Nothing in the drawers. Harvey raised his voice. "Check the laundry room and the hall closets."

Harvey glanced at the table. There was at least fifty grand worth of coke and heroin, plus some random bottles of oxy and ecstasy. At least fifty. That much meant there had to be cash in the house.

He was closing the refrigerator when Dave wandered into the kitchen. "Anything?"

"Not a damn thing," Harvey said. "You?"

"Nada except for some porn mags," Dave said as Costillo wandered in.

"Zilch," Costillo said. He stopped next to the table, looked down at the drugs. "They were in the middle of packing. Lucky again, Harvey. What we got here? Forty grand worth?"

"Closer to fifty," Harvey said.

Dave scanned the open cabinets. "No way there's fifty large in goods on the kitchen table and not a single stack of cash somewhere in the house. We missed it."

Harvey nodded. "Go over it again."

"Where are those porn mags?" Costillo asked Dave as the two of them left the kitchen.

Harvey looked slowly around the room. His gut told him if there was money in the house it was in the kitchen —it was usually close to the drugs. He'd searched every cabinet and drawer, every plastic container. What was left?

The food...

The pantry, if it could be called that, was a couple of cabinets half-full of food. He started with the breakfast cereal, pulled the plastic bags from the boxes and checked the bottoms of the cardboard sleeves.

Nothing.

A white box held nothing but rice, an open bag nothing but chips.

Then he opened a large box of Saltines and there was the cash. There were no sleeves of crackers on top, no farther attempt to hide the money. He peered inside, guessed there were at least twenty stacks. Without hesitation he grabbed the four on top and stuck them behind the waistband of his pants beneath his coat, spread them out so they wouldn't be noticed.

"So you found it," Dave said from behind him.

Shit...

Harvey turned around, held the box of Saltines up. "Cracker box. Good haul, too."

Dave gazed at Harvey for a moment, his eyes weighing, then said, "Hey, Costillo! Harvey found it."

Harvey walked to the table and put the Saltine box next to a bag of coke, started pulling out the stacks of cash. "Let's see what we got."

Dave only watched as Harvey arranged the stacks with gloved fingers.

Costillo walked in and whistled, started thumbing the cash. "This'll make Robertson happy."

Harvey finished emptying the box, avoided looking at Dave. Had he seen? If he had, would he tell? He and Dave had worked together for years, but loyalty only went so far.

At the same time, he couldn't stop thinking about the cash pressed against his hip. How much had he gotten? Would it be enough to hold off the banks for another three months? Six? He wouldn't know until he got home, and that was hours away still. They had to document everything, collect it all in evidence bags, and then take it to the station to hand in for forfeiture or destruction.

"Maybe thirty-five thousand," said Costillo as he put

down the last stack. "Lots of miscellaneous bills, so it's hard to tell. Still, not bad."

"Not bad," Harvey agreed, hyper-aware of the cash against his hip. Even if it was only enough for three months, the night was a success. "Let's get plenty of pics before we bag and tag everything. I don't want to be here all night."

EIGHTEEN

JON

Jon had imagined finding her over and over, but the scene had always cut to a shot of the man and woman led away in handcuffs. He'd never considered what he would say or do when confronted by her and so he froze.

Her eyebrows drew down as she stared and he wondered if she would recognize him, another possibility he'd never considered. If so, what would she do? But Jon saw no spark of recognition in her eyes, only irritation.

"You want a drink or not mister? It's kinda busy."

He took a deep breath and found his voice. "Sorry. Budweiser."

She grabbed a glass from the rack behind the bar, hurried to the nearest row of taps, and was back with the drink about fifteen seconds later. The expression of irritation was gone. "You running a tab?"

"Yes," he said, afraid to look her in the eye again. "Yes, I am."

———

TWO HOURS and three beers later Jon still sat there—he and Sarah hadn't discussed what to do if he actually found the girl with the tattoo. He'd thought of calling or texting Sarah, but the look on her face earlier that night made him want to figure it out on his own. For the time being at least. He could go straight to the police, but it seemed too soon—they would question her, but that was it, and all she'd have to do was say she was at home that night. As the accuser, the burden of proof would fall on him. Besides, those kinds of questions might scare her off, and then they'd never find the man that was with her.

Maybe if I follow her she'll lead me to him... There was the question of what to do then, but he'd have to figure that out later. Figure out what he had to do first, and then do it, just like his father had always said. The path forward would reveal itself with each step he took.

So he choked down beer and watched her. She worked in tandem with the other bartender, her movements economical and elegant, smooth, nothing wasted while she smiled, sneered, cajoled, cheered the patrons into round after round after round, nudging along the atmosphere toward ever greater heights of jovial drunkenness while she danced behind the bar and raked in tips, not just comfortable in her element but thriving.

Last call came at two in Virginia—a fact learned after he began the search—but he already felt flushed and a little dizzy, and if he kept drinking he'd have to be carried out of the bar, and if he sat there without drinking she would notice him and he didn't want that. So at half-past midnight he closed the tab, left her a twenty-percent tip—nothing noticeable, not too much, not too little—used the restroom and left, passed the mountainous bouncer once again on his way through the swinging doors.

Outside the entrance was an awning-covered area where a few groups of people stood smoking and cursing and flirting, protected from the rain that continued to fall. Jon passed the girls in cowboy hats from earlier, one of them puking onto the concrete while her companion stood over her smoking a cigarette and capturing the moment on her phone. Jon skirted the vomit and ran through the rain to his car.

Back in the Volvo, he started the engine, put the wipers on intermittent so he could watch the doors. The lights outside the Hill were generous and he could see well despite the steady rain. There would be at least one side or rear entrance where food and liquor would be delivered, but he didn't think the woman could slip out unseen—there was only one way in and out of the parking lot.

Jon sat in the dark and watched the door to the bar as his clothes dried, as he wished that Lee was in the passenger seat, glancing occasionally at his cell as time marched slowly toward two.

SHE CAME out at a quarter to three.

Jon had moved the Volvo across the street to a bank parking lot when the Hill really started to empty, and from that distance he wouldn't have been able to tell it was her if not for the mass of curls. She wasn't alone, hunched beneath an umbrella with another woman, and a moment later the two of them stopped next to a small sedan. They talked for a few minutes and then the woman with the butterfly tattoo got into the sedan. The one with the umbrella walked to an old Jeep Wrangler a few spots away and disappeared inside. As soon as the lights on the sedan came to life, the car pulled out of the lot and sped south. The Wrangler followed an instant later and headed the opposite direction.

Jon cursed as the sedan's taillights receded into the rainy distance. He cursed again when he realized how stupid it'd been to park front first. He backed up, watching the distance to the sedan grow and hoping he didn't hit something. The Volvo's tires spun on the wet pavement as Jon shot out of the bank parking lot, narrowly avoiding the lone car that happened to be speeding past, earning him a loud honk and a flash of high-beams. He leaned forward, his chest pressed against the steering wheel as he peered through the wet darkness toward the fading taillights.

Thanks to the late hour the street was green lights wall to wall and he was able to catch up a minute later. Half a block back he slowed, unsure how close to get, tried to think of what he'd seen on a million stupid police shows, painfully aware they'd probably all gotten it wrong.

He felt anxious, stomach roiling, and considered putting down the window in case he needed to vomit on the asphalt streaming along beneath the car, only discarded the idea because the rain had begun to fall in heavy sheets.

The sedan turned twice in the next five minutes and then pulled into Shady Acres Apartments, the sign at the entrance covered with faded paint, a couple of letters missing from the name. She parked in front of the building closest to the street.

Jon followed her into the complex and continued past

without slowing, not taking a spot until he was in front of the third building from the street. He turned off his lights before he had come to a halt, put the gearshift into neutral and killed the engine. He stepped out of the car into the rain, and his clothes soaked through within seconds as he peered over the roofs of the nearby cars and in the light from the sodium arc lamps above he saw her run through the rain toward her building.

How many apartments in each one? Ten? Twenty?

Keeping the cars between them, Jon scurried after her. Lights danced in the windows of a few apartments, televisions watched or slept before, and he worried someone would notice him, but for the most part the buildings were dark. If someone did see him the downpour would hide his features.

He lost sight of her as she stepped into the building's shadowed entrance. He forgot about being noticed and moved faster, drew near enough to see that each apartment had a wall sconce next to the door, but only a couple were turned on, lighting the tunneled stairwell that split the building in half front to back. It wasn't a lot of light but it was enough to see the woman tramping up the stairs, her back toward him. If she turned at the top of the stairs she'd be looking right at him, so he ran forward as she neared the top of the flight, her footfalls loud above. Just before she reached the top he stepped into the stairwell and halted against the wall. His heart thumped so hard he felt like the increased pressure might blow his eardrums.

Calm...

You've got to follow if you want to see which apartment she goes into...

Her footsteps continued to trudge upward. Eyes raised, he slid forward and saw her step off the stairs onto the landing far above him before she turned toward the back of the building. A moment later keys jingled, the metallic sound carried through the air.

Jon choked down the nervous bile in the back of his throat and sprinted toward the stairs. His shoes slapped quietly against the concrete as he ran, changed to muffled thumps as he took the treads two at a time.

He slowed close to the third floor landing, head swinging as he searched for her. A narrowing crack of light at the far end of the stairwell disappeared a moment later as the door met the jamb.

Jon slumped against the railing, leg muscles quivering, had to sit down on the steps so he didn't tumble down them. He was overwhelmed by what he had done, by the recklessness of it.

But he knew where she lived.

So?

The insidious question sucked away the sense of success that had filled him, made him aware for the first time that he was wet and uncomfortable. So what if he knew where she lived? The knowledge wouldn't make Lee better. It would only nurse the grudge that Jon had toward the man and woman who'd taken away his son.

Jon forced himself upright. Water dripped off his fingertips as he trudged up the last steps and walked across the landing until he stood in front of the door she'd entered. The sconce outside of the door was off, but there was more than enough light to see the number on the door.

Eleven.

Jon stood dripping before the door, torn between the desire to run and the alluring fantasy of knocking on the door and confronting her, telling her he knew what she and her friend had done, demanding that she tell him where the man was and that they turn themselves in.

He realized with a start that his fingers were just inches from the knob. He snatched them back as if from a burning stove.

Even if I did it, even if I could, Lee would still be in a coma...

Jon took a step back.

Building One, apartment eleven.

Calm...

He needed to think. That was what he needed to do more than anything. Think long and hard about what was right for Lee. Lee was what mattered. Not him or Sarah. Lee.

Jon turned away from the door and walked back to the stairs, descended to the ground floor and without hesitation walked through the pouring rain to the Volvo. He got in, unconcerned about the water that puddled on the floor and seat. He backed out of the spot, turning over the information in his head again and again as he drove home.

NINETEEN

SARAH

"They won again last night, Lee. That's seven in a row since the Red Sox."

The words brushed against the edge of Sarah's nightmare and somehow pulled her out of it. She opened her eyes and saw Jon sitting on the edge of Lee's bed, their hands touching. Dim morning light leached through the room's lone window. Huddled in the big chair and still sleep confused, she tried to forget the dream Lee lifeless in her arms as she struggled up the hill, Lee lost and injured in the darkness, Lee flying through the air and hitting the tree.

Jon's back was to her, his shirt speckled by rain. His damp hair was still as black as the day she'd met him, but he'd gained weight since the accident. No more than a few pounds around the middle, but still, it was the only weight she'd seen him put on in their thirteen years together.

He gave Lee the play by play and she found herself

listening even though she already knew what had happened, had watched the game on the television in Lee's room before she went to sleep. Lee had come along and baseball had permeated her life to the point where she kept track of every Nationals game, watched the race for the pennant, even pulled up videos for Lee to watch. Sarah Young, formerly Tate, who had avoided sports and the jocks who played them for as long as she could remember, had become a baseball fanatic. And that had been more than fine, had been wonderful, because it was part of what had defined them as a family, part of the cement that had held them together.

If only he hadn't taken the parkway...

Always she came back to it. Because of his stupid desire to take the scenic route he'd made that turn and nothing would ever be the same. She couldn't move past it. She couldn't forgive him no matter how many times he apologized. She wanted to hate herself for being unable to accept his apologies, but she couldn't, and nothing she did could change the way she felt.

Sarah sat up in the chair and the sweater she'd been knitting the night before slid to the floor with a clack of needles. Jon glanced over his shoulder at the noise and met her gaze. She realized she was still attracted to him. Even after what he'd done, even though she couldn't see a path to forgiveness, she still loved him, even if it wasn't the love it had been. It sounded like a cheesy line from one of those country records Jon's dad had always listened to, but she guessed love just wasn't enough sometimes.

She took a deep breath and said, "How long have you been here?"

Jon stared at her for a moment longer, then lowered his eyes and turned back to Lee. "Maybe ten minutes."

Sarah glanced at the clock again. "You're running late."

"I didn't get much sleep."

"Why?"

Jon let go of Lee's hand and slid off the bed back to the floor. He started toward her and then pulled up short and took half a step back, couldn't look her in the eyes. "Because I found her."

"You did?" Sarah asked. She was on her feet even though she didn't remember standing, the fuzziness of sleep gone in a flash. "You're sure?"

"Positive. I didn't remember what the tattoo was, but when I saw her, I didn't have any doubt. It was her."

Careful, Sissy. Remember what we talked about...

"Where?"

"A place in Arlington called the Hill. I stopped there... randomly... and when I went in there she was. Right behind the bar, serving drinks. It was a butterfly tattoo on her cheek. A butterfly."

"Did you call the police?"

Jon cleared his throat and shook his head. "No. I—"

"You what?"

His words came out in a rush. "I stayed at the bar until she left and then I followed her home."

"You saw where she lives?"

Jon swallowed and nodded. Sarah reached out, almost put her hand on his forearm before she pulled back.

He noticed but only said, "It's an apartment complex about ten minutes from the bar. Shady Acres. Building one, unit eleven. It's just down the road from our house."

"You're sure it was her? Absolutely sure?"

Jon nodded again. "Yes. Absolutely."

He found her. He actually found her... "Did she see you?"

"No. At least not when I followed her home. I don't think so anyway. But she saw me at the bar. I ordered from her."

"Do you think she recognized you?"

"It didn't seem like she did."

"And you didn't say anything about the accident?"

"No." Jon hesitated then asked, "What do you think we should do? Do you think we should call the police? We don't have any proof."

Careful, Sissy. You haven't seen Lee since the loading dock, and if you mess this up you'll never see him again...

"No," Sarah said with a gentle shake of her head. She hated to admit it, but her mother was right. She'd thought Lee was a hallucination at first, but she'd replayed his appearance behind the loading dock over and over and over and she no longer doubted he'd been real, that he'd come to her because she was the only one who could help him. "No, we shouldn't call the police. Not yet anyway."

"Then what?"

"I need to think about it for a couple of days."

Jon raised his eyebrows. "But what if she leaves or something?"

"She's got a job. She's got an apartment. She won't be going anywhere that quickly. I need time to think about the best way to approach her."

"You think that's what we should do? Talk to her?"

"Maybe. I'm not sure." She reached out again and this time she rested her hand on Jon's arm. "Don't go back to the bar or to her apartment. We keep away from her until I figure out what we should do. Okay?"

Jon glanced at her hand and then nodded. "Okay."

Sarah dropped her hand. "Now hurry, before you're late for work."

Jon nodded, went and kissed Lee on the forehead, and then hurried out of the room. She watched him go with a flutter building in her stomach.

Good, Sissy. Good. Now it's time to give the bartender a visit, just like we talked about...

TWENTY

HARVEY

After the bust-out Harvey stayed late at the station—he finished all the operation paperwork so he could take the next day off, then took a few minutes to look up Jon and Sarah Young's address.

He didn't make it home until after midnight, wasn't in the house for two minutes before he counted the cash. One stack was mostly hundreds—lucky indeed—and the total was just over nine grand. Not enough to get rid of Nonna's problems, but enough that he wouldn't have to worry about money for the next four or five months. Enough that he forgot about Dave, forgot about the kid, and slept through the night.

THE NEXT MORNING the rain was still coming down and the kid was nowhere in sight.

The ball... it was just the stress over Nonna and Robertson, Harvey thought as he drove away from his house. *I imagined how big it was...*

The rain was falling in heavy sheets by the time he parked outside the Young's. He squinted through the rain at the house, just another unremarkable seventies rancher on a street full of them. A green Subaru was parked in the driveway in front of the open garage.

What if they're both at work, Harvey? Not the best time to show up...

The open garage and the Subaru argued against that possibility.

What if he's in there... Some school closings had already been announced on the radio because of potential flooding. The possibility that the kid was so close made his ballsack tighten.

He'd been certain he had to confront the kid's parents, but parked outside their house it seemed like the worst thing he could do. The kid might not have told them anything yet, but if Harvey showed up at his front door surely he'd spill everything. And if he got caught, Nonna would be the one to suffer the most.

And so what if he isn't home? Anything you say will make them ask the kid... Showing up at their house was stupid. He'd just have to deal with the kid. The thought made his stomach twist, but Harvey knew it was right—he couldn't involve the parents. He was reaching for the shifter when the entry door inside the garage opened.

Harvey froze, sure the opening door would reveal the kid and his baseball.

As big as the moon...

The rain made seeing anything difficult, but Harvey could tell the person that walked down the stairs into the garage was a woman. Sarah Young most likely. He exhaled, hadn't realized he was holding his breath. Heart thudding in his chest, Harvey watched as the woman opened a red umbrella and left the shelter of the garage. She got in the sedan, closed the garage door as she backed out, and then drove away, her taillights fading quickly in the downpour.

Not really thinking about what he was doing, Harvey started the Cherokee and followed after her.

THE CAR TURNED into Rainbow Pines and pulled into a spot near the front of the facility.

Harvey followed and parked at the back, left the Cherokee running as he watched the woman head inside beneath the red umbrella. He contemplated following her immediately then decided against it.

She disappeared inside as he took his phone out of his coat and googled Rainbow Pines. The search results took a while to appear, the service no doubt affected by the rain. The first entry had the right address, had the heading *Rainbow Pines — Short- and Long-Term Care Facility.* Harvey slept the phone without reading more.

Gomer home... the kind of place Nonno might end up...

He thought of leaving, sure she was just visiting a grandparent, maybe even a mom or dad, but his gut told him to follow her. Pointless or not, he'd been a cop long enough to know it was a bad idea to ignore his instincts.

Harvey pulled his umbrella from the door and got out of the Cherokee into the rain, dodged the deeper puddles on his way across the parking lot.

Most of Rainbow Pines was low and rectangular, covered in cream-tinted stucco and lots of narrow, vertical windows, but the part of the building that surrounded the entrance was two stories of glass. The double doors whooshed aside and he stepped into a large, open atrium, the light coming through all that glass dim from the rain but still comforting as he closed his umbrella. The paint on the walls was fresh, the floor polished and clean, the air redolent with the smell of flowers that were in vases throughout the room. To the left and right were seating areas with new, modern-looking sofas and chairs, the reception area straight ahead.

This wouldn't be such a bad place for Nonno... He could only imagine the sticker shock though. The future spun out before him, the money pouring into a place like the Rainbow Pines faster than he could steal it.

Remember why you're here, Harvey...

The woman was nowhere in sight.

Harvey walked up to the reception desk where a middle-aged blond woman with beautiful eyes and an unremarkable face smiled congenially at him from her chair.

"May I help you, sir?" she asked.

"I sure hope so," he said, dialing up Harv as he gave her his best smile. "I was supposed to meet a friend and I'm running a few minutes late. Her name is Sarah Young. Do you know if she's here already?"

"You just missed her," she said, tapping a clipboard next to her. "She was the last one to sign in."

"That's good," said Harvey. He leaned closer and lowered his voice. "I promised her I'd be on time, but, you know... it's a bit of a problem for me."

"Me too," said the woman in an exaggerated whisper, winking one of those beautiful eyes. She glanced at the clipboard again. "She's only been here a few minutes, so I'm sure you're fine."

"Phew. Is okay if I go on back?"

"Of course. I just need you to sign in if you don't mind," she said, handing him the clipboard and attached pen.

"Not at all," said Harvey. He quickly jotted down a fake name and address—it was an alias he'd used during operations so it was fresh in his mind. "I'm afraid I can't remember the room number. Four-something. I'm as lousy at remembering directions as I am at being on time."

"No worries. Let me see." She typed away on her computer for a moment. "It's actually Room 198. You'll go down the hallway to your right, take the second left and go through a set of double doors. Take the next right and Mr. Young's room will be the last numbered door on the left, just past the waiting area. If you make it to the door marked storage you've gone too far."

"Thanks so much," said Harvey with another smile. "Have a good day!"

"You too. Enjoy your visit to Rainbow Pines!"

Visiting her in-laws, Harvey thought as he followed the receptionist's directions down the wide, spotless corridors, passing well-scrubbed orderlies and a few nurses, the doors to the rooms closed.

Harvey stopped just short of room 198. The muffled sound of a voice came from the other side. He listened for a moment then walked back to the waiting area he'd just passed, sat down on the couch, picked up a random magazine, and waited.

PERHAPS TEN MINUTES later Sarah Young emerged

from Room 198, her red umbrella at her side. Seeing her sent him back in time to that night on the Accotink Parkway.

She walked past Harvey without a glance, her face set and determined. She was pretty, but a bit plain, her hair straight, her body slim but not curvy. She moved quickly away and a moment later disappeared around the corner that led to the building entrance.

Well, you've seen where she went, Harvey. What now?

Instinct had told him to follow her inside Rainbow Pines, but he felt no such compulsion to see where she went next. That left only one option.

Harvey put down the magazine, walked to Room 198 and paused outside of the closed door. He looked down the corridor to the left, but the only person in sight was a retreating janitor pushing a mop bucket. There was a small desk farther down the hall, perhaps a nurses station, but it was abandoned. To the right the hall ended at an emergency exit.

Harvey depressed the door lever, envisioned a wrinkled old man staring vacantly at the ceiling, and prepared a lie in case the occupant was aware of his presence. But when the door swung all the way open there was no old man—only a boy whose skull was flat on one side, a boy with his eyes closed.

A boy Harvey recognized.

TWENTY-ONE

ELLE

Elle was halfway through her third screwdriver of the morning—she'd woke early for some reason, didn't have a damn thing to do with Harvey's visit to the Hill the night before—when someone knocked at the door.

If it's Harvey at the door door door gonna knock him to the floor floor floor...

But when she opened the door it wasn't Harvey—and if she felt a twinge of disappointment it was just too much vodka onboard—only a woman beneath a dripping red umbrella, the steady rain falling from a sky so dark it looked more like evening outside than almost noon. The woman stared at Elle, her eyes wide.

"If you're a Jehovah's Witness you best just turn around," Elle said. "Nobody here needs saving."

"I was hoping I could speak to you for a few minutes," the woman replied, her words as stiff as her back. As she spoke her eyes narrowed in a way that Elle didn't care for. It gave the woman's unremarkable face a pinched, shrewy look.

Two screwdrivers ago she would've slammed the door in the woman's face, but drunken boredom prevailed. "About what?"

"My son," the shrew said after a brief hesitation.

"I'm not following, lady," Elle said as she raised her glass only to find it empty. She let her hand drop with disgust.

Too much think think think need another drink drink drink...

The shrew's thin lips pursed. "My husband saw you last night. He recognized you by the..." She trailed off and touched her cheek.

It took Elle a moment to realize the shrew meant the butterfly, the shitty tattoo she'd gotten after a drunken birthday party when she was fifteen.

Recognized... ? What? Then the various ethanol-soaked cogs in her head turned and aligned and she remembered the Asian guy staring at her from across the bar, remembered the blood mask, remembered the kid Harvey described to her, and what the woman said—*recognized* —clicked into place.

"Get the hell out of here," Elle said as she retreated into the apartment and started to slam the door.

The shrew moved with surprising speed, dropped her umbrella and stepped into the doorway to take the swinging door on her shoulder. Elle was so shocked she watched dumbly as the door bounced off the shrew, who only gave a small grunt as she pushed farther inside.

"I'm not going anywhere," the shrew said. "Does the man that was with you that night live here too?"

"If you don't get out right now, I'm calling the police," Elle said as she backed farther into the apartment, wishing there was something she could pick up to threaten the woman. But in the sparse apartment there was nothing. She thought of throwing the empty glass at the shrew's head, but she'd probably just miss.

"You're not," said the shrew and Elle could only watch the apartment door close, the umbrella abandoned outside. The shrew wasn't a large woman, shorter than Elle and maybe thinner, but she stepped forward as if she topped Elle by a foot or more. "If you do, I'll tell them what you did."

"I don't know what you're talking about, lady."

"*Don't you dare lie!*" the shrew hissed, spittle on her lips, her whole body shaking. "You know exactly what you did to me. To my son!"

Elle stared at her and backed farther away, tried to think of what to do. But she couldn't. Every thought was a dead end, except one. "I need a drink."

Disgust filled the shrew's face. Elle ignored it and turned toward the kitchen. The shrew followed her part of the way then stopped.

At the counter, Elle picked up the bottle of cheap vodka —using it as a weapon didn't cross her mind—and poured a shot into her glass. Then she thought about how there was no landline and she didn't know where her mobile was, and added a second shot. She looked at the shrew, her face full of rage, then raised the glass and swallowed the booze in one long pull. She'd have to talk the shrew back out the door.

"Do you want a drink? I don't have a lot to mix with here, but I can stir you up something if you don't like it neat or with orange juice."

"Of course I don't," the shrew barked.

Elle nodded. "Okay. Tell me again what you want and why you think I can help?" Even if she'd known where to find Harvey, she wouldn't have given him up so quickly. Partly because he'd warned her—she didn't think he was as hard as he tried to come off, but she suspected he was hard enough to make her life miserable—but mostly because she knew Harvey wouldn't think much of someone who folded that easy.

The shrew's mouth tightened, and when she spoke she sounded like she was talking to a child. "We were in an accident on the Accotink Parkway and my son was injured. I don't remember much, but my husband heard your friend say something about bartending. That, and he saw the tattoo on your face. He didn't think it was a butterfly, but when he saw you last night, he knew."

What can I say say say butterfly gave me away way way...

Elle considered admitting she'd been there that night. She could claim it'd been a one night stand—*not even a claim, really*—and that she'd never even known the man's name, couldn't help. She'd met him at the bar, thought he was hot, and the two of them had gotten fucked up and then gotten in the accident. He'd been driving and afterward he'd told her not to tell anyone, had dropped her off at home, and she'd never seen him again.

She couldn't do it though. Not to the shrew. If she told the woman she'd been there then she wouldn't be able to get the shrew out of the apartment. She could see it in her face. "I'm afraid your husband got it wrong, lady. I've never been near the Accotink Parkway in my life. He must have imagined everything. Go ahead and call the police if you want. They'll bother me, but they'll find out I'm telling the truth."

The shrew's face grew angrier, but Elle doubled down.

"I'm sorry your son ended up in a coma. I am. I'm not a parent so I can't imagine what that must be like, but I'm sure it's fucking terrible. And you want the people that did it to pay. I get that too. But you're looking in the wrong place."

The vodka singing in her veins, Elle walked out from around the kitchen counter, passed the shrew and went to the door, pulled it open. She was sure it was the right thing to do. "If you need anything else come on back and ask. I'm sorry I couldn't help."

The shrew stared at Elle, her mouth clenched and hard, but she said nothing.

Elle met her gaze, knew that if she looked away the shrew would read it as a sign of guilt. After a moment the shrew's face softened. She didn't look convinced, but she didn't look like she was chewing rocks anymore either. Maybe just dirt. Elle took the slightest step backward, inviting her once again out of the door, and the shrew nodded, as if she'd come to a decision.

"Okay," the shrew said, nodding as she walked toward the door. But she paused next to Elle, her eyes staring outside the apartment. "There's only one problem."

"What?" Elle asked, the question startled out of her.

The shrew's eyes slid onto her own, glinted like hard little diamonds. "I never told you my son was in a coma."

Fuck... The curse had barely entered her thoughts before the shrew picked up the ceramic bowl by the front door and swung it toward her head, Elle's keys and money clip falling to the floor. There was no time to scream, only an instant for her alcohol-stunted reflexes to fail her. The bowl crashed into the side of her head and the world went supernovae bright, then dark as night.

TWENTY-TWO

SARAH

The ceramic bowl shattered and the woman slumped to the ground like a marionette whose strings had been cut, half in and half out of the doorway, a small trickle of blood beginning to flow down the side of her head. Sarah stood over her, a jagged fragment of the bowl trembling in her hand, her lips parted, her chest heaving.

No time to waste, Sissy. Get moving...

Sarah dropped the ceramic shard onto the cheap living room carpet. She bent over, grabbed the woman by the armpits and pulled, leaned backwards against the weight, and a moment later the woman's feet cleared the threshold and then the path the door would sweep. Sarah dropped her to carpet.

She walked past the unconscious bartender and picked up the umbrella she'd dropped outside the door, glanced outside to make sure there were no witnesses. The dim landing was still empty.

Sarah backed into the apartment and closed the door, propped the umbrella against the wall, then knelt and extended a shaking hand toward the woman's head.

She knew all along. Knew and tried to lie about it...

Sarah was sure if she'd left, the woman would've been out of the apartment within a day, probably out of the city, too. Then they would've been back where they started, with nothing. No justice for her Lee, who'd come to her so she'd know what to do.

The woman's thick curls were spread around her head like a halo. Sarah plowed her fingers through the hair until she found the impact site, a hard knot the size of an apricot, the skin split down the middle and oozing blood.

I wonder if I hit her too hard?

You saw how much she was drinking, Sissy. The bitch won't even feel it when she comes to...

Sarah doubted that. Nobody could take that kind of a hit and not feel it later. No matter.

Gotta find something to tie her up with...

The insanity of what she was doing flitted through her mind, but she didn't care—it was what Lee wanted. The whore and her friend had put Lee in a coma and she wasn't going to sit back and let them get away with it, let them live their lives like nothing happened while Lee sat in that goddamn bed day after day after day never moving. They deserved to suffer just like him.

Outside the rain began to fall harder.

SARAH WENT into the kitchen and started pulling open

drawers, searching for something to restrain the woman. On her third try she found a stack of mismatched kitchen towels. She grabbed all of them and hurried back to the woman, who still hadn't moved.

Gotta hurry... no telling how long she'll be out...

Hopefully the alcohol and the blow to the head would combine to keep the woman unconscious for a long time, but Sarah couldn't bank on it.

Sarah took two of the towels and knotted them together, then knelt and rolled the woman onto one shoulder, her head flopping. She pulled the woman's arms into place and used the knotted towels to bind the woman's wrists, her hands still shaking. Once that was done, she rolled up a third towel and stuck it between the woman's slack jaws. She wrapped the towel ends around the woman's head and tied them off.

Maybe I should keep her here instead of taking her home?

No, Sissy. A friend or family member might call or show up. Stick to the plan...

The plan made her nervous. She'd texted Jon not long after he left Rainbow Pines and told him she'd gotten a headache and then vomited, told him she didn't want to risk getting Lee sick so she was going to stay at the house until she was better. Best if he stayed away from her as well— she'd pack him some spare clothes and his bathroom bag and run them back to Rainbow Pines, would have the staff put them in Lee's room. He could stay with Lee until she was better.

You can't control anything here, Sissy. But you can manage your husband. The plan will work...

But she still had to get the woman out of the apartment and into her car.

Sarah went to the nearest window and split the dusty mini-blinds, peered out as the plastic slats quivered beneath her fingers. The rain fell in undulating sheets, pounded against the asphalt in the parking lot so hard the water bounced back into the air. She let the blinds close.

If I can get her down the stairs and out to the parking lot I'll be fine—the rain is coming down so hard nobody will be able to see a thing...

She had to go immediately though. If the rain let up or stopped the chance of getting caught would be higher.

Sarah opened the door a few inches, then went to the woman's head, bent over, and put her forearms beneath the woman's armpits and lifted. She struggled for a moment, but eventually made it upright, the woman's head slumped across one arm. Sarah backed away from the door, pulled the woman around until she could get a foot in the door and kick it open. She dragged the woman out of the apartment, almost hit her flopping head on the door frame.

The rain outside the building was so heavy she could barely see the cars in the parking lot. She left the door open and lurched to the stairs, exposed to any curious eyes until she could get into the rain.

Certain someone would see them and call out, Sarah's heart pounded in her chest as she descended the first flight of stairs, moving backwards as fast as she dared, the woman's feet thumping down every step and threatening to disrupt her balance. By the time Sarah made it to the second flight the muscles in her arms and thighs were burning, and halfway down she began to doubt whether she could make it to the ground floor, much less the car.

Stop whining and do it, Sissy. Lee's depending on you...

Panting through clenched jaws, Sarah tried to ignore her aching muscles and sped up even though it made her feel like she was going to fall at any moment. She turned quickly through the final landing and started down the last flight of steps, her arms quivering. Two steps from the bottom, her legs gave way and she stumbled backwards, turned just in time to prevent the worst of the fall with her left hand. An instant later the bartender's weight collapsed on top of her and the woman moaned.

Get up, Sissy! Now!

Sarah wanted desperately to just lay there, to let her muscles rest, but the little moan that escaped past the towel in the woman's mouth spurred her on. She shot back up to her feet, carrying the woman with her, and backed toward the parking lot as fast as she possibly could. A moment later they emerged from under the building overhang into the downpour and she was instantly drenched—it was like jumping into a pool.

Sarah dragged the woman across the flooded asphalt—her thick, curly hair now a limp towel draped over her head—and, after some difficulty, opened one of the Subaru's rear doors and shoved the woman into the backseat, only banging her around a bit before she got her inside, her face shoved against the far door. Sarah moved the bartender's feet out of the way of the door and closed her in.

Her legs still burning, Sarah trotted back to the apartment, took the stairs two treads at a time, water continuing to pour off her despite being out of the rain, and hoped no one decided to come out and watch the storm or have a smoke.

No one did and a moment later she was back in the apartment, the door closed behind her. She ignored the water dripping off her clothes, picked up the last towel she'd left on the floor and walked to the kitchen. Using the towel, she put away the orange juice so it didn't look like the woman had disappeared in the middle of what she was doing. Then she retrieved the pieces of ceramic bowl from the carpet and wiped them down quickly before throwing them in the kitchen trashcan.

Make sure she lives here alone, Sissy...

Cursing herself for nearly forgetting, Sarah ran to the apartment's bathroom. She used the towel to open the vanity drawers, but there was nothing inside any of them to suggest that more than one person lived in the apartment, much less a man.

I should check the bedroom...

No, Sissy. Just get out of here. We'll find him soon enough...

On her way back to the apartment door, Sarah picked up the keys and money clip that had fallen to the floor—carefully, by the edges so she wouldn't leave any fingerprints—put them back on the table, and grabbed her umbrella.

She took one last look around, then wiped the inside of the doorknob and opened the door. It wasn't raining as hard as before, but it was still a downpour and no one was in sight. Using the towel, she turned the door's button lock, then closed the door, wiped down the outside of the knob, and ran back to the Subaru without looking back.

TWENTY-THREE

ELLE

The pounding was the first thing Elle became aware of.

It wasn't a hangover—she'd have recognized that right away. This was a different beast. Her eyes squeezed shut, it resonated through her skull like an alarm bell and when she moved her head throbs of pain made her stomach churn. She recoiled from the queasiness, afraid to move again in case she barfed all over her bed.

Gotta get some pills...

The thought of moving was frightening but she had to get something to help with the pain. She cracked open her eyes at the same time she tried to sit up, her head pounding like a motherfucker.

But she couldn't sit up. Her arms were caught on something.

Confused, drunk, and still full of pain, she rolled her throbbing head to one side, squinted at her arm, and saw there was a rope tied around her wrist. She flexed the arm in disbelief and saw the rope raise off the bed and tighten, her arm moving no more than a couple of inches.

That's when it all came rushing back, the woman in her apartment, that *shrew* swinging the bowl at her head.

Elle jerked her arm again, harder, and still it wouldn't budge. A bloom of fear expanded in her chest as she swung her head the other way and saw that her other wrist was bound as well. The pain forgotten as adrenaline flowed into her veins, Elle raised her head and looked at her feet, saw two more ropes stretching to the corners of a bed she finally recognized as not her own.

She began to scream.

ELLE FLUNG her head back and forth, curls flying, her arms and legs jerking at the ropes that circled her wrists and ankles. Her world narrowed to the four points binding her to the bed, a world where there was no room for rational thought, only an animal instinct to escape that precluded logic. If she could've gotten her teeth to the knots at wrist or ankle she would've chewed at them until her lips and gums bled and her teeth loosened in their sockets.

The shrew ran into the room and Elle screamed louder, strained against the ropes until her muscles burned and her joints felt like they were separating.

The shrew reached the bedside and—despite Elle's thrashing—stuffed something rough in her mouth. Elle tried to spit it out but the shrew looped another piece of fabric over her mouth and then tied it off behind her head, holding the wadded cloth in.

Elle's heart raced, thumped so fast she thought it might

explode out of chest. Her breath came fast and then faster still, until she strained to breathe past the gag, unable to suck in enough air through her nose. It wasn't enough and she felt like she was drowning, there wasn't enough air, she couldn't get enough air around the gag, and so she breathed faster and harder, made it impossible to get enough. Spots appeared in her vision, shooting toward her as if they were piercing her eyes and tunneling into her brain like parasitic worms.

The shrew was talking and gesturing at her, but Elle was too far gone to understand the sights and sounds coming at her. The shooting spots grew brighter and brighter and then they too were swallowed by darkness.

ELLE WOKE the second time to find the room empty once more. She was disoriented for a moment, head throbbing, vision spinning, and then the ropes and the gag placed her squarely back in reality. Her heart—still beating fast but no longer galloping—picked up a step as she struggled to pull air into her lungs.

Get your shit together...

She breathed through her nose, inhaled and exhaled as slowly as she could. She'd never had a panic attack and the thought of it happening again scared her.

No chance of getting out of this if you can't stay conscious...

That was some heroic bullshit. How in the fuck could she possibly get out? She was tied spread eagle to a bed, could barely utter a sound because of the gag in her mouth, and had no idea where she was.

Bad morning to get shit-faced. Sober I might have had a

*chance against that maniac... or at least come to before she
could drag me all the way back to her lair.*

Not that it mattered. Done was done.

A memory swam through her mind. *She wants to know
where Harvey is...*

But she couldn't lead the shrew to Harvey, didn't even
know his last name, much less where he lived.

*I've got nothing. I can't give her what she wants and I'm
going to die here...*

No, Elle thought, shaking her head. *Fuck that and fuck
this freak...*

Feeling better, with her breathing under control and the
threat of another panic attack diminished for the moment,
she raised her aching head and examined the room.

She could hear a steady rain outside and the air was
filled with the perfume smell of powdered carpet cleaner.
A fan was motionless overhead, while a single window on
the wall to her left let a shred of pale light into the room
past the edges of blinds that looked like they might be
made of real wood. There were two doors, one past the end
of the bed, the other on her right. Both were closed, one
perhaps a closet or bathroom. A fancy dresser sat against
the wall to the right, its shiny top bare except for a glass
vase of fake flowers. The big bed had a wooden frame that
matched the dresser and a pair of nightstands. It had to be
the shrew's house. She wondered where the husband was
hiding.

Elle looked at the knotted rope around her left wrist and
started breathing fast again, closed her eyes until her
breaths evened out. If she lost control, the rag in her mouth
might shift and make her gag, and with no one to help her
she might retch over and over again until she finally puked
and drowned in her own rank vomit, heading to whatever

miserable afterlife there might be with the taste of vodka and orange juice filling her mouth.

Hell if I'm making this easy for her...

The rope was thin, maybe a quarter of an inch, but still too large to break. That left the knot, which pressed against the inside of her wrist. She was no Boy Scout, but there didn't seem to be anything exotic about it. Nothing but a couple of square knots with an inch or two of leftover rope sticking out. She bent her wrist and flexed her fingers toward the knot, was able to touch it but not enough to do anything other than feel it brush against her fingertips.

I shouldn't have thrashed around before...

She'd probably tightened the goddamn knots. Her wrists and ankles sure as hell hurt where the ropes dug into and dimpled the flesh. She flexed her fingers again, wondered if she was getting enough blood supply past the rope. There was no deadness or pins and needles, but she didn't think she'd been tied up long. She looked at her other wrist, couldn't even graze that knot.

For the first time in her life she wished she was one of those double-jointed freaks.

I'm not getting out of these damn things...

Not by herself. Anything she did to try and loosen the knots would only tighten them more and then she might be looking at losing a hand or a foot if the shrew left her restrained for a long time.

Elle felt panic brushing against the edge of her mind again and forced herself to breathe deeper. She looked up at the fan, inhaled and exhaled slowly, tried and failed to ignore the rag in her mouth. She attempted to force it out with her tongue, but the loop that ran behind her head made it impossible.

She was about to raise her head to get a look at the ropes

binding her ankles when the door past the end of the bed opened and the shrew came in again.

Ding dong dead dead dead tied to the witch's bed bed bed...

The shrew stared at her for a long time, her eyes narrow, her mouth set in a straight line. There was a hardness to the woman that reminded Elle of her father, a man whose face held the same blank expression whether he was teaching you how to throw a ball or beating you senseless.

"I'll take the gag out," said the shrew after a moment. "But if you scream it goes right back in. Do you understand?"

Elle wanted to tell the shrew to go fuck herself, but she nodded.

The shrew bent over and jerked the looping gag down around Elle's neck, then she grabbed a corner of the rag that was in her mouth and plucked it out. Elle gulped in a huge rush of air, reveling in the feeling of a clear mouth.

"There was a man in the car with you that night," the shrew said as she looked down at Elle. "Tell me who he is and where I can find him."

The only way out of the ropes was if the shrew untied her, but the vodka and her tongue betrayed her as usual. "Look lady, I'm sorry about what happened to your kid. But he's okay now, so why don't you just let it go?"

The shrew's eyes narrowed.

"*Okay?*" repeated the shrew, her voice quiet. "Okay." She spoke as if she were tasting the word, trying to understand what it meant. "My son is lying in a hospital bed, unresponsive, with a piece of his skull removed so that his swollen brain won't be damaged even farther. He has a feeding tube stuck into his stomach. He's got a catheter and a urinary tract that keeps getting infected. He has to be moved so that he doesn't get bed sores. And you have the nerve to say he's... *okay?*"

Elle answered without thought, admitted what she couldn't tell Harvey the night before. "I just saw him the other day at the park. He was playing baseball." *Ah fuck...* Her jaws hadn't clacked shut before the shrew leaned forward and slapped her so hard across the cheek that Elle's head lifted off the mattress. The throbbing in her skull ratcheted up a few notches and—feeling almost sober—she wondered if she would pass out again.

"How dare you," the shrew said from between clenched teeth, her chest heaving, the hand that slapped Elle balled into a quivering fist. "If you ever say anything about my son again, I'll kill you. Do you understand me?"

Elle stared back, her mind a knot of anger, fear, and confusion, all blurred by vodka, but if she knew anything it was how to survive. She nodded.

"Good," the shrew said. "Now tell me where I can find the man that was in the car with you."

Elle swallowed, and—drunk or not—could barely believe the words that came out of her mouth. "How do I know you won't just kill me once you find him?"

"Were you the one driving?"

"No."

"So—assuming you're not lying—you don't have anything to worry about. Help me find him and I'll let you go."

That didn't mesh with the expression she saw on the woman's face, the expression that reminded her so much of her father. Elle didn't believe a word the shrew was saying.

So there she was, tied to the damn bed, forced to choose between two losing options. Well, the bitch had hit her over the head, abducted her, tied her up and then slapped her, so damn if she'd do what the shrew wanted. She'd out-toughed her father and he made this crazy bitch look like a saint. She'd sooner die than give the shrew what she wanted. "Look, I don't know where he lives. I don't even know his last name. But his first name is Harvey. That's everything I know."

"That's not good enough. It's not enough to find him."

"It's all I know."

"Then you'll be here for a while."

Elle held the shrew's gaze for a moment, then said, "Rot in hell, lady."

TWENTY-FOUR

HARVEY

Harvey walked out of Rainbow Pines in a daze. The rain had eased while he'd been inside, but it still soaked his hair and coat in moments, his umbrella forgotten in his hand.

If Lee Young is in there, then who's been following me? Does he have a twin brother? A cousin?

He wondered again if he was losing his mind, had been seeing things that weren't really there. *You knew he was still in that bed. You knew and so you kept seeing him. Him and that baseball...* He'd met more weird people than he cared to think about in his years on the police force, and weird people had weird things happen to them. It was just natural for them, a sort of magnetism—perhaps that's what he'd become. Another weirdo who saw things that weren't there.

No.

No, he wasn't the weirdo type. He didn't have visions.

He didn't believe in those kinds of things. He hadn't seen a ghost or some kind of spirit.

He'd seen a kid.

The question was, what kid?

HARVEY SAT in the Cherokee and watched the rain bead on the windshield.

Worrying about the kid following him around had been bad enough, now he wouldn't be able to stop thinking about the boy slowly rotting inside Rainbow Pines. The boy he'd put there.

I've got to end this somehow... He had to focus on work. On Robertson. But he knew he wouldn't be able to do that until the kid left him alone.

He needed to talk to Elle again. Fidgety as she'd been the other day, she'd known something. He was sure of it.

It was time to find out what.

HARVEY MADE it to Shady Acres just after noon, parked right in front of Elle's building a spot away from the beater she'd tossed a bag into before their disastrous trip down the Accotink parkway.

He ran through the rain and climbed the stairs swiftly, thought of how he'd tell her the news. But when he knocked, she didn't answer.

"Wake up, Elle!" he shouted, banged even harder on the door as the wind-driven rain slashed into him. "It's Harvey!"

Still no answer. *Probably sleeping off some kind of binge...*

He tried the door and was surprised when it turned smoothly beneath his palm.

"Elle?" he called as he pushed inside the dark apartment. "Elle!"

When there was still no answer, Harvey groped for a switch. The light illuminated a scene much the same as he remembered from his one night there, the apartment spare and depressing.

Not wanting to draw an audience he closed the door behind him, water dripping off his clothes onto the worn carpet.

Harvey didn't call out again, walked to the bedroom where he expected to see Elle passed out. But when he looked through the door there were only rumpled sheets on the bed and discarded clothes on the floor. He checked the bathroom, but it was empty as well.

He went back to the kitchen and looked around. There was booze on the counter but that wasn't unusual. There was some water on the floor but in this weather that didn't mean a damn thing. No, what was unusual was her car out front and the door unlocked. It was unlikely she'd decided to take a walk on such a nasty day, but she might be in a friend's nearby apartment. But if either of those things had happened, Harvey thought Elle would've locked the door. Even if she didn't own a big TV or a computer, the residents of a place like Shady Acres would be just as likely to steal food or booze.

Harvey was about to do a second search of the apartment when his cell phone buzzed.

It was Dave.

Shit...

"What's up?" Harvey asked as his eyes continued to scan the apartment.

"You got time for lunch and a beer?"

Dave sounded normal enough, but Harvey sensed something in the undercurrents of his partner's voice and any doubts he'd had about what Dave saw evaporated. "I've got lunch plans already, but I can swing a beer."

"Good enough," Dave said. "Macho Burrito in half an hour?"

"Yeah," Harvey said. He hung up, tried to ignore the tightening of his guts.

One thing at a time...

He walked through the apartment again, was about to give up when he noticed keys and a money clip on the table by the door. Harvey went closer, saw that the clip held a few bucks and Elle's driver's license.

She should be here, Harvey thought. *Something's wrong...*

DAVE SAT in their regular booth when Harvey made it to Macho Burrito. There were two Pacificos on the table and the obligatory chips and salsa, which looked untouched. Add that to the little something that was off in his voice earlier and Harvey felt his guts tighten even farther.

"Forgot your umbrella on a day like this?" Dave asked as Harvey dripped into the booth. He didn't smile.

"Been one of those days," Harvey said. He took a long swig of beer, resisted the urge to chug it in one go and order another. "What's up, Dave?"

Dave took a gulp of his beer and scrubbed one hand

through his thinning hair. "I had a meeting with Robertson this morning."

His mind leapt to the worst, but Harvey was determined to let Dave spin out the story on his own terms.

Dave swallowed. "He didn't beat around the goddamn bush. He told me internal affairs had evidence you were on the take and wanted to know if I'd ever noticed you do anything odd."

Oh Nonna...

Harvey forced himself to take just a sip of beer. He'd known the moment might come. Had hoped it wouldn't, but still, he'd known. "What'd you tell him?"

"That I'd never seen anything and that you've never said anything that made me think you were."

Harvey wondered if Dave was wired. It was certainly possible. Internal affairs wasn't above trying to sting one of their own. He didn't think Dave would ever agree to it, but Dave had a wife and kids and Harvey knew who came first.

He looked into Dave's eyes. "You're not sure though, are you?"

"Jesus, Harvey," Dave said. "Are you?"

"In case you haven't noticed, I'm not exactly living a life of luxury," Harvey said.

"Good," Dave said, although the look on his face said he knew Harvey hadn't denied anything. He took a gulp of beer. "He's planning to talk to you tomorrow morning."

"He ask you to tell me that?"

"No, you prick!" Dave barked as he rocked back in his seat, finally sounding like himself. "I'm telling you because you're my partner. I don't know what you did to get their attention but you'd better make sure it was just a misunderstanding."

He had to stay calm, shouldn't assume internal affairs

had enough on him to cause real trouble. He'd lay low and go along with what they asked of him. Sometimes if you didn't dig yourself in any deeper, you could come out on the other side not much worse for wear. Internal affairs scared him a lot less than Robertson. "Robertson tell you what kind of evidence they had?"

"No details. But he said the amounts the dealers have been reporting hasn't been squaring with what's been turned in lately."

"Doesn't mean a damn thing," Harvey said. "They lie all the time. Robertson knows that."

Dave nodded. "Yeah. But you remember Crazy Tom?"

They'd busted Crazy Tom about three months ago for cooking and selling meth. "What about him?"

"It came out later he had a thing for numbers. Had all these notebooks filled with crazy records about everything— the weight of every batch he cooked down to the milligram, the amounts of final product, how he divided it up, how much he sold it all for. *Everything*. Numbers out the ass. Kept real close track of his cash the same way."

"So?" Harvey said, but he already knew what Dave would say next.

"So he said he knew exactly how much was in his place when we busted him, down to the penny. And what we turned in was quite a bit less."

More than Four-thousand less..."That's it?"

Dave shrugged. "That's all Robertson mentioned."

"Okay. Good to know." Harvey finished his beer and slid back out of the booth, took a five dollar bill out of his wallet and set it down on the table, resisted the urge to spill everything to Dave—not just the skimming, but the kid, Elle, everything. He didn't like lying to his partner, especially when Dave probably knew he was lying. They were too close, too familiar. Well, he could keep him out of at least. "Thanks for the warning, Dave. I appreciate it."

Dave stared at him for a moment, then rolled his eyes and finally picked up a tortilla chip that he loaded with salsa. "You'd do the same thing for me, asshole."

TWENTY-FIVE

ELLE

When the shrew left, Elle abandoned the idea of not struggling. If the ropes tightened enough that she cut off the blood supply to a hand then so be it. She wasn't sitting and waiting for the crazy bitch to come back and do god knows what else to her. She'd pissed the shrew off, which might have been a mistake, but fuck it and fuck her.

Gotta be smart... gotta be patient. She didn't have much of either trait, but hey.

Her head still aching, she looked at her right hand again, turned her wrist to check each side of the rope and knot. The rope was smooth, not the rough sort. She supposed that meant it was made from nylon or some poly-something shit. She didn't know if that made any difference in how easy or hard it would be to get free. Maybe since it was smooth she'd have a better chance of sliding a hand out. The knot, like she'd seen earlier, was plain and tight, no gaps. The other end of the rope disappeared below the edge of the mattress, anchored out of sight.

She flexed until the rope was just tight and then twisted her wrist slowly, saw that the rope was still while her wrist spun.

That's gotta be a good thing...

She ignored the urge to pull right away and turned her head to look at the other wrist. She flexed and twisted as before, but the rope moved with her, tighter than the other side. Maybe from when she'd panicked, or maybe because the shrew had tied that knot a bit tighter.

She raised her head to look at the knots around her ankles but couldn't see them very well. A slight wiggle of each leg told her the knots were pretty tight. Unlike the ropes around her wrists, the two binding her ankles were tied around the bedposts where she could see them. She lay her head back down, her neck muscles already tight.

It's the right hand or nothing...

She forced herself to breathe even slower—thank god she wasn't congested or she might be dead already. She listened for sounds of the shrew but heard nothing. She could be gone for all Elle knew, though she doubted the shrew would leave her alone, gagged or not. She wondered where the husband was and if he knew what his insane wife had done.

When she felt calm—which was probably amped up compared to most people—she pulled gently against the rope on her right side, rocking her wrist back and forth at the same time. The rope slipped from her wrist to the base of her hand, the knot against the heel of her palm, and then bound there. She touched her thumb to her pinky finger to narrow her hand and the rope slipped another half an inch before it stuck. Still breathing slow, she pulled harder, continued to rock her wrist, willing the rope to slip past the fat part of her hand and off, but it didn't budge. She felt herself breathing harder, gave into it, and strained as hard as she could, a muffled grunt escaping her mouth as the pain increased.

The rope didn't budge.

Tears started to leak from the corners of her eyes, trailing down her cheeks onto the mattress, and she lost it, thrashed and jerked against the bindings until her muscles ached and she could barely breathe.

Nothing gave way.

TWENTY-SIX

JON

Jon's cell died right before lunch—after spending half the night at the Hill, he'd been so tired he forgot to put it on the charger when he got home.

I should've noticed when Sarah texted me this morning... but he'd been distracted, still wound up about finding the bartender. The entire night was hard to believe, his trip to the bar and her apartment surreal.

He didn't want to risk missing a call from Sarah or from Rainbow Pines, so rather than eat at his desk as he'd been doing lately, he trotted through the rain out to the Volvo and started home. Sarah might have brought his charger to the office, but she didn't need to be out of the house when she was sick. She'd be mad when he showed up, worried about Lee, but he'd dart in and out and everything would be fine.

WHEN JON GOT to the house the garage door was up and Sarah's Subaru was parked in the middle of the double bay—they usually left the garage open since Lee went in and out so often to rifle through his bin of baseball equipment. The neighborhood was safe, so they only put the door down at night and when the house was empty.

He shut off the Volvo and hurried through the rain into the open garage, only slowing when he reached the door to the kitchen. He turned the knob quietly, not wanting to disturb Sarah if she was sleeping on the living room couch.

"Sarah?" he called out in a quiet voice as he stepped into the kitchen. But the only sound that returned his greeting was the ticking of the old clock.

Jon closed the kitchen door gently and went through the living room to the hall, walked quickly past the closed doors of the guest room and Lee's bedroom.

Will he ever sleep in there again? Ever listen to ESPN on the radio while he tosses a baseball up and down on the bed?

Jon quickened his pace, suddenly anxious to be out of the house and away from the memories. He quietly opened the door to the master bedroom, pushed inside expecting to see Sarah curled up in the bed, reading a book or snoozing as she waited to get better.

But the bed was made and their small en suite bathroom was dark.

Maybe she felt like taking a walk or something... That seemed unlikely because of the rain, but he couldn't think of anywhere else she might go.

Still wondering, Jon unplugged the charger that lived on his nightstand and wrapped up the cord. Sarah had a charger in Lee's room at Rainbow Pines, but her cell was a different brand.

He left their bedroom and was on his way down the hall

when he heard a strange noise. He stopped, unsure where the sound had come from, and heard it again a moment later. A muffled sort of grunt. Snoring? Sarah didn't snore, but if she was sick...

He heard the noise again and realized it was coming from the guest room.

Why would she use the guest bedroom?

He stood there for a moment, staring at the door to the guest bedroom, the power cord forgotten in his hands, and the noise came again.

Not snoring.

What is she doing in there?

Jon walked over to the door and opened it.

THE BARTENDER WAS LYING on the bed, bound to the frame by ropes that ran from her wrists and ankles. She raised her head to look at him, her chocolate curls framing the gag in her mouth, started thrashing on the bed, grunting behind the gag, her eyes wild. He heard a sharp noise and it took him a moment to realize it was the sound of the power cord clattering onto the wooden floor at his feet.

What—

"Jon!"

Sarah's voice shocked him out of the stupor that had wrapped around his mind.

He looked over his shoulder and saw her striding out of Lee's bedroom, her face contorted. "Sarah? What—"

"Get out of there. Now!"

Startled by the anger in her voice, he took a step away from the door. Sarah scooped up the phone charger and slammed the door closed.

"Sarah—"

"No! In the kitchen. Right now."

CALM...

Sarah drove him forward, her hand on the small of his back, his thoughts a whirlwind of questions and disbelief. She didn't stop pushing until he stepped into the kitchen. Jon tried to sort his thoughts into some semblance of order.

"How... how could you do this?"

Sarah threw the charger to the floor at his feet and scrubbed her hands through her hair, started pacing across the living room, her hands balled into fists, her face still contorted. "It was the only way."

Jon pressed his hands against his face, covered his eyes and tried to convince himself it was all a dream. But his hands fell to his sides and nothing had changed. "You *abducted* her, Sarah? Do you realize what that means? She was the criminal and you've made her a victim. You've destroyed any chance we had of getting a conviction against her for the accident."

Sarah shook her head, her lips pursed as she paced. "No. No, there was no chance of that anyway. It was nothing but a dream, just our word against hers. It would never be enough."

"There was a chance at least. Now that's gone. Don't you realize you could go to jail because of this?"

Sarah stopped pacing and shocked him by laughing, an edge of hysteria dancing through the sound. "You think I care about jail? Have you *seen* Lee?"

Calm... need to calm down...

Jon tried to slow his breathing, tried to slow his racing heart as Sarah continued.

"No. You're wrong. She won't tell the police anything, because she's guilty and she'll be worried about going to jail."

Jon finished a series of deep breaths. Yelling wasn't going to help, arguing wouldn't solve anything. "We don't even know if she was the one driving."

Sarah stopped pacing and her hands relaxed at her sides. "She said she wasn't. Not that I believe a word she says. But driving or not, she's guilty. They both are."

Jon shook his head. "It doesn't matter if she's guilty. This is *wrong*. This isn't who you are."

Sarah's hands clenched into fists once again. "I'm just doing the best I can for Lee with what I've got."

"But this isn't what Lee would want."

She crossed the space between them in two large strides and her slap caught him flush and full on his left cheek, rocked his head backwards. He blinked against the pain, gathered himself in time to catch her wrist and stop a second hit.

"Don't you dare... " she said as her arm shook and strained against his grip, her voice breaking.

Her arm went slack and she started to cry. He let go of her wrist and pulled her toward him, ready to hold her, ready to forgive her despite what she'd done, ready to feel loved for the first time since the accident. Her lips quivered, she wouldn't look at him and the tears came harder as he put his arms around her. But before he could pull her close she planted her hands against his chest and shoved him away.

"Don't you dare," she said between sobs, backing away from him. "You can't make this all better, Jon. This isn't something you can make go away with a hug and a kiss and whispers about how much you love me."

"But Sarah—" he said as he stepped toward her. She moved to put the kitchen island between them and Jon stopped, afraid she might run away.

"No buts," she said, shaking her head, watching him the way you would a poisonous snake that was within striking range. "I know what I've done by bringing that woman here. I know. And I don't care. Our son is stuck in that bed and I'm scared to death he's never getting out of it. Scared to death he'll be just another one of the gorks the staff talks about when they don't think we're listening."

"I understand that, Sarah. I do. Trust me, there's nothing that frightens me more. But still, it doesn't make this right. Nothing can make this right. We have to let her go. Now."

Sarah's face abruptly changed, the tension in her jaw and around her eyes melting away.

"She won't get hurt," Sarah said, her voice soft.

She swiped at the tears on her cheeks and left the protection of the island, walked up to him and cupped his face in her hands the way she'd always done before the accident. Her eyelashes were damp from the tears, her blond hair damp from the rain and smelling of lavender.

"I promise. We've just got to keep her here for a little while, Jon. Just long enough to convince her to tell us how to find the man who was with her. We have to. I couldn't live with myself if we missed the chance to put away these people. Could you? Could you face Lee if you did that?"

Jon wanted to look away but couldn't, transfixed by her eyes gazing up at him, by the feel of her hands against his cheeks. He wanted to tell her it didn't matter, that punishing the people who'd hit them wouldn't make Lee better. He was angry about it, devastated, but sending them to jail wouldn't change Lee's past or future. Either Lee would wake up or he wouldn't. If he did wake up, either he'd be normal or he wouldn't. The woman in the bedroom couldn't change that. But he knew it wouldn't matter to Sarah. He could see it in her eyes. To her it would be the same thing as giving up on Lee. And he couldn't ask her to do what he'd already done.

"What if she won't tell?" he asked, despising himself for the capitulation inherent in the question.

Sarah's face relaxed and her thumbs traced the arc of his cheekbones. "She'll tell us. Hold her a little while longer, maybe let her get a little hungry, and she'll tell us."

"It's wrong."

"We won't hurt her, Jon. Being a little hungry never killed anybody. It might take her the rest of the way toward telling us how to find the man. That, or wanting a drink. She's an alcoholic, I'm sure of it. She'll be dying to tell us just so she can get another drink."

Jon closed his eyes, the feel of her touch sinking into him. "I—"

She kissed him then, nothing passionate, just a lingering of her lips against his before she moved away, her fingertips trailing down his jaw. It was the first time she'd kissed him since the accident.

"It'll work, I promise," she whispered.

Jon tried to think of something else he could say that might change her mind and couldn't, could only remember the feel of her lips against his. "This is wrong."

Sarah answered without hesitation. "Probably. But the world isn't always black and white, Jon. It's not always good and evil. We live in the gray between because sometimes there isn't any other way. This is one of those times. Lee deserves justice."

He thought of Lee chasing down fly balls, of Lee smashed at the bottom of the tree next to the Accotink. "If we haven't gotten an answer in twenty-four hours this ends."

Sarah nodded in agreement, her face grim. "Fine. Twenty-four hours."

TWENTY-SEVEN

ELLE

The faint light coming through the window had grown even dimmer and she'd stared at the ceiling fan for what felt like an eternity—the hope she felt at the appearance of the shrew's whipping-boy husband first withering and then dying—when the door opened and the shrew entered carrying a shopping bag.

The shrew walked to the side of the bed and looked down at Elle for a long time, her face angry one moment and scared the next. Elle didn't know if that was comforting or frightening.

"You've been crying," the shrew said.

Elle wished the gag was gone so she could curse the bitch and spit on her, bitterly aware that the woman and whatever was in the bag made her nervous. She'd spent too much of her childhood nervous and hated the feeling even as it fell into place like a well-worn coat.

"Are you ready to tell me more about the man who was with you?"

Elle did nothing. Fuck if she would nod or mumble. If the shrew wanted any kind of answer she'd have to take the gag out first.

The shrew's lips tightened but she said nothing. Instead she put the bag on the floor. Whatever was inside clinked when she set it down, sending a paroxysm of fear down Elle's spine as her mind leapt to pincers and pokers.

The shrew sat on the bed next to Elle, between an arm and leg, and tucked her hair behind her left ear. She stared at Elle and after a moment the shrew's face smoothed out, the anger and fear gone.

"Do you understand what you did?" the shrew asked, her voice calm and dead flat. "You didn't just take my only child. You took my husband from me. You took my whole life away. I've got nothing now. Nothing except a chance to see justice done."

Elle tried to keep her face blank as she returned the stare. It wasn't easy, but she'd done far harder. Her father had seen to that. Had, in a way, prepared her. The thought made a laugh rise up in her belly, though it died behind the gag. The bastard hadn't done much else for her.

"Is something I said funny?" the shrew asked.

Elle knew she should shake her head no. That was the wise response. But fuck her, so she nodded.

She expected the shrew to lose it again, maybe slap her around some more. Instead the shrew only pursed her lips and reached into the hardware bag. Elle's muscles tightened against the ropes.

I won't thrash around. I won't. I survived my father and I can survive this...

There was more clinking and a moment later the shrew

withdrew a length of chain from the bag. The links were on the thin end, nothing heavy duty, and it was only a few feet long. Three at the most. But when the shrew set it down on the bed Elle flinched away as if a snake had been placed there instead.

The shrew—her face calm still—reached into the bag once more and this time came out with a couple of padlocks, keys still inserted. She tossed the padlocks between Elle's splayed legs, then picked up the chain and walked to the end of the bed.

Elle jerked her head up, her eyes on the chain. The shrew pushed one end under Elle's left ankle, looped it back on itself, and then picked up a padlock. She unlocked it, slid the hasp of the lock through two links of the chain to complete the circle, then closed it with a quiet snick that sounded like a thunderclap in Elle's ears. The key stayed in her hand.

Elle's heart hammered in her chest. Ropes already held her but for some reason the chains made the situation more real. More permanent. Suddenly she could see herself growing old in the room, years passing as the shrew kept her hidden away from the world, like one of those sad fucks the authorities find every now and then caged in someone's basement. She strained her head higher and garbled through the gag.

"You'd like to talk now?"

Hating herself for it, Elle nodded.

The shrew looked at her for a moment then said, "If you scream the gag goes right back in. Understand?"

Elle nodded again. The shrew came around the bed and pulled the gag down, removed the wad of cloth from Elle's mouth. Again Elle felt that sense of relief, of freedom that her mouth was clear. It was crazy that something so simple could feel so damn good. "Why chains?"

The shrew had already moved back to the foot of the bed and was studying the length of free chain. It wasn't long enough to reach and then wrap around her other ankle. "I'm sure you need to use the bathroom."

She did, and badly, but she said nothing, her thoughts jumping from one useless idea to another until they settled on being quiet.

"The only way I can get you to the bathroom is in shackles so you can't try and run."

Shackles. Elle decided being quiet could take a flying fuck. "What'll you do if I just shit and piss in the bed?"

The shrew's face stayed blank. "I can't stop you if you want to do that. But I think you might regret it after sitting in your own filth for a few hours. Don't you?"

She's a real bitch underneath that boring face... "Look lady, I'd tell you where to find the guy if I knew. I told you his name already. I don't know anything more than that. It was a one night stand, okay?"

"Have you seen him since that night?"

Elle hesitated, then said, "He came by the bar once."

"So you've talked to him a couple of times, which means you probably know more about him than you think. You just haven't remembered it yet. Probably because you drink too much."

"There's nothing else to remember goddammit. I've told you everything I know."

Instead of answering the shrew started untying the knot next to the chain. After a brief struggle the knot came loose and Elle's leg was free.

Elle didn't hesitate, kicked out immediately at the shrew's

head. The shrew dodged backward, the foot missing her by inches, and with surprising reflexes grabbed the chain that flailed behind Elle's leg. Elle jerked the leg, hoping to yank the chain free, but before she could even tighten the slack the shrew yanked Elle's leg back onto the bed. Before Elle could react the shrew jumped onto the bed and sat on top of the free leg. She wasn't a big woman, but Elle had no leverage and it might as well have been a three-hundred pound man on the end of her leg. Her legs were closer together than they had been and the shrew wrapped the free end of the chain around Elle's other ankle and then snicked a second lock into place.

I won't cry. I won't...

She bit her tongue until it bled.

"YOU SHOULDN'T HAVE DONE THAT," the shrew said, her chest heaving as she took a second chain and two more locks out of the bag. She walked to the right side of the bed and repeated what she'd done with Elle's ankles, except that she freed the right arm, leaving Elle tied to the bed's opposing corners so that she still couldn't move much. Elle didn't struggle, her head full of visions of how she would use the chain to choke the life out of the bitch on the way to the bathroom.

But that fantasy was quashed when the shrew pulled yet another chain from the bag. She locked it to the middle of the ankle chain and then bent Elle's leg until she could lock the other end to the middle of the wrist chain, leaving Elle's body contorted. The key to the last lock went in her pants pocket while all the others went back into the hardware bag.

"Jesus, lady. I'm not a fucking mass murderer."

"No, but if I give you any opening, you'll take advantage of it. You just proved that."

"Look, I'm sorry about what happened to your son. I am. It wasn't fair and the guy deserves to pay for it. But I can't help you. I don't know anything else. I swear."

The shrew ignored her as she untied the last two knots, freeing her from the bed. She backed away, eyeing Elle warily despite the chains. "Get up."

Elle almost refused just to spite the bitch, but her bladder was really barking. *Besides, the more I see of the house the better chance I have of getting the hell out of here...*

Elle struggled to a sitting position, her shoulders aching, the chains clinking like she was old Jacob Marley. That almost made her laugh, but her head started throbbing again and her good humor died. She shuffled her legs off the bed and onto the floor, then stood. It felt good to be upright even though she hurt all over.

The shrew had positioned the chains well. Elle could stand almost straight, but she couldn't lift her arms above her waist, and she couldn't get her feet more than a foot and a half apart at best. She might be able to shuffle forward faster than a walk, but if she tried to run she'd be on her face in moments.

The shrew opened the door and stepped out of the way, gestured toward the hall. "First door on the left."

Elle shuffled into the hallway. She glanced left even as she turned right and saw a living room where the hall ended, the furniture and decorations as boring as the stuff in the bedroom. The kitchen was probably out there as well, but she couldn't see it.

Framed photos of the family—a few including the husband—were on the walls, and she noticed a large picture of the boy wearing a baseball uniform, his grin easy and natural.

That's him. The same damn kid I saw in the park...

It couldn't be though.

"Keep moving," the shrew said, and Elle felt the woman's hand in the small of her back, pushing her forward.

She doesn't want me looking at him...

The bathroom door was open, the light already on, and Elle's bladder urged her onward once the goal was in sight. She clanked like mad over to the toilet and turned around, fumbled awkwardly at her jeans until she was able to slide them to her knees. She almost fell onto the toilet and started peeing immediately.

The shrew stood in the doorway, looking away. Elle didn't care if the shrew saw her naked or saw her piss. As good as it felt to go, she wouldn't have cared if the husband came down the hall for the show.

Elle glanced around. It was the boy's bathroom, the shower curtain and towels both sporting the Nationals logo in red and white. The vanity had two sinks and next to one of them was an electric toothbrush shaped like a baseball bat.

"He really liked baseball, huh?" Elle said as she reached awkwardly for the toilet paper roll and managed to remove a few squares, and then, even more awkwardly, to wipe.

"He *does* like it a lot," the shrew said, still looking away.

"Look, lady. I'm sorry about what happened. I don't have any kids but I grew up with brothers and sisters. I know what it means to love someone."

The shrew's face flushed as she looked at Elle. "Don't you dare try to tell me you know what *I* feel. You don't know anything about me or my son or what this has been like."

Elle stood, tried to bring her underwear and pants along with her but failed halfway. The shrew glanced away again, angry or not. Elle bent over and managed to get her clothes back in place after a brief struggle, the clinking chains making her want to cry and laugh at the same time. "This is batshit crazy. You realize that, don't you?"

The shrew glanced at her sharply, then away again, and Elle thought she might have struck a nerve. But all the shrew said was, "Back to the bedroom."

Elle shuffled into the hall once more, her eyes drawn again to the picture of the boy. The shrew drove her past it and back into the bedroom, turned and shoved her roughly onto the bed. Elle, unbalanced in the chains, fell easily.

The shrew pushed her onto her back and lifted Elle's legs into place on the bed, pushing and shoving her around until she was back in the position she'd woke in. The shrew tied an opposing arm and leg to the bed just as she'd done before, contorting Elle's leg again, but then she started fussing with the knot that held the free rope by the head-board. Elle watched her, confused, then realized the shrew was adjusting the length of the rope.

"You can't leave me in these chains, lady," she said, her breath coming quicker.

The shrew tightened the new knot and dropped the free end of the rope on the bed. "Perhaps a few hours of discomfort will help you remember more about your friend in the car." She took the key out of her pants pocket and used it to open the padlock at the top of the chain that linked Elle's ankles to her wrists.

"You can't do this, you fucking shrew," Elle said as she

jerked her untied arm out of the shrew's grasp. She lashed out but the chains pulled her up short.

The shrew's open hand slammed into Elle's face and drove her teeth together so hard she felt an incisor chip. Her vision doubled and she blinked against the pain as the shrew raised her arm above her head and tied it off to the adjusted rope.

Elle tried to clear her head, succeeded in time to watch the shrew tie up her other ankle, leaving her spread eagle on the bed again, chained wrist to wrist and ankle to ankle.

"I'm gonna—" Elle's words were cut off when the rag was stuffed back in her mouth.

The shrew slid the gag into place again, then picked up the bag that held the keys, cocked her head slightly to the side as she examined Elle. "Do you believe I'm capable of hurting you?"

All Elle could do was look away.

TWENTY-EIGHT

HARVEY

"Your grandfather's having a great day," Nonna said with a smile as she ushered Harvey into the house. Her face was radiant. "He's even been talking a little. He hasn't done that in weeks."

"Really?" Harvey said, the competing worries over Robertson, the kid, and Elle fading into the background for a moment. "What did he say?"

"He asked about the rain. Can you believe that?" Nonna said, her smile growing even larger. "You remember how much he used to love the rain."

She practically pulled him into the kitchen where Nonno sat at the table.

Harvey could see what she meant instantly. Instead of staring ahead vacantly, Nonno looked up as they entered. He didn't smile but his eyes found Harvey and sparkled.

"Go on," prompted Nonna and Harvey realized he'd

frozen in the doorway. Feeling strangely hesitant, Nonna guided him forward by the elbow and Harvey knelt.

"Nonno," he said, finding it difficult to speak. "It's good to see you."

Nonno reached out and cupped Harvey's jaw, his hand rock steady. Harvey felt the roughness of his grandfather's fingers against his skin, inhaled the familiar metallic tang of the soap Nonna bathed him with, the buttery smell of the gel that held his hair back, the pungent odor of the balm that kept his papery skin moist.

Harvey smiled.

THE THREE OF them ate beside the large window that looked out on the rainy afternoon. The red sauce Nonna had simmering on the stove filled the room with the aroma of tomatoes, rosemary, and basil, and there was fresh bread on the table next to the antipasto. The kitchen was warm and familiar, filled with contentment instead of dread for the first time in a long while.

Nonno took every bite his wife offered without hesitation. He even fed himself a few things.

"You should go for a walk," Nonna said after they'd finished eating. "There isn't much he enjoys more than a walk in the rain."

"You always made me go with him," Harvey said with a smile. "You said it was good for me, but I really think you just wanted some time alone. Right, Nonno?"

"Right," said Nonno said as he looked down at his plate.

Nonna beamed and Harvey smiled back at her. Perhaps his grandfather was just parroting what Harvey had said, but Harvey didn't care.

"Let's do it then," Harvey said.

IT WAS a production to get Nonno out of the house of course. Good day or not, Nonno couldn't manage himself. He'd been wearing adult diapers for a while, but he was dry and clean when they took him to the bathroom, and he relieved himself as soon as they'd gotten his pants down and helped him sit. That sort of thing had made Harvey squeamish at first, but he'd watched Nonna do it without flinching and had realized there could be dignity even in undignified situations. After the bathroom they exchanged his house slippers for a pair of galoshes and got him into a lightweight coat.

Once that was done Harvey took out the large umbrella that was in the closet. "You coming with us, Nonna?"

"No," Nonna said with a smile and a wink. "You two enjoy yourselves."

"Suit yourself," Harvey said. "Come on, Nonno. It's been too long since we took a walk together."

Harvey guided Nonno through the door Nonna held and out onto the porch. The wind had died down but the rain was still steady. Harvey helped Nonno descend the porch steps to the sidewalk, held the umbrella with one hand and Nonno's upper arm with the other.

"Left or right?" Harvey asked when they reached the street. When he was a kid Nonno had called out the question at the end of some blocks but not others, always causing Harvey to wonder why he asked when he did. Harvey felt a little weird asking the question instead of answering it, but at the same time it felt right. Nonno didn't respond so Harvey took them left.

They didn't move fast, but Nonno was steady on his feet and they covered ground more quickly than Harvey had expected. His grandfather had always been talkative on their walks, telling Harvey what to expect from the world and how to deal with it, so Harvey filled the rainy silence with talk of the bust-out from the night before.

After they made the next turn, Harvey realized he wanted to tell Nonno about the kid and what had happened. The temptation was strong, but Harvey quashed it. Nonno was probably incapable of repeating the story to Nonna, but he might understand enough to be upset by it. Harvey didn't want that, or for Nonna to catch it secondhand.

"Left or right, Nonno?" Harvey asked when they came to the end of the next block. The rain still fell, but not too hard and they were staying pretty dry beneath the large umbrella.

"Left," Nonno said, already turning.

Surprised, Harvey followed along.

When he looked up, he saw the kid.

AS BIG AS THE MOON...

Harvey jerked to a halt, stopping Nonno at the same time, his fingers digging into his grandfather's thin arm more than he'd intended. Nonno came to an obedient stop.

The kid—brother, cousin, whoever he was—stood facing them halfway down the block, a ball darting between his hand and glove. He wore the Pirate's hat and uniform. Harvey couldn't tell for sure because of the distance, but he was almost certain the kid had on cleats.

"Wait here, Nonno," Harvey said. He offered his grandfather the umbrella and to his surprise, Nonno grasped it. It drooped a bit when Harvey let go, rested against the top of his grandfather's head, but Nonno held it in place. "Don't move. I'll be right back."

Harvey started forward without waiting for an answer, the rain cool on his face. He felt drawn to the kid, like metal shavings to a magnet, and he had to fight the urge to run. He glanced back once to see Nonno standing motionless on the sidewalk where Harvey had left him, the umbrella still covering him.

He turned back toward the kid only to see him trotting away down the sidewalk, the ball visible in front of him periodically, arcing above his head before falling into his glove.

"Hey!" Harvey yelled, speeding up. "We need to talk. Now!" The kid didn't look back and a moment later he turned a corner and disappeared behind a hedgerow.

Harvey started to run, his feet splashing through puddles on the sidewalk, soaking the cuffs of his pants. He didn't notice as he sped onward. He turned the corner as fast as he could and then halted when he saw the kid standing just fifteen or twenty feet away, the rain not yet visible on his white jersey and dark hat.

The kid wasn't tossing the ball anymore and he stared calmly at Harvey without moving.

He's not frightened at all…

That made Harvey nervous—most kids would be at least a little scared if an adult was chasing them. Anger wouldn't have bothered him, but in the face of that peaceful gaze Harvey took an involuntary step backwards, tensing in expectation of another ball thrown at his head.

"I checked on Lee today," Harvey heard himself say, as the rain picked up and started to trickle down his face. A slight buzz filled his ears. "What is he? Your brother? Cousin?"

The boy didn't answer, but he cocked his head to one side as if he were listening intently. There was something wrong about the way the kid looked, something important, but Harvey was too agitated to figure out what.

"Whatever Lee is to you, he's in a coma and not going anywhere. I don't know if you think I've got something to do with that or what, but you're wrong, kid."

The wind picked up and the kid started toward him. The gust blasted into Harvey, chilled him, made his damp skin goosebump beneath his wet sleeves. Startled and scared, Harvey stepped aside and the kid went past as if he was carried along by the wind. Part of him wanted to reach out and grab the kid, to shake him and demand that he stop following him. But at the same time, the thought of touching the kid frightened him in a way he hadn't experienced since he was a child, sure that there was a monster in his closet and torn between a desire to open the door and discover the truth and an inability to bring himself one inch closer to the knob.

The kid stopped at the corner and turned to face Harvey. Harvey wondered if he'd speak—the thought made his skin scrawl for some reason—but instead the kid placed the ball in his glove and used his free hand to point back down the sidewalk toward where Harvey had originally seen him.

"What?" Harvey asked, afraid to move closer to the kid even though he still felt that magnetism toward him. "What are you pointing at?"

Then he remembered.

Nonno...

Trying to ignore the panic spreading throughout his

body, Harvey ran past the kid and looked down the side-walk. Besides the rain, the only other thing that shared the block with him was the umbrella, lying upside down in the rain.

Nonno was gone.

TWENTY-NINE

JON

Still in shock, Jon called out sick for the afternoon, spent a half hour trying and failing to forget about the woman tied to their spare bed.

He sat at the kitchen table and attempted to read a magazine, but that was absurd and futile and he quit after he'd been over the same page at least a dozen times. He couldn't focus on the words, couldn't stop thinking about *her*.

He tried television next, watched a few minutes of a documentary about Norwegian sled dogs and wondered what jail would be like. How long until Sarah and he would be arrested? The question should've disturbed him, the prospect of incarceration should've frightened him. It didn't. What could be worse than the way things already were? His son would never wake from the coma he was in. His wife had left him in almost every sense of the word.

And now there was a captive in the bedroom. Their family had begun to disintegrate the night of the accident and abducting the bartender was the final phase of that dissolution. His family, his marriage, his life were gone. What difference if he were in jail or free? None, except where he spent his time living in the past, regretting what should've been.

He couldn't stay in the house. He thought of taking a drive, but he was too distracted and might get in an accident in the rain, and where would that leave the woman in the bedroom? He thought of visiting Lee, but that made the guilt inside swell to overwhelming proportions. His son had always been so good, so nice to everyone. Pure. Lee would never understand tying up a woman in the spare bedroom, never comprehend a world where that might be the right thing to do. And that would only make Jon feel worse about what he'd agreed to. So when Sarah had once again circulated to the back of the house, Jon left by the front door.

THE RAIN STILL FELL, as heavy as before. If the forecasts were to be believed it would continue to fall for at least another day. Flooding, the meteorologists proclaimed, was inevitable.

Jon left the house without a raincoat, without an umbrella, and the rain drenched his clothes for the second time that day. He wandered the neighborhood streets, hoped clinging clothes and water streaming down his face would drive the woman out of his head, but of course they didn't. He stopped trying and all his thoughts were the same horrors as before, nothing revelatory, everything as worked over as a mouth sore.

He walked without direction or forethought, took lefts and rights at random, waded through water flowing down the sides of the streets, didn't try to avoid the arcs of spray whenever a car passed, and a half-hour later found himself outside the nearest convenience store. He thought of turning around, remembered what he had to go back to, and pushed through the door.

THIRTY

There were no other customers. Jon went straight to the coolers and picked up the first twelve-pack of cold beer that wasn't Budweiser, walked to the register, rivulets of water flowing from him onto the floor, his shoes squelching with each step.

The clerk—a too thin woman with bad hair and worse makeup—looked him over and frowned, but her voice was sympathetic when she spoke. "You okay, mister?"

"No," Jon said as he put the beer on the counter.

The clerk leaned on the counter and nodded as if that was the answer she'd expected, made no move to scan the box of Miller High Life. "It's this rain. Talk about depressing. Ain't gonna let up neither. You hear what they're sayin' it's gonna do?"

Jon stared and she raised her eye-liner eyebrows in expectation. There would be no transaction without an answer. "Flooding?"

She brought one spidery hand down on the counter with a smack. "Flooding! Damn straight. You remember the last time it flooded around here?"

"No."

She shrugged. "Neither do I. Thought you might. This all you gettin' sweetie?"

Jon grunted and she gunned the box of beer, shook her head when the price rang up. "Champagne it ain't. Natty light's cheaper *and* tastes better. Just my two cents."

Jon fished a ten out of his wallet, the cash dry but the outside of the leather dark with water. He took the change absently, dumped the coins into the Take-a-Penny, Leave-a-Penny jar, and shoved the damp wallet in his rear pocket.

"You take care of yourself, okay," the clerk said, a sad smile on her face. "Go home and dry off before you get too far into that twelve-pack."

"I'll try," Jon said and he squelched back outside into the still falling rain.

He stood outside the door, rain beating against his face as he looked up at the sky, wondered if the day would feel any different if the sun were out, decided it didn't matter. It was what it was. He tore open one end of the already soggy box of beer and fished out a can, popped the top and took a large gulp and fuck the open container law. The beer tasted terrible and that was fine. He only wanted to forget the woman, or at least cloud his mind so much he didn't care, so he tipped back the can, gulped until it was empty.

A car pulled up, wipers slapping fast, and a moment later a lady huddling beneath an umbrella gave him a wide berth as she entered the store. He stared her down and threw the empty into a nearby trash can, got out another beer, the box cradled in the crook of his arm like a baby—he could remember carrying Lee that way, when Lee could finally hold his head up and Jon had gotten brave enough to hold him that way—and started walking back toward the house, drinking as he went.

THIRTY-ONE

Jon wandered, swapped out empties for fulls as he walked, did his honest best to think of nothing, and by the time he made it home he was on his sixth can.

He stood in the rain outside the house swaying, soaked, stared at the front door, and knew he couldn't go inside. He didn't want to confront Sarah—she would just disapprove, right? Of course she would—but really he couldn't go inside because he'd be closer to the woman.

So he trudged into the foundation plantings, set his nearly collapsed box of beer down on the weed-ridden mulch, unzipped and pissed on the porch foundation, his dick small and shriveled after all the cold rain, the relief so profound that his head rocked backwards, his mouth gaping and filling with rain.

When his bladder was blissfully empty, he zipped, picked up the disintegrating box of High Life, and walked to the garage, which was closed again. He used the outside keypad to run up the garage door—only getting the code wrong once—and then the door rumbled and squeaked upward on its tracks, loud despite the nylon wheels that had cost so much more but were of course so much better.

Jon wasn't one of those guys that liked to hang out in garages. Never had been, never would be. But at that moment sitting in the garage with his beer and watching the rain falling on the front yard seemed like the best decision in the world.

Jon turned on the radio he and Lee listened to while they washed the cars—it was tuned to the classic country station his father had loved so much—and then started to extract a chair from the mess at the back of the garage. A moment later the door to the kitchen opened and Sarah peered out. Jon straightened and licked his lips, considered making an excuse, then decided he didn't need one. She'd given him the excuse.

"What are you doing, Jon?"

"I needed a drink," he said, raising a can towards her. He took a large gulp. "So I got one."

Sarah's eyes narrowed. "I meant, what are you doing in the garage?"

Jon looked around, wondered if she was trying to trick him into saying something wrong. "I'm going to watch the rain and listen to some music. There's nothing else to do."

Sarah's eyes were hard. "You'll attract attention. Don't you think that's a bad idea right now?"

Jon shrugged. "There's nobody to notice, Sarah. Only an idiot would be out in this weather."

Sarah raised an eyebrow. "Exactly."

Jon saluted her with his beer and took another gulp. She pursed her lips and he thought she would lecture him, but she only receded into the house, her face stony as the kitchen door swung closed.

He went back to digging and a moment later spotted a

lawn chair. He was reaching for it when his eyes fell on the plastic bin that held Lee's bats, extra gloves, helmets, batting gloves, more balls than Jon could count. He froze, overwhelmed by an avalanche of baseball memories, of catch in the park, of batting practices, of games lost and games won. Drunk or not, god but the memories hurt.

Jon gritted his teeth and grabbed the chair, stalked around his car and shook it out until he could sit. He dropped into it, the sodden box of beer still cradled in his left arm.

The driveway, the front yard, the street, the neighborhood were all shrouded by a wall of rain that blurred before his eyes. Sarah's car sat in front of him, water bouncing off its hood, and Jon stared at the Subaru unseeing and drank, listening to Hank Williams and remembering baseball.

The bound woman in the spare bedroom was finally absent from his thoughts.

JON WOKE, lids heavy, the steady drum of rain at first confusing and then familiar. He straightened his neck, winced at the pain of sleeping in an awkward position. In the light of the overhead fluorescent, Jon stared at the back of the garage door, tried to decide how long he had been asleep and wondered if it was still daytime or not. It didn't occur to him to wonder why the door was closed.

His head swam. He fumbled at the collapsed box of Miller on his lap and found there was still unopened beer left in the bottom. He considered grabbing another, but decided he needed to piss first.

He stood and the box of beer finally gave way, crushed empties and four or five fulls falling to the floor. Jon ignored the cans rolling around and stumbled past his car to the kitchen door, found it locked. He leaned his head against the door for a long moment, the world spinning, then dug his keys out of his pocket, found the right one, and opened the door.

The kitchen was empty, all the lights but the pendant over the sink turned off. Back in a room with a window, he saw that it was late in the day. Hard to tell how late because of the weather, so he glanced at the clock on the microwave, squinted until he saw that it was quarter of seven.

The house was quiet. There was that sense of emptiness that meant Sarah was gone. With Lee no doubt. Where else would she go? He listened longer to be sure, swayed on his feet. Yes, she was gone. Probably closed the garage door on her way out so the neighborhood didn't have to witness the weekday drunk in the Young house.

Jon used the toilet in the powder room off the kitchen and then walked to the back of the house where he stopped in front of the door to the spare bedroom, his clothes dripping on the floor. He heard nothing from behind the door.

Maybe she's gone... Maybe Sarah decided to let her go and that's why the house feels empty. They drove back to her apartment...

He latched onto the fantasy, delighted in imagining the weight lifted from him if it were true. Funny that it'd be nice to go back to the way things had been, horrible as they were. He wondered if it was just his life that was fucked up or life in general.

Part of him wanted to walk away from the door, to play out the fantasy as long as possible, but he couldn't avoid the room any more than he could avoid thinking of Lee a thousand times day. So he grabbed the cool metal of the doorknob and pushed inside.

Jon stared in disbelief.

The ropes still held her on the bed, but chains now bound her wrists and ankles together.

Chains.

He thought the woman might be asleep but she turned her head and met his gaze, her eyes full of fear above the gag that rested in her mouth.

He almost left, doing what Sarah would want, but he couldn't.

The chains were too much.

He walked to the bed and collapsed more than sat next to her, her eyes following every movement he made. He hesitated a moment and then pulled out the gag.

"Untie me," she said, her voice harsh. Not pleading though. "Untie me now before she comes back and I'll walk out of here and you'll never hear from me again, I swear."

She said it with such conviction.

"Where can we find the man who was driving the car?" he asked.

"I don't know. I don't know where he lives or where he works. It was a one night stand. All I know is his first name is Harvey. If I knew more I already would've told your crazy-ass wife." She closed her eyes and bit her bottom lip after that last part.

The comment didn't upset him. Instead he wondered if she was right. He remembered Lee in the passenger seat and thought maybe he was crazy, too. Nothing had been right since the accident. Nothing. That they might have lost their minds was not a big stretch of the imagination.

"I know you're scared," he said. "I'm sorry. But I promise you won't get hurt."

She surprised him by laughing. "A useless promise. We both know your wife is running the show."

Jon shook his head. "She just wants to do the right thing for our son."

"You're drunk, heel-licker," she said laughing.

The laughter and change of subject startled him and he responded without thought. "It was the only thing left to do."

She stared at him, her eyes intense, weighing. "Look, mister. I know what happened was terrible. But this—" she rattled the chains bound to her wrists, "—is not the answer. Get these ropes and chains off me, we'll go to the police, and I'll tell them everything. I'll tell them what I know about Harvey, about what happened in the car. Everything. And I won't say a word about this. I promise. Just get me out of here before she comes back. We can go right now. Straight to the station."

Jon decided no one in her position could be that good of a liar. Sarah might not agree, but the woman's offer was everything they needed. Besides, those chains were wrong. He didn't know how he would explain it to Sarah, but he'd find a way. He nodded.

"Thank you," she said. "Hurry."

Jon didn't move. "I don't know where the keys for the locks are."

"It doesn't matter," she said, shaking her head. "Just untie the ropes. We can stop at a hardware store on the way to the station and you can get some bolt cutters to get the chains off."

"Okay," he said. It felt right to agree. Explaining what he'd done to Sarah wouldn't be that difficult. He stood and moved to the head of the bed where he could get to the ropes that held her arms above her head and started fumbling at the knot.

"Hurry," she said, and for the first time there was pleading in her voice.

"I'm trying. You must have pulled on the ropes. The knot is really tight." The bigger problem was that he could barely focus, his vision swimming. He finally got one loop loose, and soon the entire knot came undone. "Move your arms toward the other corner, it'll make the next knot easier to get undone."

She complied as he walked around the bed, and as Jon started on the second knot he felt his head clear a bit. Another indication he was doing the right thing. He began to imagine what he'd say at the police station, how happy Sarah would be when the woman helped them find the man who'd hit them. "What's your name?"

She hesitated, then said, "Elle."

"I'm sorry, Elle. This is all my fault. I shouldn't have let it happen. There."

She pulled her arms forward over her head, raised her torso at the same time. She winced in pain as she made it upright and the chain around her wrists clanked as she moved. "My ankles. My fingers are too numb to do it myself."

Jon moved to the foot of the bed and had just touched the knot on Elle's left ankle when the garage door started to rumble again.

He froze.

"No. Don't stop," Elle said as she leaned forward and started plucking ineffectually at one of the knots. The rumble paused briefly then started again. "Help me. Please."

Jon shook his head. "No. No, we've got to tie your arms back up. It'll be better if I just try again later." He moved around the corner of the bed, the rumble dying.

"No. You've got to do it now. Now," she said, panic edging into her voice.

"I'm sorry. It's too late. She'll stop us."

He took hold of her left arm to lower her on to the bed once again, but she jerked as soon as he gripped her. Surprised and still wobbly on his feet, Jon stumbled and fell to his knees by the edge of the bed. "I promise I'll get you out," he said, voice low. "Just not now."

Instead of acquiescing, Elle swung her joined fists around and smashed them into the side of Jon's head, the loops of chain connecting with his temple in an explosion of pain. He wobbled on his knees and she prepared to hit him again, but he started to fall. The last thing he saw were her fingers reaching for the knots that still bound her ankles to the bed. He hit the floor, skull rebounding off the hardwood, and then there was darkness.

THIRTY-TWO

HARVEY

Harvey sprinted down the sidewalk, tried to ignore the images that popped into his head, the myriad disasters that could befall a demented old man wandering the streets alone in the rain.

He'll be fine, Harvey told himself as he grabbed the fallen umbrella on his way past. *He's just walking down the sidewalk, or trying to get into somebody else's house because he thinks it's his...*

He stopped at the intersection, closed the umbrella as his eyes darted every direction except for the way he'd come, the kid behind him forgotten. Nonno was nowhere in sight.

He's not fast, no matter which way he went. Pick a direction, check it out for a block and then come back to here...

He chose the way they'd come first, on the off chance that Nonno actually remembered the way back home. He pounded down the sidewalk, breath ragged in his ears, head swiveling as he checked yards and porches on both sides of the street. He made it to the next intersection and saw nothing.

Retrace.

He made it back to the intersection just as a stopped car began to pull through, its wipers slapping across the windshield. Harvey ran in front of the car and smacked his free hand down on the hood. The sedan honked and jerked to a stop as Harvey raised his hand and the umbrella in a placating gesture, hoping the driver wouldn't think he was a carjacker.

"Have you seen an old man walking?" Harvey yelled as he approached the woman driver. But as soon as he was no longer in front of the car the woman sped away, nearly running over his feet as she fled.

Harvey ran across the intersection, choosing the opposite direction he'd first gone, reasoning that if the driver had seen an old man in distress she would've stopped.

He was halfway down the block when he spotted Nonno face down on the ground, one leg in the road, one leg on the sidewalk, sprawled and still, a few feet from a parked car. No moving cars were in sight.

"*Nonno!*" he shouted as he ran faster, already sick at thought of telling Nonna what had happened.

Harvey dropped the umbrella and fell to his knees next to his grandfather's head, which was turned to one side, only half his face visible. Nonno's eye was closed, his limbs absolutely still. Rain ran down his cheek into his gaping mouth.

He's breathing though...

Harvey leaned over far enough to shield Nonno's face from the rain and got out his phone. He dialed the emergency number, used his free hand to touch his grandfather's throat. The pulse there was regular and strong.

The operator picked up and Harvey said, "I need an ambulance to the five hundred block of Wickenham Ave right away."

THIRTY-THREE

Once the paramedics were on the way, Harvey examined Nonno more closely. He couldn't see any injuries but that meant nothing. It was the bones that mattered in the frail. He knew how bad the recovery statistics were for the elderly when they broke a hip.

Harvey was running his hands gently along his grandfather's right arm—his left was pinned beneath his body—when Nonno's one visible eye fluttered open, rolling in its socket. His papery lips parted. "Nonna... "

"Shh, Nonno," Harvey said. "You fell. An ambulance is on the way. Don't try to move. You'll see Nonna in just a minute."

Nonno's eye closed again.

But Nonna didn't know. A stab of guilt pierced Harvey. *I left him to go after the kid... I left him...*

His chest feeling like it was full of lead, Harvey dialed another number and a second later Nonna picked up. "Hello?"

Harvey swallowed. "Nonna."

"What's wrong, Harvey? Did something happen? Is

Nonno okay?" Every question came faster than the previous one as her words gained an edge of dread.

"Nonno fell. I... I let go of him for a second and he tripped." Harvey was disgusted with how easily the lie came to his lips.

"Is he okay?"

"I don't know. An ambulance is on the way already."

There was a choked sound and then a heavy sigh. When Nonna spoke again her voice was calm and businesslike, but beneath that facade Harvey could hear tightly reined in fear. "Where are you?"

"Wickenham and Hardwick."

"I'm coming," Nonna said and the phone went dead.

THE AMBULANCE ARRIVED before Nonna but only by a couple of minutes. She wasn't running, but she was walking at a pace that would've inspired someone in their fifties. She wore an unbuttoned raincoat, the hood thrown back, her hair slick from the rain.

Nonna rushed to her husband's side just as the paramedics were rolling Nonno gently onto a collapsible gurney, his neck already braced. The rear doors of the ambulance were open, the lights flashing. A couple of neighbors had appeared on porches, no doubt held to that distance only because of the rain.

"Are you his wife, Ma'am?" one of the paramedics asked, a young hispanic woman who looked like she could bench press more than Harvey. He'd already told them what happened—the lie again—and filled them in on Nonno's history.

Nonna covered her mouth with one hand as she saw the

scraped and bruising skin of the left side of Nonno's face. She reached out and grabbed his near hand, but Nonno's eyes only gazed blankly up at the sky above, oblivious to the rain falling on his face, the plaques that filled his mind gumming up the works yet again. "Yes. Has my grandson told you that my husband has late-stage Alzheimers?"

"Yes, Ma'am," the same paramedic said with a nod as her partner strapped Nonno to the gurney. "Is there anything else we should know about his health?"

"He had lung cancer about five years ago. There haven't been any relapses."

"Okay. We're taking him to the emergency department at Fairfax Hospital. One of you can ride with us, but it might be best if you just meet us there. Is that okay?"

Nonna looked at him and Harvey said, "Of course, we'll be right behind you."

"Good," the paramedic said. The two paramedics began to wheel Nonno toward the rear of the ambulance. "We'll take good care of him, Ma'am, and we'll see you in a few minutes."

Nonna looked as if she were about to cry. Perhaps she already was, but there was no way to tell in the rain. Harvey felt a burning sense of shame, felt as bad as he had as a small child confessing to stealing cannoli from the refrigerator.

"Nonna, I'm so sorry. I didn't think he—"

"Oh, shoosh," Nonna said as she wrapped trembling arms around him. "He's tough. I'm sure he'll be just fine. I know you'd never hurt him on purpose."

"THE GOOD NEWS, Mrs. Aiello, is that while your husband does have an injury to his spine, it isn't overly serious and can be treated." Dr. Burnett was pretty, her brown hair framing a round, young face. If not for the white coat Harvey would've thought she wasn't old enough to be a physician.

"Thank goodness," Nonna said, and Harvey saw the tension leave her shoulders, felt some of it leave his own as well. She gripped Nonno's hand in her own, just below the I.V. poking out of his wrist. "Thank you so much for taking care of him, Dr. Burnett. You and the rest of the staff have all been magnificent."

Dr. Burnett smiled. "We're glad to help. Now let me tell you a little more about what happened. Your husband has a compression fracture of one of his lumbar vertebrae. This injury is common in patients with osteoporosis, which your husband shows some evidence of. He may even of had a minor fracture there before the fall, but we'll never know. Does that make sense?"

"Yes," Nonna answered.

Dr. Burnett nodded. "Good. Your husband's chart says he has Alzheimer's? Is that correct?"

"Yes."

"And he still lives at home with you as the primary care giver?"

Nonna nodded. "Yes. I have some help a few times a week, but mainly just with household stuff. For now I'm still able to take care of him."

"And it looks like you've been doing an excellent job," Dr. Burnett said. "But this injury can't be treated at home. If he isn't rehabilitated correctly, he'll have a lot of pain and trouble walking, which we want to avoid. Because of that, he needs to spend some time in a recovery facility. Someplace that can help with the rehab, help him get in and out of bed in a manner that doesn't aggravate the injury. Things like that. Does that make sense?"

Nonna nodded, though her face looked more grim than it had before. "Is there someplace that you recommend?"

"Yes," Dr. Burnett said, and Harvey felt a cold certainty flow into him. "There's an excellent facility not far from here that specializes in exactly this kind of care. You might have heard of it. It's called Rainbow Pines."

THIRTY-FOUR

SARAH

You think you can hurt her, Sissy? You drowned Adam to save yourself, but are you hard enough to do what's coming for Lee?

She was sitting outside the guest bedroom listening to the woman, listening to her mother, when her phone rang. Her cell was in the kitchen, but there was no mistaking the ringtone she'd set for Rainbow Pines.

Lee...

She sprinted into the kitchen and answered the phone. "Hello?"

"Hi, Mrs. Young, this is Janet."

"Is Lee okay?" Sarah asked. Janet was one of Lee's nurses.

"Yes. More than okay actually. He's opened his eyes. Can you come over?"

LEE...

She had trouble focusing as she ran through the Rainbow Pines parking lot, water splashed from puddles soaking her legs, her umbrella barely protecting the rest of her from the blowing rain.

You shouldn't have left Jon alone with her, Sissy...

Her mother was right, but staying at the house hadn't been an option, not with Lee's eyes open. *He agreed to twenty-four hours. He won't go back on his word. Besides, he's passed out...*

She signed in quickly and ran to Lee's room, her heart pounding in her ears.

Janet—a short, pretty young brunette just out of school, who liked her sweaters pink—was leaning over Lee and cleaning the surgical wounds on his head when Sarah stopped in the door, breathing hard, suddenly filled with reluctance. Janet heard her and turned, smiled and beckoned her over with the hand holding a bottle of antiseptic.

"Come see, Mrs. Young."

Sarah walked slowly to the bed, one hand covering her mouth, tears already trailing down her cheeks.

"I KNOW it's a term that bothers many people, Mrs. Young," Dr. Kamarti said as he stood next to the bed examining Lee, "but it's also fairly accurate."

Sarah felt numb, the rush of elation she'd felt when seeing Lee's eyes open replaced by uncertainty. "How long could he stay like this?"

"The vegetative state is similar to the coma itself, Mrs.

Young. It could last a few days. It could last for months. There's no way to predict what will happen or what might pull Lee out of it. Time maybe. Perhaps a lot of verbal attention. We have no way of knowing. The important thing to remember is that this is a positive development. It means Lee's brain is healing."

Sarah nodded even though she didn't feel very positive. But when she looked at Lee again, at his open but vacant eyes, she was surprised to realize that she did feel a little better. Looking at him helped. She'd seen his eyes of course, every time Dr. Kamarti or one of the nurses thumbed up his lids and shone their probing lights into his pupils to see if they were reactive, but that was hardly the same as seeing them open on their own.

They were such beautiful eyes, so dark and liquid. Jon's eyes. But the concave patch of skin that covered the left side of his head where the bone had been removed made his face look different. He was Lee but not Lee.

"Do we need to do anything differently now?" Sarah asked.

"He'll be cared for in much the same way he has been," Dr. Kamarti said as he stepped away from Lee and faced her. "But the staff will add new therapies to his regimen based on the premise that Lee will see what is happening, even if appears he is not. They will show him objects, try to get him to follow things with his eyes. These are the small steps, the beginning steps, that could lead to farther recovery. You can show him pictures he might recognize. Anything that he sees might help. And the staff and you will need to be on the lookout for any signs of increased awareness."

"Is it okay to have the television on?" Sarah asked.

Dr. Kamarti smiled and nodded, his big ears bobbing.

"Of course, of course. He may watch as much of the Nationals as you like, Mrs. Young. Anything that could stimulate his brain, his memories, will help."

It's all lies, Sissy. Lies, lies, and more lies...

Sarah reached out and took Lee's hand, gazed at his open, staring eyes, and wondered if her Lee was still in there at all.

SARAH DIDN'T WANT to leave Lee but she had to check on the woman, whose presence in her home was more confusing than it had been before Lee opened his eyes.

Nothing has changed, Sissy. She's still guilty. Her and her boyfriend. You can't let them get away with what they did to Lee...

Sarah pulled up outside the garage and raised the door, the rain only a drizzle for the moment as the weatherman on the radio talked about cresting rivers and more rain to come. It had only been a little more than an hour since she left the house, and Sarah was surprised when the rising garage door revealed an empty folding chair.

Sarah forgot about Lee for the first time since the phone call. She got out of the car and sprinted into the house, slapped the button on her way past that would close the garage door as she imagined the woman trying to run away, then ran through the empty kitchen and down the hall to the spare bedroom.

The woman was sitting up on the bed, her still chained hands working frantically at the knotted ropes that held her ankles to the bed. Jon lay on the floor, a thin trickle of blood trailing down his cheek.

"Help!" the woman screamed when she saw Sarah, her

eyes frantic as she tried to unravel a knot. "Help me! Help me!"

Sure the screams could be heard blocks away, Sarah ran forward without stopping to think and drove a balled fist into the side of the woman's head, the impact making a sharp pain bloom in her hand. The woman's head snapped to the side and she fell onto the mattress, the screams replaced by a moan.

Good, Sissy!

Sarah hurried around the bed. The woman wasn't unconscious, but her eyes rolled in their sockets and Sarah knew she only had moments before the woman gathered her wits enough to put up a fight. Grunting, she ignored the pain in her hand and shoved the woman back into the middle of the mattress, threw her limp arms back over her head. She knelt on the bed and tied up the woman's wrists once more, then searched for the gag. She spotted it on the nightstand, so she scooted off the bed and grabbed it.

"Fuck," the woman muttered, blinking hard. Sarah shoved the twisted gag between the woman's jaws and pulled the loop over head. The woman began to struggle harder, speaking garbled curses through the gag. It wouldn't keep her as quiet as the rag that had been stuffed in her mouth earlier, but Sarah didn't think she'd be able to make enough noise to alert the neighbors. She checked the knots at the woman's ankles and found they were fine. She hadn't had much time to try and undo them apparently. A glance at the head of the bed told her the new knots at the woman's wrists weren't great but they were holding well enough. Sarah would know soon enough with the way the woman was thrashing.

Sarah slumped to the floor, shaking as the adrenaline bled out of her system. The pain in her hand was intense and it was already starting to swell around her knuckles. She needed to get ice on it but that couldn't happen until she stood up. The way her legs felt suggested that wasn't a good idea yet.

She crawled over to Jon and tapped him on the cheek to see if he would stir, but he didn't budge. Was that because of the hit to his head or because of how much he'd drank? She had no idea.

Taking a deep breath, she used the side of the bed to get to her feet, wincing at the pain in her hand as she pushed upwards. She felt a little light-headed, but after a couple of deep breaths her legs felt steadier and she was fairly certain she wouldn't faint.

Sissy...

I know. You were right, I shouldn't have trusted him...

Shaking, Sarah walked to Jon's feet. She grabbed his ankles and pulled, her hand throbbing like it'd been clamped in a vise. He was heavy, but he slid easily across the hardwood. She dragged him out of the bedroom and down the hall to the bathroom.

SARAH DUMPED a cup of cold water on Jon's face. He didn't sputter and shake like they did on television, but his eyes peeled open a moment later. Then he promptly rolled onto his side and vomited on the floor. When he was done heaving, he made it to his knees and rocked onto his heels, stared at her as spittle dangled from his lips. He had trouble focusing.

"What happened?"

Sarah grabbed a hand towel from next to the sink and tossed it onto his lap before she sat on the edge of the tub, her injured hand cradled against her stomach. "She hit you I guess. Did she get loose on her own or did you do it?"

You already know, Sissy...

Jon blinked a couple of times as the cogs turned slowly in his beer-addled brain. "I did it," he said after a moment. He picked up the towel and scrubbed his mouth.

"Why?"

"We aren't that kind of people," Jon slurred as he dropped the towel. "Least I thought we weren't."

Lee didn't come to him, Sissy. He doesn't care about Lee the way you do...

"Lee deserves justice," Sarah said. "Any decent parents would do the same."

Jon opened his mouth but then shut it again with a clack of teeth. He shifted around until his back was against the side of the tub and then rested his forehead on his drawn up knees. "I just want things the way they were."

"They'll never be that way again," Sarah said. "Even if Lee makes a full recovery. There's no going back, and no amount of drinking will make the problems we have right now disappear."

Jon was silent for so long before he answered that Sarah thought he might have fallen asleep. "She shouldn't be here, Sarah."

It was old territory, so she changed the subject. "Lee opened his eyes."

Jon's head snapped up, his eyes wide. "He's awake?"

"No. He's in a vegetative state. We'll have to start trying to stimulate him visually."

Jon wobbled to his feet. "I want to see him."

"No. You're still drunk."

"I'm fine," Jon said, even as he had to shift his feet around to steady himself.

"You're not," Sarah said as she stood. "And you're still bleeding. You can't drive and I'm not taking you there when you're drunk. Take a shower. Clean up the mess you just made on the floor. Drink some coffee. Do whatever you have to do to sober up. Then we'll go." Whatever mistakes he'd made, he deserved to see his son's eyes open once more.

I hope you've learned from your mistake, Sissy...

I have...

———

SARAH PEERED into the spare bedroom, hoped to get an unguarded look at the woman. She wasn't thrashing around anymore, her head tilted backward, her chin pointed up at the ceiling. Tears ran down her temples and into her thick curly hair.

It's working, Sissy. She'll talk soon...

Seeing the woman suffer didn't make Sarah happy. But she didn't feel any pity for her either.

Sarah entered the room and the woman glared at her with watery eyes as Sarah made sure the ropes were still secure. "You shouldn't have taken advantage of my husband like that." The woman's eyes were filled with hatred. Well, let her hate. "Have you remembered anything else?"

The woman uttered an expletive around the gag.

"Your choice," Sarah said. "You can have some water later, but don't expect any food. A little hunger might change your mind about talking."

Sarah left the lights on as she exited the room.

THIRTY-FIVE

HARVEY

Dr. Burnett recommended sending Nonno directly from the emergency room to Rainbow Pines. "He'll be cared for well there," she told Nonna, "and he can start therapy immediately."

Harvey listened, but heard little. *Rainbow Pines... It's where the boy is. Maybe that's what the kid wants. He wants me to be there with him...* The kid and the boy were still separate in his mind, but their paths were converging—he kept forgetting which one he was thinking about, and when he thought of one, he thought of the other.

"Harvey?"

Nonna's voice was concerned. Harvey looked up and realized the doctor had gone, leaving the three of them alone in the room. Harvey tried to recall what he'd heard and failed.

"Yes, Nonna?"

"Are you okay?"

Harvey nodded. "Sure. Just upset."

Nonna gave him a tiny smile and patted his knee. "It's fine, Harvey. These things happen. Nonno wouldn't be mad at you and neither am I. Okay?"

Harvey nodded, but her words did nothing to ease his guilt. His gaze kept returning to a scrape on Nonno's cheek.

"Can you go home and get some clothes for Nonno and I, and bring them to Rainbow Pines? I don't want to leave him during the transfer but we'll need them."

Harvey nodded. "Of course."

"Can you get Nonno's medicine as well? Do you remember where it is?"

Harvey nodded again. "I'll get everything you need."

"EXPECT another eight to twelve inches overnight, folks. It just keeps coming and there's no end in sight until Thursday at the earliest. Make sure you stay away from all the local waterways as they start to rise above—"

Harvey turned off the radio, tired of hearing about the flooding that was going to hit the city. Harvey didn't care if they were in the middle of a hundred-year flood or a thousand.

It was him... but which one?

I shouldn't have left Nonno...

Once he was back in Nonna's neighborhood he drove down the street where he'd seen the kid. It was dark of course, the lights fragmented through the drops of rain, but Harvey half expected to see the kid standing on the same corner.

He stopped outside the house but didn't kill the engine, instead stared at the rain illuminated by the headlights. Nonna hadn't said much, but Harvey knew she was worried. She'd done her best to keep Nonno out of managed care, not only because she wanted to care for her husband herself, but also because she'd always worried about how many patients got ill in those facilities. Now she was faced with the prospect of an indeterminate amount of time in Rainbow Pines and the very real possibility that Nonno might die sooner than she'd expected.

All because I tried to chase down the kid...

That sent his mind off toward the boy again, which led back to Nonno, which led—

Do what Nonna asked you to do, came a thought. *Do at least that much for her...*

Harvey got out of the car and trudged down the sidewalk, unconcerned about the water that soaked his shirt and hair.

The porch was dark, unlit because of Nonna's hurried exit. She'd remembered to lock the door though and it took him a moment to find the right key. Once inside, he found the house lit only by the kitchen fixture, a wash of light that spilled weakly into the hallway ahead of him.

Harvey closed the front door and blocked out the sound of the rain. He dripped down the hallway to Nonna and Nonno's bedroom, didn't bother to turn on any lights as he went—he could've made his way to their bedroom even without the kitchen light.

Harvey switched on the stand lamp in the corner of their bedroom and went to the small closet. He dug out a brown leather overnight bag that must have been as old as he was, set it down on the bed, then walked to the large bureau that housed Nonna and Nonno's clothes. He went through the drawers and gathered enough for each of them for two days.

When he turned around, the kid was on the bed.

THE CLOTHES DROPPED from Harvey's limp hands and landed in a pile at his feet. The buzz filled his ears again.

The kid sat right in the middle of the bed, his legs crossed beneath him. He was dressed in full Pirate uniform, everything from the hat down to the socks and cleats, even the blue and red piping trim. Again there was something wrong about his appearance, but Harvey still couldn't put his finger on it.

When Harvey spoke his voice was rough. "What do you want?"

The kid's only answer was to take the ball out of his glove and begin to toss it in the air. It went just up to the ceiling, so close Harvey thought it would surely hit, but then fell right back into the glove again without the kid shifting an inch. He did it again. Then again. Up to just kiss the ceiling, then right back down to catch it in the glove.

It's as big as the moon, Harvey thought as he watched the ball go up and down, and finally he realized what was wrong about the kid's appearance. The house had been locked and the kid must've followed him inside, but from the blue brim of his hat, to the crisp white of his jersey and pants, the kid was dry from head to toe.

There's not a speck of water on him anywhere...

"You're really him," Harvey said, and the knot that'd been tied inside of him on the night of the accident finally

unraveled. "You're in my head. Have been ever since I realized you were in the car that night. That you got hurt."

The corner's of the kid's mouth turned up a hair. And
all the time the ball still went up to kiss the ceiling, then
down to catch, and Harvey couldn't take his eyes off of it.

As big as the moon...

"I tried to avoid your car," Harvey said as his eyes
followed the ball up and down, up and down, as the buzzing
in his ears increased. "But it was too late. Then I thought
everyone in the car was okay. Your dad. Your mom. I didn't
know about you until later."

It was the first time he'd spoken the words aloud and the
admission... eased him. There was no soothing away of the
guilt, no lessening, just a lightening of the burden of denial.

The ball, which had been rising and falling as regular as
a metronome, landed in the glove and was left there.

The buzzing in Harvey's ears ceased.

And the kid smiled.

HARVEY PICKED the clothes up off the floor and packed
them in the overnight bag. He grabbed the bag and went
across the hall to their bathroom, added everything he
thought his grandparents would need.

When Harvey came out of the bathroom the kid stood
in the hallway, the ball tucked away in his glove. They
stared at each other for a moment and then the kid used the
glove to gesture toward the kitchen. Harvey nodded and
walked past, glanced back once to see the kid watching him
but not following.

He didn't bother to sort through the meds on the corner
of the kitchen counter, just shoved them all into the bag,

maybe a dozen pill bottles. Some might be Nonna's, but she'd need her meds as well.

The kid was nowhere in sight when Harvey walked out of the kitchen. Harvey left the house, locked the door behind him, and wondered if that was that as he headed through the darkness and rain to his car.

It wasn't though, because the kid was in the back of the Cherokee when Harvey slid into the driver's seat and tossed the overnight bag onto the passenger seat. The kid sat in the middle of the rear bench, his face dimly lit by the street lights. To Harvey's surprise his presence was comforting. He pulled away from the curve, sliced through the rain as he drove back to Rainbow Pines.

THIRTY-SIX

JON

Jon's head throbbed from the hit he'd taken. Or perhaps from too much beer. Probably both. Didn't matter which because Lee had opened his eyes.

The news resurrected the hope he'd thought dead for good.

His eyes are open...

He cleaned up the vomit first, unfazed by the filth, his muddled thoughts all on Lee. When that was done he pawed through the medicine drawer until he found some ibuprofen, poured what looked like two or three or maybe four into his palm and choked them down dry. Once the pills were safely on the way to his stomach—which felt normal despite its recent purge—he slurped cold water from the tap until he couldn't hold anymore, hoped he wouldn't barf it up, hoped it would help sober him up.

He got in the shower next, and while the hot water did

nothing for the throbbing in his head, it did help steady his hands a bit.

His eyes are open...

The news couldn't make him forget the woman. If anything it made him feel more guilty. But he still wanted to see Lee right away, and Sarah was right that he needed to sober up first. So he stayed in the shower until the hot water was gone and when he got out his head throbbed a bit less. He dried off and went into the bedroom where he only fell down once trying to pull on his underwear and pants.

He sat on the bed to put on his socks.

SARAH LEANED against the kitchen counter next to the sink, a bag of frozen vegetables on her hand, and a blank, distant expression on her face. She didn't notice Jon and he stopped, examined her in a way he hadn't done since Lee was injured.

She looked tired. No, tired was inadequate. She looked exhausted. There were dark circles beneath her eyes, accentuated because she'd gotten thinner since the accident. Too thin, her cheekbones too prominent. Her color wasn't healthy, her skin as washed out as sun-bleached upholstery. She wasn't getting enough of anything. Enough sleep. Enough food. Enough love.

All my fault...

She noticed him and her lips thinned.

"Is your hand okay?" he asked before she could speak.

"It's fine."

"Good. Listen I'm sorry about—"

"It doesn't matter, Jon."

"I thought I could do it. Leave her in there for a day. I don't think I can though."

"I'll deal with her. A day and she'll tell us where to find the guy she was with and we'll let her go. I promise."

With her eyes on him all he could do was agree. "Where do we go from here?"

"We go to see Lee."

THEY SIGNED in at the front desk of Rainbow Pines and hurried to Lee's room, umbrellas dripping at their sides.

The closer they got to Lee's room the better Jon felt, the pain of Sarah's words replaced by the anticipation of seeing his son's eyes. Such a small thing, but enormous when stacked against the positive developments that had occurred since Lee entered the hospital.

They rounded the final corner, and as they neared the end of the long corridor Jon took a deep breath. He was excited but all too aware how easy it would be to let himself believe that more was to come, that soon Lee would be up and talking, smiling, tossing a ball again.

Stop worrying about the future and just enjoy this moment for what it is...

The door to Lee's room was open—the therapists believed it was good for him to hear noise from the hallway and often left it open after their visits—and Jon walked in first. He came to an abrupt halt, raised a hand to the doorframe to steady himself as he caught his breath. Lee's eyes were indeed open, and they stared straight at him.

He cleared his throat. "Lee?"

Lee didn't respond, and as Jon started moving again Lee's eyes didn't follow him, only continued to stare straight ahead to where Sarah stood in the doorway, an anguished expression on her face.

Jon sat on the bed and took Lee's hand in his, barely noticed as Sarah moved to her chair in the corner. "It's so good to see you awake, Lee." It was so easy to pretend that Lee could hear him, especially when Lee's left arm spasmed and jerked. Jon caught his breath, but of course Lee's eyes never moved, never reacted, and a moment later the spasm passed. "There are so many things I've got to tell you."

"CAN I HELP YOU?" Sarah asked a few minutes later as she stood from her chair.

Jon looked up from Lee and saw a man standing in the doorway. He wore a casual suit, the damp blazer unbuttoned. He was tall and thin, his dark hair cut short above a handsome, confused face.

"No. No, I'm sorry," he said, "I didn't mean to interrupt. The door was open, and I didn't really think... " He trailed off, avoided their eyes as his cheeks flushed. "My grandfather's a patient here and when I walked past the room I thought recognized your son. It was a mistake. I'm sorry. I hope he gets better soon."

"Thank you," Sarah said, and she did sound grateful. She walked to the door and put her uninjured hand on the man's back, gently turned him toward the the nurses station. "I hope your grandfather gets better soon as well."

The man looked as if he wanted to say more despite the obvious dismissal, but his eyes widened and he left without another word.

Sarah watched the man walk away and then turned to Jon and said, "I need to speak to the nurses. I'll be back in a few minutes and we'll go home so you can sleep. You've got work tomorrow."

Jon didn't acknowledge what she said and she left. No doubt what she said was true, but she probably wanted to check on the woman too. And he knew she wouldn't leave him home alone after what happened earlier.

Jon took Lee's hand once more, determined not to waste their time together. Lee still gazed at the doorway, his expression blank. Jon didn't think he'd blinked since they'd arrived. They would need to ask the nurses about that, if there was some kind of drops he should get to prevent his eyes from drying out.

"So let me tell you about the Nats game the other night..."

THIRTY-SEVEN

HARVEY

When Harvey left room 198 he thought the kid might stay behind, but as Harvey plodded down the corridor the kid followed along in his wake, there every time he looked back.

The boy's eyes are open, but the kid is still mine. Just mine...

He'd delivered the overnight bag to Nonno's new room —the kid behind him ever since he'd entered Rainbow Pines —and once things were settled, he told Nonna he was going to the cafeteria to get her some tea. But as soon as he'd stepped out of Nonno's room he'd been overwhelmed by a desire to see the boy again.

His eyes are open, but he's not quite awake. Does that mean he'll wake up soon? Does it change anything?

Harvey didn't know. The presence of Lee Young's parents had surprised him, but not as much as seeing the boy's eyes open.

A few minutes later he walked into the cafeteria in a daze. Only a few of the round tables were occupied and the room was quiet except for the sound of the rain falling on the skylights. Harvey stood just inside the entrance, his mind still outside of the boy's room. *The kid didn't even look at the boy. Why wouldn't he look at him?*

"Can I help you, sir?"

"What?" Harvey asked, startled back into the present.

"Can I help you find something, sir?" The young woman wrung her hands together as she spoke. "I'm afraid we don't have anything hot at this time of night, but I could make you a sandwich."

"No, I'm fine," Harvey said with a shake of his head. He glanced over his shoulder to make sure the kid was still there. "I just need tea. Do you have some?"

"Of course!" the woman said with a smile. "Let me show you what we have."

"YOU NEED TO GO HOME, Harvey. Don't you work tomorrow?"

Harvey looked away from the kid in the corner of the room, thought of the voicemail he'd finally checked. Dave had been right—Robertson wanted to see him first thing in the morning. "You shouldn't be here alone, Nonna."

"Nonsense. Nonno's here and I've got everything I need since you went to the house. There's no reason for you to stay here. Besides, I can tell how tired you are. You've had trouble having a conversation ever since you got here."

"Are you sure?"

"Of course I am. Give me a kiss and go home and get some sleep. We'll see you tomorrow."

HARVEY DROVE HOME, the wipers slapping in the dark, the kid's face a pale sliver in the rear view mirror, his eyes sometimes locked onto Harvey's but more often than not gazing out of the window into the night.

The kid was sitting in one corner of the living room when Harvey made it inside, throwing the ball into his glove over and over. Harvey froze when he saw him, so startled that he forgot to close the front door until the wind gusted and blew a sheet of rain inside.

The kid was wearing a different uniform. Gone was the Pirates outfit, replaced by Dodgers blue and white, the cap on the kid's head solid blue with a white B.

Harvey stared at the kid for a long time, thought about putting on dry clothes, then decided instead to get the bottle of whiskey off the top of the refrigerator. He poured himself three fingers, then took the drink and sat on the couch.

He watched the kid and drank. The ball—once as big as the moon—no longer held his attention.

Why did he change uniforms?

The question was passing and didn't draw him in the way it would have the day before. His natural curiosity had been dulled by the day's events, his mind gravitating toward the image of Nonno lying on the sidewalk, the rain running into his open mouth.

"Why me?" he asked the kid after he'd emptied the glass, and for the first time since arriving at Nonna's that afternoon, he thought of Elle. "I wasn't the only one in the car."

The kid ignored him.

Harvey wondered if Elle was back at the bar. He thought of getting up, of getting into the Cherokee and driving to the Hill. No doubt the kid would follow. Would she see him? Perhaps he could pass the kid along to her. But for some reason, he knew that wouldn't work, was certain of it. The kid was his, like it or not.

"If the boy wakes up will you leave me alone? Is that what you want?"

The kid stopped throwing the ball into the glove and looked at him, his head tilted slightly to side. The pose reminded Harvey of the way a raven eyed its prey before plunging its beak ahead. The kid looked away after a moment and the ball started moving again.

Harvey watched the kid for a few more minutes and then got up for a refill. The meeting with Robertson in the morning was the last thing on his mind.

THIRTY-EIGHT

ELLE

Elle felt betrayed by her tears. She'd thought she was hard, thought she was done with them, but after another failed attempt to free herself, sobs wracked her body again.

The tears were few and small though and she wondered if she was dehydrated. Her head ached, but that could just as easily be from the hit she'd taken as from dehydration.

She'd gone a long time without water. There was no clock in the still lit room, but the darkness outside the window told her enough.

I probably haven't been here twelve hours and it feels like forever already...

She fell into a daydream, imagined Harvey bursting through the door to rescue her. *Here comes the white knight, shrew won't put up a fight fight fight...*

Pain brought her back. Her jaws ached from the gag, her tongue coated with dried mucus. Her ankles burned.

Her wrists were raw and bloody but if anything the ropes around them had only grown tighter, made her fear that if she kept at it she might lose her hands.

Assuming you even get out of this room alive...

That possibility seemed smaller and smaller as time passed. If only the heel-licker had been a little quicker, or could grow a set of balls and deal with his wife. The first possibility was past, the second nothing but a hope.

I don't want to die. Not in this fucking bed. Not in this fucking house, with that goddamn shrew laughing over me...

She tried to embrace the anger, to let it fuel her and replace the fear, but it wouldn't take, not strong enough to overcome the thirst and the hunger, much less the deep, gnawing desire for alcohol.

At first she hadn't thought much of that feeling, figured it was just part of the fear and pain. But instead of stepping back as the fear had—no one could stay amped up that long, not left alone in a room—or staying constant as the pain had, the gnawing had grown, made the hollow feeling of hunger in her stomach seem like the bite of a no-see-um compared to the hornet's sting of her desire for booze.

Nothing more than a dime-a-dozen alcoholic...

Somehow she'd held it in check before the accident, but since then it'd been one more drink, and then one more, and then one more until she passed out. She'd tried to remember the last time she'd fallen asleep sober and couldn't.

Because you didn't want to think about what you'd done...

She hated her mother for abandoning her, and had tried so hard, for so many years, not to be like her, but the harder Elle tried, the more like her mother she'd become—just another deadbeat that ran from any obligation or responsibility. It had to be the biggest fucking joke in the world.

She hadn't known about the boy though. She hadn't. Not that it mattered. Even if the boy hadn't been there, they'd left the parents behind.

You deserve this bed. These ropes and chains. This gnawing in your belly and mind. The shrew was right...

THE SOUND of a slamming door roused her from a half-asleep stupor.

Please let it be the husband...

But when the door opened, the shrew came in. She stopped, her eyes roaming Elle's body, her face unreadable, her right hand cradled against her belly. After a moment she spoke. "You'll regret doing that to your wrists."

Elle only looked away, afraid the shrew would see her pain, her longing for booze.

The shrew left and returned soon with a glass of water that she set on the nightstand by Elle's left hand. The shrew lowered herself onto the bed next to Elle and said, "Same as before. I'll take your gag out so we can talk. If you start screaming it goes right back in. Understand?"

Elle wanted to refuse, to curse the bitch, but the glass of water was so close she could smell the slight tang of chlorine in the air. She wouldn't have thought that was possible, but the smell was unmistakable. She nodded, already imagining what the water would feel like as it flowed into her mouth and ran down her throat.

The shrew pulled the gag free and Elle's jaw muscles began to ache even harder after suddenly being released from the position they'd been locked in for hours. Still, she lifted her head and spoke, her voice thick and rough. "Can I have a drink? Please?"

The shrew used her left hand to pick up the glass and tilt the contents toward Elle's open mouth. Elle sucked greedily at the water that dribbled past her dry lips, but before she could get enough for a second swallow the shrew pulled the glass away. The cool water that flowed down her throat felt like it was gone before it even reached her belly.

"No. Please let me have more. *Please.*"

The shrew's expression didn't change. "I need you to think about everything this Harvey ever said to you. Everything you noticed about him. Anything he mentioned that might be a clue about where he lives or what he does. Anything."

Desperate for another drink, Elle tried. "He never said what he did. I... don't like to know, so I didn't ask. But he's always wearing a suit. I don't know what that means. Businessman or something I guess."

"What else?"

Elle closed her eyes as she tried to remember. "He didn't wear any jewelry. No wedding ring or anything."

"What about his car?"

"It was older, nothing fancy or anything."

"What kind was it? What color?"

Elle couldn't remember, those details lost in the haze of that night. She almost lied, but was worried the shrew would be able to tell. "Some kind of SUV. Dark colored."

The shrew pursed her lips. "What did he do with the car after the accident?"

"I don't know."

"Was he driving the same car when he came to the bar?"

"I... I don't know. He came in, we talked for a minute outside and then I went back in before he left. I never saw his car."

The shrew scrubbed at her face with her left hand, the other lying still in her lap, and Elle sensed her chance to get another drink slipping away.

"I'm sorry," Elle said, her voice cracking, her mouth already dry again. "I'm trying. I just... there isn't much. I barely know him."

"There's got to be something else," the shrew said without even raising her head.

She thought of Harvey's claim that he'd seen the boy twice, that he was trying to find him. But the shrew said her son was still in a coma and claiming otherwise would just piss her off. "I'm sorry. There's not..."

The shrew returned the glass to the nightstand and picked up the gag again, the rolled up fabric brushing against Elle's chin as she lifted it.

"*No*," Elle said, ashamed by the whimper that emerged from her mouth but unable to stop herself. "No. *Please.*"

The shrew paused with the gag held against Elle's chin. "When you remember something else, you can have another drink."

"Please," Elle said, shaking her head. "I can't. I can't. *Please.*"

The shrew said nothing as she advanced the gag.

"*Please*. One more drink of water. Just one. Or just a little vodka. Anything. *Please. Plea—* "

The shrew slid the gag into place and cut her off.

THIRTY-NINE

HARVEY

Harvey's alarm blared through the fitful, alcohol-laced sleep he'd suffered for a few short hours. He groped for the clock and found the button by instinct. For a moment he just lay there, one arm out of the sheets, nose congested, mouth dry, his head not pounding but swimming.

Maybe he'll be gone. Gone with the morning...

When Harvey went to sleep the kid had been sitting in the corner of the bedroom, his gloved hand cradled in his lap while his free hand balanced the ball on the backs of his fingers.

He fought the urge to close his eyes again. *Robertson is expecting you. You've got to visit Nonna. And there's still Elle, wherever she is...*

Harvey took a deep breath and sat up slowly in the bed, his eyes going immediately to the corner where the kid had been the night before.

He wasn't there.

Harvey looked with disbelief around the room, certain he would find the kid nearby. But the room was empty.

Harvey was getting out of bed when there was a whisper of noise outside his bedroom. He felt surprisingly calm as he walked to the open door.

A baseball sat in the hallway.

Harvey thought about picking it up, but what if it was really there and he could touch it? Perhaps worse, what if the ball wasn't really there and his hand caught nothing but air? What would that do to him?

He left the ball where it was.

HARVEY CHANGED INTO FRESH CLOTHES— THERE wasn't time for a shower—and walked into the living room.

The kid sat in the same corner as he had the night before, still in the Dodger's uniform. The glove was in his lap, and in the glove was a baseball, a sliver of white nestled in brown leather.

Harvey felt the pull of the ball in hallway. Was there more than one? Or was it the same? Much like trying to touch the ball outside of his bedroom, the thought of going back to the hallway terrified him. He didn't want to know if the ball was gone or still there. Either possibility was knowledge he didn't want—better to leave it an unknown, like Schrödinger's cat in a box.

He picked up his keys and wallet from the kitchen counter, avoided looking at the hallway, avoided looking at the kid, hoped but didn't expect the kid to remain behind when he left the apartment. He locked the door behind him, picked up the umbrella from where he'd left it on the porch, and then trudged out to the Cherokee in the downpour.

Inside, he leaned his forehead against the steering wheel, enjoyed the solid and reassuring feel of it against his skin. *Everything's come undone. Work. Money for Nonna. Nonno. Everything. All because of the kid...*

"It was wrong to leave you," he said as he raised his head. "But I can't change it now."

The kid looked back at him from the mirror, his eyes serene and unperturbed. *You're right,* those eyes said, *so what are you going to do about it?*

"THE GODS ABOVE HAVE SPOKEN, Harvey. You're on desk duty for the foreseeable future." Robertson loomed across from him, his meaty hands steepled before him. He watched Harvey, but his gaze wasn't searching. "Not my decision of course. But I gotta do what the assholes upstairs tell me to do. Sometimes I can convince them otherwise. Not this time."

"Why?" Harvey asked, because there was nothing else to say. Robertson knew what Dave had known—and more, no doubt—and was probably just fishing for a confession.

Robertson shrugged. "Hell if I know. Maybe you can tell me."

Harvey said nothing, only watched as the kid paced behind Robertson, tossing the ball close to his boss's head.

"Everything all right, Harvey?"

Harvey stared at the name on the back of the kid's jersey. Vaughan. Thinking back, he couldn't remember if he'd seen a name there before or not.

Robertson leaned forward. "Harvey?"

Harvey blinked, tore his eyes off the kid and focused on Robertson. "Yeah, boss. Desk duty."

Robertson's face tightened. "This is serious shit, Harvey. You realize that, right? When internal affairs comes knocking, somebody's head rolls. If you know why they're interested in you, then it'll be better for everyone if you tell me right now. We can clear the air, get it all out there, then we can move forward and see how much of your career can be salvaged. You understand?"

"I understand, boss."

When Harvey didn't say anything more Robertson leaned back once again. "They'll let you cool your heels for a day or two. That's what they always do. So finish any paperwork you've got, pass your outstanding cases to Dave, and then sit tight. Okay?"

"Do you need anything else?" Harvey asked.

Robertson arched an eyebrow. "I suppose I don't. Look, I know this is difficult, Harvey. But it'll pass. And hey, at least you don't have to run any ops in this god-forsaken weather. The way things are going, one of those Weather Channel bastards will be here any day now looking for a drowned neighborhood to wade through so they can get some footage and bump their ratings."

"Sure, boss," Harvey said as he stood. He closed Robertson's door on his way out—the kid didn't need it open to follow.

FORTY

ELLE

The nightmares came whether she was awake or asleep.

She would doze off, overwhelmed by exhaustion, and find herself in the utility closet cowering behind the pinging bulk of the water heater as her father stomped around the house searching for her, as he screamed that she had to come out and get what she deserved, only to jerk awake to the ropes and chains, to the thirst and hunger, to the pain, to the biting need for booze. She would lay in the dark shaking, too dehydrated to cry, until the adrenaline burned off and her heart slowed, remembering where she was and what had happened. The waking minutes passed in an agony of sensation, only dulled by the fear of what the morning would bring, until sleep took her again and sent her once more into the past.

THE RUMBLE of the garage door tugged her out of another nightmare. She lay still and listened, no longer confused to wake up and find herself bound to the bed.

The light coming around the edges of the blinds was dim but no longer dark, the long night over.

Let it be the shrew that's leaving... The heel-licking nutless wonder was probably the only chance she had left.

She was disappointed but not surprised when the door opened a few minutes later to reveal the shrew, who flicked on the overhead light and then stood at the end of the bed examining her. There were dark circles under her eyes and Elle hoped the shrew's sleep had been as shitty as her own.

"Did you remember anything else during the night?"

Elle, still gagged, didn't attempt to answer. She'd tried rabid defiance. She'd tried begging. Neither had gotten her anywhere.

"Time to pee then," the shrew said.

Elle's shoulder muscles cramped as the shrew shackled her wrists to her ankles again and she had to bite the gag to stop herself from moaning. She had trouble getting to her feet once she was free of the bed, but the shrew only watched, her face blank, until Elle was able to stumble down the hall to the bathroom.

The bit of pee she was able to produce was a disturbing dark yellow, almost brown. Elle said nothing though, only wiped and pulled her pants back up awkwardly. She hoped the shrew would see it and realize how dehydrated she was.

She looked for an opportunity to attack on both ends of the trip, but the shrew was wary and took no chances. Not that it mattered—she was already too weak to have much of a chance. A few minutes later she was back on the bed, spread eagle again.

The shrew sat down but Elle refused to look at her, stared at the ceiling instead.

After a few minutes the shrew spoke, her words slow and careful. "I want to be done with you. But it isn't my decision to make. It's yours. We can't move on from here until you tell me what I need to know."

Elle ignored her and after a moment, the shrew got up and left the room, leaving the door open on her way out. Unable to stop herself, Elle stared after her.

What in the hell is she doing?

She got her answer when the shrew returned a minute later with a paring knife.

ELLE JERKED INVOLUNTARILY when she saw the knife and the muscles of her left shoulder started to spasm. She bit down hard on the gag in her mouth as she waited for the spasm to pass, her eyes locked on the shrew.

The shrew held the knife in her left hand, her right no longer cradled against her belly but still held awkwardly. She stared at Elle, her face flitting between anger, fear, and disgust. Mostly anger. When she spoke her words were almost a whisper. "Do you think I'm capable of using this on you?"

Oh jesus... Elle's heart felt like it might explode out of her chest, her nostrils flaring as she tried to suck in enough air. She nodded, afraid to provoke the shrew by refusing to answer.

The shrew walked to the right side of the bed where she sat next to Elle, so close that her hip pressed against Elle's hip. Elle shied away but it got her nowhere, the ropes holding her tight. She couldn't take her eyes off the knife, its sharpened edge gleaming with reflected light.

The shrew moved the knife toward Elle's face, the blade trembling ever so slightly.

Oh jesus fucking christ...

Elle wanted to close her eyes but it was impossible.

The shrew and the knife both got closer and Elle shook her head, slowly at first, then with more speed. She garbled around the gag, her body tensed against the coming pain.

The knife paused an inch from Elle's cheek and the shrew's voice was a hiss. "I *need* you to tell me. Tell me his last name. You must've seen it. On a credit card. On a forgotten piece of mail in his car. If you just think, you'll remember and we won't have to do this." The shrew reached forward with her free hand and tugged the gag out of Elle's mouth, her face wincing in pain as she did it. "*Tell* me."

"I don't know," Elle croaked, her mouth and throat so dry they felt cracked.

"You do," the shrew said. "*You must!*"

Elle's lips trembled as she babbled, hating the weakness of it, unable to stop herself. "*Please.* Please, don't do this. We'll figure out something. Some way to find him. He'll come back to the bar. Just let me go and he'll come back and I'll tell you he's there."

"Not good enough," the shrew said, her words barely audible. She moved the knife closer and Elle turned her head away as far as she could, her left ear pressed against her outstretched arm as she closed her eyes. The tip of the knife pressed against her cheek and there was a flash of pain.

Elle cried out but stayed still, afraid to move and risk driving the knife into her flesh. Pain radiated across her face and she felt a warm trail of blood creep down her cheek toward her neck.

"*Tell me!*"

Elle couldn't speak. Eyes still closed, her cheek burned, throbbed, and all she could do was sob.

The shrew jerked the gag back into place.

Oh god thank you she's leaving...

Elle opened her eyes reflexively, expected to see the shrew stand up. Instead the shrew yanked up Elle's shirt, baring her stomach and breasts, and dragged the knife across the valley of skin between two ribs.

FORTY-ONE

SARAH

The woman's eyes went wide with pain but the gag muffled her screams.

Hard, Sissy. Be hard for Lee...

Sarah pulled the knife away where the woman's ribs ended by her stomach. She didn't think she'd pressed hard enough to slice into the muscle below, but a lot of blood still welled out of the cut, started oozing down the woman's side toward the sheets. Sarah pulled the woman's shirt back into place, pressed it against the wound to sop up the blood. The cotton would help stop the bleeding.

The woman stopped screaming, began to pant and whimper around the gag, her chest heaving.

"The longer you breathe like that, the longer it'll take for the bleeding to stop."

The woman's breathing slowed as her eyes darted

between her ribs and Sarah's face, her eyes wide with fear and pain.

She'd worried she wouldn't be able to go through with it. But she hated the woman so much, hated what she'd done to Lee, that she'd felt a thrill pulse through her body as the small rip appeared in the middle of the butterfly, bisecting what should have been a line of symmetry but was only a jagged smear of blue that separated one badly inked set of wings from another.

When the woman's breathing was almost back to normal, Sarah slipped the gag from her mouth yet again. She expected more pleading or perhaps curses again, but the woman wouldn't even look at her. Maybe she'd finally broken. "How do I find him?"

Nothing.

Again, Sissy. Cut her again...

Sarah clenched her jaw, contemplated the knife in her hand, then made her voice as cold as possible. "The next time I come in here, you'll tell me how to find him. It'll be your last chance."

YOU SHOULD'VE CUT her again, Sissy...

Sarah tossed the knife in the kitchen sink, then turned around and leaned against the counter, scrubbed her good hand across her face. *It wouldn't matter. She doesn't know anything. If I cut her again she'll just start making stuff up to stop the pain...*

She knows! You just have to be harder, Sissy. Think of my son. My Lee...

Sarah's fists tightened, the pain in her injured hand flaring. *He's mine! Not yours. He is not Adam! My Lee...*

She had to get away.

You can't leave her here alone again. That slant-eyed husband of yours—

It doesn't matter! She doesn't know anything. She's useless—

She isn't. You need to cut her again. She—

SHUT UP! Sarah beat her good fist against her head until her knuckles ached. *SHUT UP, SHUT UP, SHUT UP!*

Panting, Sarah cradled her throbbing hands against her chest and rocked back and forth. *I need to see Lee. I need to...*

Go on, Sissy. You killed my son so go ahead and fail your own...

Sarah fled the house, hoped seeing Lee's open eyes again might calm her, might drive the voice out of her head.

FORTY-TWO

JON

Jon spent the night on the couch.

He woke—only a little stiff, only a little hungover—and pretended Elle wasn't in the house. He passed Sarah in the bedroom, in the hall, in the kitchen. Never said a word. Left the house at the usual quarter past seven and drove through a deluge, passed more than a few flooded and barricaded streets on the way to Rainbow Pines. He talked to Lee, eyes still open, and then struggled through the rain to an office that was half-staffed at best. He worked on an overdue project for three hours and then asked his boss if he could take the rest of the day off because of some intestinal distress that was still left from calling out sick the afternoon before. His boss—a hypochondriac who was especially fearful of vomiting—told him not to come back until he was better and promptly brought out the bottle of hand sanitizer he always kept near at hand.

Driving through rain so heavy he couldn't see more than fifty feet, Jon went to the nearest hardware store and bought a pair of bolt cutters. They were bigger than he expected, perhaps more than he needed, but he didn't want to go after the chains around Elle's wrists and ankles with an inadequate tool.

The decision to free her was obvious after he'd seen Lee. His son's open, unseeing eyes had bored a hole straight through him, set free all of the unease and doubt and guilt he'd felt ever since finding Elle in the house. He'd left Rainbow Pines the night before filled with the clear understanding that what they'd done had to come to an end. It was what Lee would want.

An umbrella provided little protection as he left the hardware store, and he soaked his shoes and socks when he missed the jump over a particularly wide puddle. Dripping, he listened to the car radio as the weather woman said the rain would end soon, but god it was coming down hard right now and if you lived on low ground and weren't flooded already, then you'd best leave it right away because holy shit this was a thousand-year storm.

SARAH'S CAR wasn't in the driveway where it had been that morning.

She's taken Elle somewhere...

Calm...

Jon sent the garage door up from two houses down and pulled inside, rain streaming down the windows as the wipers flicked the last of the water off the windshield. He grabbed the bolt cutters and got out of the car, feet squelching as he hurried inside, one terrible possibility after another running through his head.

FORTY-THREE

HARVEY

Harvey sat in the Cherokee outside of the station, the rain pounding against the roof, Robertson forgotten. His phone sat on his lap, open to the Wikipedia entry about Vaughan. With all the rain falling, the page had taken a long time to load, the reception flitting between no service and a single bar, but once it was all there Harvey had learned that a guy named Arky Vaughan had indeed played for both the Pirates and the Dodgers before retiring. Those were the only two teams. Not long after he retired, Vaughan was fishing with a friend in a Northern California crater lake when their boat capsized and both of them drowned.

What's it all mean, Harvey? Does it even matter?

Harvey let it go, gave up the new information to his subconscious to figure out.

He glanced at the kid in the mirror—he was balancing the ball on the back of his glove—then scanned through the stations on the radio. Nearly all of them were talking about the rain, about cresting rivers and high ground, but eventually he found the local ESPN station, turned up the volume as the talking heads argued about the Nat's chances of a pennant. He figured the kid would like that.

THE RAINBOW PINES parking lot was a sea of puddles large and small. He parked in a big one near the front, unconcerned about the water that lapped over the tops of his shoes when he got out of the Cherokee.

The receptionist with the pretty eyes gave him a warm smile as he approached, his presence now familiar. "Still coming down out there, huh?" she asked as she handed him the visitation log.

"Cats and dogs," Harvey said, channeling Harv as he handed back the log. "But the weather geeks are saying it's almost over."

"Thank heavens," the receptionist said. "My husband was joking about needing to build an ark."

"Might want to tell him not to put the hammer and nails away yet. The flooding is only gonna get worse," Harvey said with a smile as he left, the kid trailing behind him.

THERE WERE two ways to Nonno's room—one that went past the cafeteria, one that went closer to room 198, the boy's room. Harvey took the former, his thoughts bouncing from Nonno lying on the sidewalk to what the kid might want to how he'd get Nonna the money she'd need.

When he made it to Nonno's room, he found the door

open and the bed empty. Nonna sat in a big chair in the corner, her hands folded in her lap.

"Hi, Nonna," Harvey said as he went to his grandmother and kissed her on the cheek. The kid went to an empty corner and began to toss the ball. "Is Nonno already in therapy?"

Nonna raised her eyes and for a second Harvey was sure she didn't recognize him. Then her face crumpled. "I tried to call you, Harvey. I tried. But it was already too late. He's gone."

"HOW?" Harvey asked, his voice a croak.

"A head bleed from the fall," Nonna said, her own voice hollow. "They checked him at the hospital, but it must have been too small to detect. One minute he was lying there just fine, and the next he was—."

She started to cry.

The fall, Harvey thought as he stared at the kid in the corner. He was no longer tossing the ball in the air, instead he stared at Harvey, his eyes calm. *Because I left him...*

Harvey fell to his knees, his voice breaking. "I'm so sorry, Nonna. It's all my fault. I—"

Nonna leaned forward and took his head in her hands, her flesh cold and dry. "Don't you dare say that, Harvey. Don't you dare..." Then she collapsed against him, sobs wracking her body as Harvey took her in his arms.

This isn't how it's supposed to be, Harvey thought as he held Nonna. *This wasn't supposed to happen...*

NONNO LAY on a gurney in a room a few halls down, a sheet tucked neatly across his chest and beneath his naked arms. There were no signs of any life-saving measures, no lines going into his body, no breathing tube in his mouth. But instead of looking lifeless, his face looked almost vibrant, more alive than he'd appeared before death, as if in dying some part of the disease that'd robbed him of the last two years had finally been cast out.

The kid entered behind Harvey as usual, but instead of planting himself in a corner, he walked around to the head of the gurney and looked down at Nonno.

Harvey stared at the kid in surprise. The uniform and the glove were gone, the kid dressed in jeans and a t-shirt.

Why did he change? Why, after wearing the uniforms for so long?

For a moment Harvey thought the kid would finally speak, but he said nothing as he gazed down at the body.

Nonna, her cheeks damp with tears, stepped forward and took Nonno's right hand in her own, caressed the wrinkled, spotted skin between his fingers and wrist, oblivious to the presence of the kid. "Not long after he found out he had lung cancer, he told me he had to go first because he knew that if I died before him, he wouldn't be able to bear the pain, that he was too weak live without me."

Harvey stepped up beside her and put his arm around her. It was hard to talk. "He was never weak. Do you remember that fishing trip he took me on when I was twelve?"

Nonna nodded but didn't look up.

"We were on the lake in that little green canoe he had and this crazy storm came out of nowhere. We started for the shore, but the canoe flipped. I could swim, but the waves and the clothes I had on made it hard. But it didn't

272 M. D. THOMAS

matter, because Nonno grabbed me and swam me all the way to shore. It must've been a quarter of a mile or more. And he pulled me all the way in."

Nonna finally looked up at him, her watery eyes wide.

"He never told me that," Nonna said, disbelief filling her voice. "He said he didn't bring the canoe home because it fell out of the truck crossing the mountains on the way back and broke in half."

Harvey surprised himself by laughing. "That was his idea. He made me promise never to tell you, because he was sure you'd never let me go fishing with him again."

Nonna laughed too, her tears falling harder at the same time. "That rascal. I should've known it would never fall out of the truck with as much rope as he used to tie it down."

At the head of the gurney, the kid's eyes finally left Nonno's body and met Harvey's. His eyes had always been calm before, deep and dark and placid, full of peace. But looking at Harvey they danced with excitement, as if there was a light inside of him that was shining out. And beneath that gaze, in that moment of reminiscence, all of the pieces —the kid's uniforms, Arky Vaughan, Harvey's own past— clicked together in Harvey's mind and he knew what the kid wanted.

Harvey watched as the kid left the head of the gurney and went to the hall door. The kid turned around and beckoned to Harvey. *Follow me*, the gesture said. And Harvey knew he didn't have a choice—he'd abandoned Lee Young once and now he'd lost his grandfather because of that decision. He wouldn't abandon the kid a second time and risk Nonna.

"I'll give you some time with him," Harvey said, patting Nonna gently on the shoulder. "I have to take care of something."

"I love you, Harvey," Nonna said as she reached out and squeezed his hand, then let go, her fingers drifting back to her husband.

"I love you too, Nonna."

When Harvey stopped at his side the kid looked up at him, his eyes deep and liquid, as if he were thinking, *"It's time..."*

I'm ready, thought Harvey.

FORTY-FOUR

ELLE

The pain reawakened her belly. She'd never been so hungry before, never realized that nausea and hunger pangs could leave her writhing, could be more painful than the fiery line of the cut across her ribs.

And on top of the screaming need for food was still the burning desire for booze.

How long before she comes back? Elle wondered as she stared at the ceiling, trying to gauge how long ago she'd heard the garage door. *How long before the cravings go away?*

She was stuck in a loop—the desire for food and booze the only thing that could overwhelm her fear, and the fear the only thing that could overwhelm her desire for booze and food.

Over over over.

Have to lie to her… have to keep her away from me for as

long as possible...

It was the only way.

Her last chance.

THE GARAGE DOOR RUMBLED AGAIN.

The noise sent a spike of fear through Elle, made her tense so hard she felt the wound on her ribs break open again, felt warm blood trickle down her side. And despite the fear and the pain, she fantasized the shrew would bring food, envisioned being spoon-fed like a baby.

Her entire body was quivering when the door opened. But instead of the shrew carrying a knife or a plate of food, the heel-licker came in. Elle was so startled that it took her a moment to notice he was carrying bolt cutters. When she did notice them, she howled around the gag and jerked at the ropes even though it burned her wounded wrists and ankles, made her side blaze with pain.

"Calm down," the heel-licker said as he closed the door. "You need to be calm."

Elle went limp even though she wanted to scream and thrash, certain it was a trick the shrew had planned. She couldn't stop herself from whimpering.

The heel-licker sat on the side of the bed, the bolt cutters resting casually between his legs. She wondered if he was about to start lopping off her fingers one joint at a time instead of the chains. *I should've been afraid of him the whole time... the two insane fuckers probably cooked it up from the beginning...* make her fear and hate the shrew, make her believe the nutless wonder was sympathetic, then switch roles on her in an effort to get her to talk.

He reached out and Elle flinched as he touched her

side. He pulled away, staring at the fresh blood on his fingertips. "She cut you... "

He stared at the blood a moment longer and then rubbed the fingertips clean on his pants. When he spoke his words were slow and quiet. "I'll let you go. But I need you to understand what you did to my son. I need you to see Lee with your own eyes."

Elle nodded because that was what he wanted.

FORTY-FIVE

SARAH

Sarah was rearranging Lee's blankets for the fifth time when she heard the door open behind her. She spoke without stopping—her movements more erratic than the injuries to her hand could account for—determined to finally get it right. "Time to roll him again?" There were so many things to worry about with her Lee

my Lee, not yours... mine...

and bedsores were always at the top of the list.

"We need to talk."

Sarah turned at the unfamiliar voice, expecting a new nurse or orderly, saw the man in the suit who'd stopped by the room the night before. The man whose grandfather was in the facility. The man's eyes had a wildness in them that instantly put Sarah on alert.

"Excuse me?"

The man didn't speak as he closed the door softly behind him, pausing oddly as he did so.

Sarah's nervousness notched up a level and she moved closer to Lee's bed. "I'm sorry, but you need to leave."

The man said nothing as his eyes darted back and forth between Sarah and Lee and the other side of the bed.

Sarah didn't like it. She reached for the buzzer on the side of Lee's bed.

"Don't," the man said as he drew a gun from beneath his coat.

Too slow, Sissy...

Sarah froze, unable to take her eyes off the gun, her thoughts racing but getting nowhere. "I'll scream. I'll scream and they'll come."

"Not before I kill him."

She withdrew her shaking hand. She wouldn't have if he'd pointed the gun at her. But he'd pointed it at Lee. She thought of charging him, screaming as she attacked to alert the staff, but she felt an awful certainty he would brush her aside like an annoying bug and then there would be no one to protect Lee. "Why are you doing this? What do you want?"

The man's eyes flicked across the bed again. "I've got to take your son."

The words hit her like a blow to the head. "Why? Why would you do that?"

Because you were too weak, Sissy...

"I'm sorry, but I have to. It's what he wants. Away from the bed."

Sarah's knees trembled. "No. Please. You can't. I won't let you take him," she said, moving toward the bed. The buzzer was forgotten. Screaming was forgotten. Her world had been reduced to the man and her son, and all she had left was to put herself between the two, to try and act as a barrier between them.

The man's face hardened. He started toward her side of the bed and Sarah huddled over Lee. She wanted to scream, no matter what he'd said, but her throat had locked up and all that emerged when she tried was a low keen.

"I'm sorry," he said as he approached, the gun still aimed at Lee. "But I don't have any choice."

She knew she should attack him but she couldn't risk Lee. What good would it do if he just shot Lee after he'd dealt with her?

He must have seen right through her because he used his free hand to brush her lightly away from the bed. The pain in her right hand flared as she bumped against the wall, tears streaming down her face.

"If you try to call security, I'll kill him. If you go to the police, I'll kill him. If you budge from this room, I'll kill him. Do you understand?"

Sarah nodded. Her head felt like it weighed a ton.

"Do you believe me?"

She nodded again.

"Good." He pulled a blanket from the bed, revealing Lee's wasted legs, and draped it over his shoulder before he took her by the arm and dragged her to the corner where he shoved her into the knitting chair. He stuffed a corner of the blanket in her mouth, filling it until her jaws were spread so far apart they ached, the rest of the blanket draped across her chest like a giant napkin. One hand locked on Sarah's shoulder, he set his gun down on a nearby table and reached into his coat, came back out with a piece of plastic that looked like two loops joined in the middle. He shoved her left hand through the arm of the chair and then slipped the loops over her wrists and pulled them tight, the injured hand throbbing in a steady rhythm.

Sarah gawked at the restraints, then up at the man, and it came to her.

The suit. The gun. The handcuffs.

It's him. She said he's always wearing a suit. But he's not a business man. He's a policeman...

Sarah thrashed in the chair, strained against the plastic restraints, but they only dug into the flesh of her wrists and made her hand throb even harder. She tried to yell around the blanket but hardly any noise emerged. The man ignored her as he retrieved his gun and replaced it in the holster hidden beneath his coat.

Sarah tried to push the blanket out of her mouth with her tongue, but the cloth was shoved in so far she gagged. Her body spasmed forward, her stomach heaving, and for an instant she was sure she'd vomit. When the feeling passed, she tried to get enough purchase on the bottom of the blanket to pull it out with her arms or legs but the angles were all wrong.

The man searched Lee's arms, perhaps for IV lines, but the port there was disconnected. He lifted Lee's gown and saw the feeding tube port in his belly, which was similarly disconnected. The catheter was still in however, and the man gazed at it for a moment before he reached down and slid it free. The man stared at the bedside monitor for a moment, then reached out and depressed the power button, shutting it down. Sarah didn't know if that would alert the nurses station down the hall or not.

The man ignored her pleading mumbles as he untucked the sheet from the base of the bed and wrapped it around Lee from the torso down, leaving only his neck and head exposed. He picked up the small bundle that was her son, carefully cradled his head as he did so, and even in the middle of the fear and panic she felt blooming inside, Sarah wondered why he would be so gentle if he just planned on killing Lee.

The man turned to Sarah once more, Lee tucked against his chest. Lee's eyes were still open and lifeless. "Remember what I said." The man's voice was quiet and clear. "I'm sorry, but I promise it's what he wants. He helped me figure it out."

What—

No. Lee couldn't have shown himself to that man. Not her Lee.

Why not, Sissy? You're the one that let him down...

Sarah jerked against the restraints as her heart galloped, pounded her feet ineffectually against the floor as the man opened the door. He paused for a moment to peer down the corridor toward the waiting area and nurses station, and then stepped out of the room, closing the door behind him.

You failed my Lee again, Sissy...

FORTY-SIX

ELLE

"Will you do it?" the heel-licker asked.

She'd have done a hell of a lot more, but no need to tell him that. "Yeah. But you've gotta get me out of this bed. Now."

He stared at her for a moment. "I need you to promise you won't run."

"Promise," Elle said without hesitation.

He propped the bolt cutters against the bed and stood, started to untie the knots around her wrists. Her hands tingled with pain as the ropes came free.

She lowered her arms slowly, scared her muscles would start to cramp, but they only ached. The cut on her ribs burned and a strong hunger pang passed through her belly as she sat up, but she ignored both as she fumbled at the rope around her left ankle.

Gotta get out these things before the shrew comes back...

before he changes his mind... She didn't trust him any more than the shrew. They were both fucked up to the nines, just in different ways.

He made it to the end of the bed and freed her right ankle before she'd even loosened the other knot.

"Let me," he said. "I can do it faster than you."

She moved her hands aside, tried to decide if she should wrap the chain at her wrists around his throat and choke him to death. His neck was only inches away from her as he focused on the knot.

What if I'm too weak to use the bolt cutters? Then I might be helpless if the shrew comes back before I can get outside...

The decision was made for her, because a moment later he loosened the knot and her ankle was free.

She started to swing her legs around to the side of the bed but was stopped by a cramp that spread though her left calf. She cried out in pain and tried to massage away the cramp.

The heel-licker dropped the bolt cutters and pushed against her toes to stretch out the cramping muscle. "Better?"

She only nodded as the muscle started to relax.

Fuck if I'm gonna thank him...

He let go of her foot and picked up the bolt cutters again. "Move your legs a little to stretch the chain."

Elle did and he placed the bolt cutter jaws carefully around a chain link by one ankle. He closed the handles and the link snapped easily. A second cut and her other ankle was free.

Elle swung her legs over the side of the bed and held her arms out for the heel-licker. Two more cuts and the chains clinked to the floor.

That might be the best fucking sound I've ever heard...

She stood, wobbling a bit on her feet, and checked her wrists. The flesh was red and raw, bloody in places, but was nothing compared to the right side of her shirt, which was a kaleidoscope mix of new and old blood.

The shrew's husband stared at her shirt. "We've got to get a bandage on that."

"No," she said as she limped past him toward the door. "Get me a coat. I just want out of here."

SHE WENT LEFT down the hallway, the heel-licker at her heels now and wasn't *that* goddamn hilarious.

"I'm sorry she did this to you," he said as they left the hall and entered into the living room and kitchen end of the house. "She's just desperate and having trouble accepting what's happened to Lee."

Elle spun on her heels—her knees nearly buckled—and poked the surprised heel-licker in the chest. "Bullshit. People feel *desperate* all the time when they lose someone. They don't all go out and get a fucking hostage to deal with it."

He dropped his eyes.

Jesus what a pansy...

She wanted to run—and fuck the promise—but she knew she wouldn't make it far. Pansy or not, she was pretty sure the shrew's husband wouldn't just let her go.

She shuffled over to the fridge and yanked it open, pain and the knife she'd seen in the sink almost forgotten at the prospect of food. Her stomach twisted when she saw that it was almost empty inside.

"There's some cheese in the drawer at the bottom," he said. "Sorry, we haven't been eating here much."

Elle stooped to pull open the drawer and grabbed a package of sliced cheddar. She tore it open and pulled a few slices out, nearly lost her shit trying to get the goddamn wax paper dividers out so she could stuff the cheese into her mouth. A moan escaped her mouth as she chewed just enough to swallow.

"Got that coat?" Elle asked as the heel-licker watched with fascination as she devoured another half a dozen slices of cheddar, more wax dividers falling to the floor. "The coat?"

He nodded and walked over to a closet near the front door. As soon as his back was turned, Elle went to the sink and grabbed the knife the shrew had used to cut her and palmed it in her left hand, concealed the blade along her forearm as she went back to the package of cheese.

The heel-licker came back a moment later, a lightweight blue raincoat in his hand. He walked over and held it out to her. "Can you get it on by yourself?"

Elle contemplated stabbing him. Even if she got picked up by the police later, she probably wouldn't get in trouble for that at least, not after what they'd done to her. But she could feel the hand holding the knife shaking—she was still too sore and weak. So she took the coat with her empty hand, wincing in pain as she held it by the collar and slipped the knife-hand into the sleeve. She tried to get her right hand in the other sleeve, but realized immediately that she wouldn't be able to do it unless she dropped the knife. "Can you hold it up? My side hurts too much."

He held the coat in place and Elle slid her right hand inside, winced at the very real pain in her side. She couldn't zip the coat, not while she held the knife, but it covered up the blood stain on her shirt well enough anyway. *I hope I don't need fucking stitches...*

The heel-licker looked at her for a second, then got a paper towel and wet it, wrung out the excess water. He held it out to her. "Your... cheek. You should probably clean it up before we go."

"I'll do it in the car," Elle said as she grabbed the damp paper towel. "Let's get the hell out here."

FORTY-SEVEN

HARVEY

The boy was shockingly light.

Harvey felt like he was carrying a doll as he followed the kid down the corridor and away from the room where he'd left the boy's mother bound and gagged. He felt bad about leaving her that way, about taking her son, but it was what the kid wanted.

They walked the opposite direction from the waiting area where he'd first seen Sarah Young, on past the storage room and a few unmarked doors, and a moment later reached the emergency exit at the end of the corridor. The kid paused next to the door, waited for Harvey to catch up. When Harvey reached the door he hesitated, eyeing the sign that warned of an alarm if the door were opened. The kid gestured at the door anyway, so Harvey turned and backed into the bar that opened it. He expected the alarm to go off, but nothing happened and he pushed all the way outside, careful not to hit the boy's head.

Harvey halted outside the door and stared dumbly up at the sky.

The rain had stopped.

THE KID WALKED down the short flight of metal stairs that descended to the asphalt below and Harvey followed. The kid had his glove again and he started tossing the ball in the air, Harvey watching as the ball arced gracefully up and down.

As big as the moon...

They walked past the corner of the building and then strode across the large expanse of grass that bordered the parking lot. They reached the Cherokee a moment later and Harvey awkwardly opened the rear door, slid the boy onto the back seat where his eyes stared vacantly at the ceiling, his chest rising and falling with regularity. He used a shoulder belt to hold the boy awkwardly in place, closed the door and hurried to the driver's side.

When Harvey got behind the wheel the kid was in the passenger seat. It was the first time he'd ever sat there. Harvey started the Cherokee, ran the wipers across the windshield once to clear the last of the rain, and turned to the kid as they started toward the street.

"It's not far to the creek. We'll be there in a few minutes."

FORTY-EIGHT

JON

The rain was little more than a drizzle but Jon still had to change routes twice on the way to Rainbow Pines. Flooded streets were everywhere. Some were minor, puddles no more than a few inches deep stretching across the road, some severe, the water more than halfway up the road signs, the houses inundated by a cosmic game of topographic fuck you. If he cared anymore, he'd be glad they lived on high ground.

They drove down mostly empty streets, the only noise in the car the sound of Elle eating, gorging her way through an entire sleeve of Saltines he'd grabbed from the pantry on their way out of the kitchen. Clasped between her thighs were two Miller High Life's they'd found in the garage—another was already empty on the floor, and a second close behind.

Jon had trouble keeping his eyes on the road.

BY THE TIME they reached Rainbow Pines, Elle had finished everything except the final beer, which she'd been nursing. "I never thought beer could taste so good."

Despite her injuries, Jon had expected her to run, surprised she hadn't fled the house as soon as he freed her. She didn't seem the type to wait around for trouble and he guessed by the next day, she'd be a state or two away, looking for some new place to hole up and make enough money to stay blissfully drunk.

He found a spot, and as the car came to a halt she finished the beer and tossed the can to the floorboard after the first three. He got out of the car and waited for her to bolt. Instead, she slammed the passenger door shut and stood next to the Volvo gazing at the sky, her curls halfway down her back, her left hand in the pocket of the coat, her right hand hanging limp at her side.

"The goddamn rain finally stopped." She lowered her gaze to Rainbow Pines, inspected the care facility for a moment. "Let's get this the hell over with."

She strode toward the entrance, left Jon behind.

BEFORE THE DOOR to Lee's room was all the way open, Jon saw the empty bed. His first thought was that he'd gone to the wrong room—but there was Lee's Pirates hat on the bedside table and there was the Nats flag hanging on the wall behind the bed where Sarah had hung it not long after Lee was moved to Rainbow Pines. His second thought was that Lee must be in therapy—but the therapists usually came to Lee and if they didn't, they moved him in his bed. Then the door opened the rest of the way and he saw Sarah in her chair, a blanket covering her torso, one corner of it stuffed in her mouth, her hands bound to the chair arm.

Before Jon could even react, Elle screeched and rushed past him holding a knife, ran straight toward the chunky chair.

"*Sarah!*"

Sarah—eyes wide—raised her right leg at the last moment and Elle crashed into it, went down, swung the knife wildly as she fell and sliced Sarah's thigh, the denim parting beneath the blade.

Jon jumped onto Elle and she collapsed under his weight, her mouth a snarl until they hit the floor, the air in her lungs escaping in one great whoosh. Jon grabbed the arm that held the knife and slammed it against the floor. The knife came free with a clatter and slid under Lee's bed as Elle gasped and wheezed beneath him.

Jon scrambled to his knees as Elle contorted on the floor, struggling for air, and Sarah started grunting and jerking her head repeatedly toward the open door, her eyes wide. Jon understood and grabbed the blanket from Sarah's lap and yanked on it, pulled it free of Sarah's mouth.

"Gag her," Sarah said, her voice harsh as her chest heaved. "Hurry! Before she can scream."

"Where's Lee?" Jon asked as he shoved some of the blanket into Elle's mouth and pulled the rest around her neck, twisted her arms behind her back. She tried to resist but was unable to put up much of a fight.

"*He* took him!"

"Who?"

Sarah thrashed in the chair, her voice a shriek, and Jon noticed that her leg was bloody where she'd been cut. "*He* fucking took him, Jon! Her scumbag friend. *He took our son!* Now get me out of this goddamn chair!"

Jon glanced down at Elle, who garbled against the gag, her eyes wild and rolling. He turned back to Sarah and said, "I'm getting security."

She shook her head. "He'll *kill* Lee."

"What?"

Sarah spoke quickly but her voice was surprisingly calm. "He said he'd do it and I believe him. He just left. He can't have made it far. Get that knife or the scissors out of my knitting bag, cut me loose, and we'll go after him and end this. *Now!*"

Jon couldn't see where the knife had gone, so he put a knee in the middle of Elle's back to hold her down and with one hand grabbed Sarah's knitting bag from next to the chair, the sack bulging with yarn and needles and pattern books. Rather than search through it, Jon dumped everything out. Balls of yarn rolled everywhere, half-finished scarves and socks littered the floor, and there in the middle of it all was a pair of orange-handled scissors. Jon picked them up and stretched to reach the chair. He slid one blade beneath the zip-tie that bound Sarah's right wrist, noticed how swollen her right hand was as he accidentally stabbed her with the tip of the scissors. Her skin dimpled around the metal but didn't give way and a moment later she was free, the restraints dangling around her left wrist.

Sarah ran past them without a glance and turned left outside of the room.

"You're coming with us," Jon said as he dropped the scissors and yanked Elle to her feet, the blanket like a giant scarf around her neck. She tried to run, but Jon squeezed her arms behind her back to control her and drove her into the hall in front of him.

There must be a mistake... why would he take Lee?

Sarah pushed through the emergency exit at the end of the corridor and Jon followed as fast as he could, driving Elle ahead of him.

Why?

"Mr. Young?" called a voice from the corridor behind him—he recognized it as one of the nurses. "Is something wrong? I just saw Mrs. Young run outside."

Jon resisted the urge to turn around, hoped the nurse couldn't see Elle well enough to realize what was going on.

"Mr. Young?"

"Keep moving or you'll regret it," Jon said in a low voice to Elle as he pushed the struggling, moaning woman faster. A moment later they made it to the emergency exit and Jon slammed open the door so hard with his foot that it rebounded off the wall, jarring his shoulder as they passed through. He ignored the pain, drove Elle down a short set of stairs to the asphalt below.

Sarah ran across the wet grass ahead of them, toward the parking lot, screaming and waving her hands at a man closing the rear door of a Jeep Cherokee. "Stop! *Stop!*"

Jon didn't stop moving and when he saw the Jeep leaving, he turned toward the Volvo. *If we'd come a couple of minutes sooner, we would've made it here before it happened. If she hadn't wanted food, I would've been in the room with Lee when the man came...* Elle cried out in pain and he realized he was squeezing her even harder. He eased up and pushed her even faster. She stumbled and he held her up, her knees never hitting the pavement, like she was a toddler who had tripped while holding his hand.

"Give me the keys," Sarah said, breathing hard as she caught up just as Jon reached the Volvo.

Elle picked that moment to try and break free, turned

and brought a knee up toward his crotch. He shifted and her kneecap slammed into his thigh with a burst of pain. Without thinking, he grabbed a fistful of curls and slammed her forehead into the Volvo's roof. Her knees buckled and she slumped to the ground.

Jon gave Sarah the keys and she sprinted around the car. Thigh muscle aching, he pulled Elle out of the way, a trickle of blood running down her face, opened the rear door, then picked her up and shoved her inside the Volvo's backseat. She tried to go straight through to the other door—the blanket working free in the process—but Jon grabbed the waist of her pants and held tight as she scrabbled at the door handle. He crawled inside, the car already moving, and her screams of protest meant nothing to him.

FORTY-NINE

SARAH

A Rainbow Pines security guard was running out of the main entrance waving his hands when Sarah drove past, and by the time she shot out of the parking lot she was doing thirty-five. The man who had Lee had gone right, so Sarah didn't have to cross traffic, but she still caused one car to swerve and another to slam on its brakes, their horns blaring. Somehow no one collided with her or each other. In the back seat, the woman cursed as she was slammed into the door.

"Do you see them?" Jon asked, his voice harsh.

At first she didn't, disoriented after the near accident she'd caused coming out of the Rainbow Pines parking lot. Then she spotted the Jeep a few hundred yards ahead, passing through an intersection, the light above turning yellow just as he passed beneath it.

Sarah—the cut on her thigh burning—stomped the

accelerator to the floor, something she'd never done before. The car hesitated for a moment as it processed what she'd done, then it dropped a couple of gears, the engine revving as it leaped ahead.

"Stop you crazy bitch," the woman shrieked as they hurtled toward the intersection. "You're gonna kill all of us!"

The light turned red and Sarah's knuckles went white on the wheel as she swerved past a slowing car. Her right hand felt like a ball of fire, but she gripped the wheel even harder.

"*Jesus Christ!*" the woman said, and Sarah felt the seat at her back bulge as the woman braced herself. Jon said nothing.

Sarah tensed, eyes on the cars in the cross-street. She peeled one hand off the steering wheel and laid into the horn, holding it down. The blare spread ahead of them as the Volvo continued to accelerate.

She took in the approaching traffic and came to the rapid conclusion that if anyone was going to hit them it would be the truck pulling out from the right, a behemoth Ford with dual tires in the rear, the exhaust pipes rising from behind the cab.

Sarah veered slightly left, hoping to give them a little more room. They rocketed into the intersection, going what felt like two-hundred miles an hour but might have been sixty. She kept her eyes ahead, locked on the Jeep that held Lee, and the woman in the back screamed.

Too slow, Sissy. Too late...

If they hit us, they hit us. I'll keep going as long as this piece of shit keeps moving...

But they didn't get hit, the big truck's horn going off as it slammed on its brakes. At the same time a car from the other direction swerved behind them, missing by what couldn't have been more than inches.

"It won't do Lee any good if we die trying to catch them, Sarah," Jon said as the woman laughed hysterically.

Sarah ignored them both. The Jeep was within reach and she was getting closer. She swerved into another lane, caused more horns to go off. She didn't care.

I'm coming, Lee. I'm coming...

FIFTY

HARVEY

Not a lake, but it'll have to do, Harvey thought as he stopped the Cherokee just up the hill from the end of the Franconia-Springfield bridge, the span blocked by Road Closed signs topped by blinking yellow lights. Sandbags thrown across the metal feet kept any wind gusts from blowing them over.

Harvey jumped out of the Cherokee, left it running. He'd seen the Volvo following him, had known who it must be. It didn't matter. He was a few seconds ahead of them and that was enough.

He opened the rear door and freed the boy from the seatbelt—he'd shifted around a bit on the ride over, but not much, his eyes still staring vacantly at the ceiling. Harvey pulled him out of the Cherokee, let the sheet fall from the boy's lower half onto the ground, and then cradled Lee Young against his chest.

Harvey turned to find the kid standing there, ball and

glove gone, his hands limp at his sides, his eyes shining with excitement.

The Volvo screeched around the final turn as Harvey followed the kid past the Road Closed signs. He clamored over the guardrail and walked toward the swollen Accotink, the creek less than a foot from the bottom of the bridge and at least three times wider than normal.

The kid stepped lightly across the grass and stopped in tall weeds inches from the roiling water. Harvey followed carefully so he wouldn't stumble—the ground felt soft and rotten and his heels sunk into the soil with every step.

He reached the edge of the creek and halted next to the kid, the two of them looking at the Accotink. The boy in Harvey's arms didn't stir, his eyes gazing upward. A light rain began to fall, and a moment later the sun broke through the clouds, turned the falling drops into a shower of diamonds.

"Are you sure?" Harvey asked the kid as the screams began behind them. "This is what you want?"

The kid looked at him, his eyes intense, and nodded.

Harvey stepped into the Accotink and the muddy, silt-laden water tugged at his calves.

Facing upstream to resist the force of the current, Harvey slid another foot sideways toward the middle of the creek. The kid wanted the boy drowned, but Harvey was certain he shouldn't rush, that the moment demanded a certain pace. He had no idea when the ground beneath him might drop off, plunging the two of them into the rapidly moving water.

"Just a little farther," Harvey said as he gazed at the boy's face. He slid sideways another step, and the water slipped toward his knees.

FIFTY-ONE

SARAH

"*Stop! Please stop!*" Sarah screamed as she clamored over the guardrail, her eyes never leaving the man who held Lee as he entered the water.

She tripped no more than two strides from the guardrail, her feet sinking in the soft dirt, and when she broke her fall, her injured hand felt like it would explode.

He'll finish what he started, drown him this time, and I won't be able to stop him...

The Accotink terrified her, reminded her of the pond, of the feel of smooth gray skin sliding across her thigh, of Adam's eyes as she'd pushed him under the final time, and she wanted to run screaming away from the flooded creek.

I can't go in there...

Half-submerged trees rose out of the water like the fingers of the drowning, and she could imagine how they would clutch at her as she was swept into them, dragging her down into the choking darkness. Down to where the fish lived and the bottom was covered in muck.

I can't...

But there was Lee, curled against the man's chest.

Her Lee.

The water was past the man's ankles and Sarah knew that at any moment he could lose his footing and slip into the water, that the current would take them and her Lee would be lost to her forever.

But she couldn't move.

I always knew we were the same, Sissy. Neither one of us could save our son from drowning...

Sarah yelled in fear and rage and ran into the water, didn't make it two steps toward Lee before she stumbled and went down, before the current swept her downstream. She opened her mouth to scream, felt it fill with the cool tang of filthy water. She expelled the mouthful in a great whoosh, most of the air in her lungs going with it.

Heart racing, logical thought gone in a film of terror, she flailed, unsure of what direction was up, her lungs already burning, and felt herself thump against the bottom, only to roll across it as the current tumbled her along. She kicked blindly, felt her feet connect with something solid, and a moment later her head popped above the surface, mouth sucking greedily at the air. She churned her arms and legs to try and keep her head up, tried to scream for help but got another mouthful of the Accotink that gagged her before she spit it out.

No not again no... Lee...

She tried to look for him, but her head kept bobbing above and below the surface and seeing anything other than brown, muddy water was impossible.

Gotta get out...

Sorry, Sissy. No one here to save you this time...

FIFTY-TWO

JON

When the car stopped and Sarah leaped out, Jon yanked Elle from the Volvo's backseat, pulled so hard she cried out in pain. Fighting her, he dragged her around the car, reached the driver's side in time to see Sarah hesitate and then plunge into the water after the man who held Lee cradled against his chest.

Sarah didn't make it far before she went down with a cry, her body disappearing beneath the surface of the water still feet from the man and Lee.

Jon screamed, not just at Sarah, but at the man, at Lee, a howl of terror and confusion as he dropped Elle to the pavement, forgotten.

He took two long strides, planted one hand on the metal guardrail and swung his legs over, cleared it easily, hit the ground running. He moved fast, leapt ahead in big bounds.

"*Sarah!*" he screamed as his right foot planted in the

soggy soil for the last time, sunk to his ankle. It wasn't enough to stop him, his forward momentum sucking him out of his shoe and the muck. His left foot—still clad in its shoe—entered the water and too late he realized his mistake. His foot failed to find the ground where he'd expected it and he pitched forward into the creek. The shallow water closed over his head, took hold of him with surprising ease, and swept him downstream.

There was no time to think about Lee or Sarah, no time to think about what he should do next, only the dirty water blinding his eyes, roaring in his ears, filling his mouth. He bounced across the bottom, just beneath the surface, was trying to get his mouth clear when his right leg got snagged in some kind of vegetation and the current flipped him over and dragged him farther down. Lungs burning, mind demanding that he breathe, Jon tried to reach his foot, but he couldn't even get his hands past his waist against the crush of water. He tried to push himself upward far enough to get his mouth above the surface, but couldn't, his body strung out in the water like a flag in the wind.

Jon knew he was about to drown in only a few of feet of water, couldn't accept it with Sarah and Lee still in danger. He was about to draw the Accotink into his lungs anyway, when his foot came free and he tumbled downstream once more. He stopped the breath and spots of light popped in his eyes as he clawed toward the surface and emerged facing downstream to suck in air so sweet it was painful.

The current pushed him toward the center of the creek as he fought to keep his head above water, carried him along so fast that before he could react he slammed into a tree trunk, the impact like a sledgehammer against his chest. Somehow he managed to wrap both arms around the tree and hold on. The water pulled at him, raked the flesh of his forearms down the bark as his feet were swept past him and he was tugged to the downstream side of the tree trunk. He lifted his chin, raised his mouth above the surface, and sucked in another breath.

He clung there for a moment, the rough bark of the tree pressed against his chest and throat, devoid of thought. Then he remembered Lee and Sarah and the man, looked back up the creek in time to see Lee and the man disappear beneath the water.

FIFTY-THREE

ELLE

Elle stood in time to see the shrew go under, the heel-licker not far behind.

I hope they both drown, she thought, her head throbbing where she'd been slammed against the car, the cut between her ribs still burning.

There was a car behind the barriers on the other end of the bridge, a man and woman standing behind the open doors yelling and pointing. No doubt they'd call the police if they hadn't already.

I need to get the hell out of here. Off this bridge, out of this city, out of this goddamn state...

But the sight of Harvey with the boy in his arms stopped her.

I can't just run and leave him there...

Her mother had run from her responsibilities over and over, and, in her own way, so had Elle.

Cursing her own stupidity, she ran farther onto the bridge.

"Get out of there you fucking idiot!" she screamed, her body pressed against the barrier rail.

Harvey looked up at her and his face was so much more open than she'd ever seen it before, almost innocent.

"It's okay," Harvey yelled. "He wants to drown just like Arky Vaughan!"

"What the fuck are you talking about? He's in a goddamn coma! He doesn't want anything!"

Harvey said nothing, only stood there facing Elle for a moment longer, somehow resisting the push and pull of the river, then he looked down at the boy in his arms and the two of them disappeared into the water.

"*Harvey!*" Elle screamed, but it was too late.

They were gone.

Got to do something... help somehow...

She spun around on the bridge, unsure what she was even looking for, and that was when she saw the kid standing in the grass beside the water, decked out in a baseball uniform from head to toe.

Watching her.

No. No it can't be him...

But it was.

The kid didn't notice or didn't care what was happening in the flooded creek, just stared at her for a moment that seemed to last an eternity. Then he started walking toward her, his eyes never leaving hers.

It's him. He's in the water with Harvey, but it's him...

Elle's mind resisted, but there was no denying the kid before her. Just as there was no denying that Harvey had held the shrew's son in his arms moments ago. She'd seen the picture of the kid in the hallway, and she'd seen the kid from Rainbow Pines in Harvey's arms. There was only one —the shrew didn't have twins.

It's the alcohol... straight to my head because I haven't drank since the other morning...

She'd almost convinced herself that was true when the kid... shifted. One moment he was in a Pirates uniform, the next he was in a Dodgers uniform.

No... it can't—

Shift. He was in jeans and a t-shirt.

No...

Elle couldn't move. Every ounce of her body screamed at her to run, but she couldn't.

Not with his eyes on her.

Shift.

No... please...

Elle felt locked in place, as if her feet had sunk into the concrete.

The kid—back in the baseball uniform—approached the guardrail, was on the grassy side one moment and on the road the next. He didn't step over it—he was simply in one place and then the other.

Please...

He walked toward her and the shifting accelerated, his clothes changing so fast they became a blur, the only constant his eyes on hers.

I'm sorry. Please. I'm so sorry...

The kid was five feet from her when he disappeared.

One second he was there—eyes on hers, the rest of him a blur—the next he was gone.

Elle gaped, blinked in horror and confusion as her heart felt like it would erupt from her chest, her mind reeling from the impossibility of what she'd just seen.

It wasn't real... wasn't—

Except that was bullshit.

She backed away from the guardrail, away from the Accotink and the boy drowning in its waters.

"You okay, Ma'am?" a voice behind her asked.

Elle's heart leapt in fear and she spun around, expecting to see the kid reaching out to touch her.

A girl stood a couple of feet away. She looked twelve or thirteen, her long blond hair framing a round face dominated by large, calm blue eyes.

"You know the guy that took the kid in the creek?" the girl asked, as if she saw such things all the time, her thumb hiked toward the water.

What if she's really him? What if it's just a trick?

Elle shook her head. Afraid to turn her back on the girl, she took a step away.

"Guy must be crazy or something," the girl said.

Is it him?

When Elle kept backing away the girl frowned. Elle didn't give her another chance to speak, only turned and ran as if death were on her heels.

FIFTY-FOUR

HARVEY

When the water enveloped his head, Harvey closed his mouth by instinct and left it that way, content to go slowly. He curled his arms around the boy, pressed the boy's face in close against his chest, as tight as he could hold him. He wondered if the boy held his breath as well, if there was enough primal instinct left in his empty mind to do at least that much.

I wonder if the kid is still watching...

His lungs began to ache.

Don't let go...

Harvey didn't know whether the thought was his or the boy's. It didn't matter. It was time to let the creek claim the boy the way it had his idol, time to let it claim Harvey as well for what he'd done, for leaving the boy and his parents behind, for causing Nonno's death.

Don't let go...

Harvey's legs caught against something, a submerged tree perhaps, but he remained limp, only the muscles holding the boy tense. They were held against the current, the force against their bodies increasing as they stopped moving, tugging at the boy. The brown of the water began to turn black before his eyes, his lungs burning, screaming at him to open his mouth.

It's time, Harvey thought and he loosened his grip, water filling the gap between their bodies as the current tried to pull the boy away.

Something thumped against Harvey's chest, hard points that jerked and beat against him, and even though he couldn't see a thing, he *knew* it was the boy's hands.

He's awake...

Adrenaline surged through him and Harvey crushed the boy back against his chest before the water could take him, pushed against whatever was holding them, disbelief rolling through his body like a shockwave. For a moment there was nothing—his shoe, or pants, or whatever, still caught—and then he hurtled upwards, broke the surface and inhaled a great slug of air with a harsh wheeze.

He came up facing downstream, altered his hold on the boy, flipped him over so that he faced the sky, his mouth free to breathe, assuming he hadn't already inhaled too much water. The muscles in Harvey's legs and free arm burned as he kept them from going back under. He wished he could see the boy's face better, could really look at his eyes, but keeping the boy afloat took too much effort.

He's awake. He—

The thought died as the boy's father hurtled into them from out of nowhere, plunging all three of them beneath the surface.

FIFTY-FIVE

SARAH

The water swept her downstream, and as Sarah struggled to stay at the surface she knew that after twenty-five years she was finally going to drown.

But her body had other things in mind, fought to stay at the surface. Her arms and legs churned, her mouth beneath the water one moment, above it the next, and then she saw the maple tree—it seemed to be rushing toward her, rather than her toward it. The maple's trunk was small, less than six inches in diameter, but past it there was nothing but water for another hundred feet. She would drown before she made it anywhere near another tree.

Sarah kicked and thrashed as hard as she could, was about to be swept beyond reach of the tree when she threw out her left arm and hooked her elbow around the narrow trunk. The creek swung her around and she grabbed hold with her other arm as well, the current streaming her body past the tree. It almost felt like she was flying, except that water poured over her chin and mouth, trying to force its way in as she held her head upright.

"*Hold on, Sarah!*"

Sarah heard the shout, saw Jon clinging to a tree upstream, his gaze already off her and searching the creek. But Lee and the man were nowhere in sight, and Jon's frantic search meant the worst had happened.

You caused this, Sissy. The moment you chose your own life over Adam's...

Oh Lee, she thought, and in that moment of unimaginable loss, she let go for the first time since the pond, let go of the anger and despair she'd felt since the hit-and-run, of the desperation she'd felt since she'd seen Lee by the loading dock behind Rainbow Pines, of the idea that a drowning little girl could be a cold-blooded killer instead of a frightened child. She let go of all of it, and with it went her mother's voice.

Fear of the water prevented her from letting go, from choosing to drown, but her muscles were wearing down and soon there would be no choices left to make. The better for it. There was no point in living with Lee gone. She found some small peace knowing that he'd drowned unaware of what was happening to him, the terror she'd lived with all her life averted. She'd die and maybe the two of them would be together again.

Sarah was starting to slip free when the man surfaced just upstream of Jon, still holding Lee as they hurtled downstream, and the absolute desolation she'd felt moments before disappeared, ceased the moment her eyes found her Lee.

She ignored the pain in her hand and pulled hard, raised one scraped arm and thrust it out of the water and around the maple, brought herself closer with a strength she didn't think she had.

Just as she got both arms firmly around the trunk again, Jon shoved away from his own tree and slammed into Lee and the man. Sarah gaped as the three of them went under, as they resurfaced and swung around wildly in the river, hurtling closer to her by the second.

She gripped the tree as hard as she could with her right arm, the wood pressing painfully into her forearm and bicep, and extended her left arm.

FIFTY-SIX

HARVEY

"Let him go!" The boy's father shouted when the three of them surfaced, clawing at Harvey's grip on the boy even as he fought to keep his mouth clear of the water.

As they struggled, Harvey saw the boy's mother stick out her hand but he knew they wouldn't make it, even if the boy's fool dad didn't drown all of them first. She wasn't directly in their path and they were moving too fast—if they kept on the way they were going they'd miss her.

He's not ready to die... he's not ready...

Harvey knew there was only one way.

"Here," Harvey grunted, and he took one last breath as the father—his eyes wide—grabbed hold of the boy.

Now...

Harvey grabbed the boy's torso and shoved him and the father toward Sarah Young with every ounce of strength he had, kicking his legs so hard his joints throbbed. He went under instantly, propelled downward by the force of his own push, but he didn't try to surface, just pushed and kicked and drove the father and son forward until a final shove propelled him in the opposite direction.

He struggled back to the surface and sucked in a lungful of air, spun himself in the water until he spotted the boy and his parents clinging to the tree at least twenty feet upstream already.

Still might all die, but at least they're together...

Harvey turned himself so that he could see where the water was carrying him. The muscles in his legs were fatigued and burning, but his arms still felt strong and he was able to stay upright. The creek turned ahead, the water shifting him toward the far bank where it moved faster around the outside of the curve, an area heavy with drowned vegetation.

Not far from the spot where I hit them, he thought as he stroked toward the bank, hoping he could use the force of the current to push him to the edge of the water before he got to the curve.

But the water carried him downstream faster than he expected, and within seconds he was swept into the trees that clogged the edge of the creek. He'd have to grab whatever he could and hold on.

Harvey was raising his hands from the water to wrap them around a promising tree when one of his feet snagged an unseen branch in the water below. Before he even had time to realize what was happening, the current swung him in a hard semicircle, headfirst into another tree.

Harvey cried out in pain as bursts of light appeared in his eyes. His right hand rose instinctively, pressed against his throbbing skull

oh god it hurts

even as his left arm flailed against the water. But his foot was still trapped and the water poured over his face, covered his eyes and filled his mouth before he could even suck in another gulp of air.

Vertigo washed through his head and the current pushed him under. Eyes rolling through the brown water, he fumbled at his pants with both hands, tried to pull his torso toward his stuck foot, but he could barely even bend at the waist.

Can't... god the pain...

Lungs burning, his head full of agony and confusion, Harvey rolled and twisted like a wild animal, but his trapped foot didn't budge.

The water darkened before his eyes, the throb in his lungs transforming into what felt like a bubble of heat in his chest that kept expanding until it took over his entire body.

Nonna...

Harvey tried again to reach his leg, couldn't even get his hands to his waist before the water streamed his limp arms past his head so that they flapped in the current, and the water grew darker still.

Can't...

Nonna...

The bubble of heat popped and a small orb of light appeared in the center of Harvey's eyes, growing, and growing, and growing, until it was as big as the moon. Harvey drew the Accotink into his mouth, filled his lungs, and the light faded.

FIFTY-SEVEN

SARAH

Just when she knew they wouldn't make it, the man disappeared under the water and somehow Jon and Lee not only came closer to the maple, but crossed to the other side of it. With no time to alter her hold, Sarah was forced to reach around the trunk toward them as they started to shoot past the right side of the tree.

An instant later, Jon grabbed hold of Sarah's wrist. He and Lee swung around the tree with so much force that they pulled her torso around the trunk, the bark grinding into her cheek and gums like sandpaper, two of her teeth digging into the wood before they snapped like glass rods. The maple bent under their combined weight as Jon's fingers dug painfully into her wrist, but that was nothing compared to the pain that bloomed in her shoulder, as if the muscles, tendons, and ligaments were being ripped apart.

Screaming with pain and effort, Sarah let go of the

trunk and grabbed Jon's forearm, the tree between her arms. She'd been pulled so far around the maple that she was able to force her left foot around the trunk, and the current locked her leg in place, Jon and Lee's weight pressing her chest into the tree so hard that her ribs creaked with bursts of pain—the thought flitted across her mind that her ribs were breaking. Struggling to breathe past the agony, she started to pull them toward her.

FIFTY-EIGHT

JON

He let go of her wrist, and somehow, Sarah—the part of her face that he could see around the maple a rictus of pain and blood—pulled him hand over hand until he was close enough to slip his free arm between her stomach and the trunk and to lock the crook of his elbow around it, Lee bobbing at his side as the tree swayed in the current. Sarah let go of him and sagged against the tree, panting, blood trailing out of her mouth and down her chin.

He spoke, barely able to get the words out around his own ragged breaths. "Help me get him closer."

Sarah only nodded and reached toward Lee with her left hand. She grabbed his armpit and the two of them tried to pull their son closer to the maple, but halfway there Sarah lost her hold and Jon nearly lost Lee altogether.

"I can't," Sarah said as she sagged against the tree.

Jon's arms felt like warm jelly despite the water that felt

colder by the second. He didn't know how long he could hold on to Lee or the maple. More spectators had gathered on the bridge upstream and a few people were running alongside the creek toward them, yelling at them to hold on. They were at least fifty feet from the edge of the water, the space between a thicket of tree trunks and branches, most of them too small to hold a person. He didn't know how rescuers would reach them.

Forget that... just hold on...

"Press on my arm, Sarah."

Sarah shifted without speaking, pinning his arm tighter against the trunk. It was just enough to ease the strain on his arm muscles.

Calm... just focus on holding him...

That's what he did until the tree trunk cracked, the pop of the splitting wood shooting through his arm like the lash of a whip.

FIFTY-NINE

SARAH

Sarah screamed, certain the maple trunk would give way and the current would sweep the three of them downstream to their deaths. But after one sickening lurch the popping stopped, leaving them a little deeper in the water, the tree bobbing farther than it had before.

Jon looked around, but a glance told Sarah there were no other trees close enough.

"You'd never make it," she said. "Not with Lee."

Jon's eyes were bleak despite his next words. "Help is coming. We don't have to hold on much longer."

Sarah looked over her shoulder, her face, her mouth, her entire body blazing with pain. Jon was right. A rescue vehicle was sliding to a stop on the wet pavement outside the bridge barriers, lights flashing. As she watched another vehicle pulled in behind it and men started pouring out of both, grabbing equipment and running toward them.

Sarah looked back at her husband and son. One of Jon's arms was close around Lee's neck, the other wrapped around his back. Lee's head was still, the water streaming across his bare shoulders where the gown had slipped, his face turned slightly toward hers, the flat part of his head pointing toward the sky where more blue was beginning to appear through cracks in the cloud cover.

Lee looked at her.

He wasn't just gazing blankly in her direction. She was certain Lee was *seeing* her.

"*Lee?*"

She let go of the tree trunk with one hand and extended it toward him, the pain forgotten. Lee didn't answer, but his eyes followed her hand when it passed in front of him.

"What?" Jon asked.

"He moved his eyes, Jon. I sa—"

There was a hollow pop dulled by the water and the maple lurched again.

No. No, not now...

"It'll hold," Jon said, but he didn't sound like he believed his own words. The rescue workers were almost there, sprinting across the soggy ground, carrying ropes and poles and floats. "It will."

"We're too heavy," Sarah said as she gazed at Lee.

"It'll hold," Jon repeated, but Sarah no longer listened.

Too heavy...

She stretched as far as she could and touched Lee's cheek. Beneath her, another pop vibrated through the tree. Not as big as the last one. But there. "I love you, Lee."

"Get back against my arm," Jon said, his eyes darting between Lee and the rescue workers.

"Tell him about me," she said as she ran her fingers

down Lee's cheek. Then she slipped around the trunk and let the current take hold of her.

"*Sarah!*" Jon screamed as the maple rebounded away, freed from her weight.

She hoped it would be enough to let it hold until they were rescued.

Jon stretched a hand toward her, unable to do more while he held onto the tree and Lee. "*Sarah!*"

The people on the bank shouted. One of them threw a flotation ring but it came up short and was quickly beyond reach as Sarah picked up speed. She tried to swim, but her arms and legs felt like lead weights hanging from her body, her chest a band of pain where she'd been crushed against the maple trunk.

Her Lee was the last thing she saw before she went under.

SIXTY

TWO YEARS LATER

JON

"Tell me again," Lee said.

The two of them sat on the leaf-littered ground beneath the budding maples that lined the western bank of the Accotink, the afternoon sunlight gold ribbons that slanted through the trees, the air cool but not cold as winter gave way to spring.

"We caught up right before he took you into the creek," Jon said. "Your mom went in after him... "

As he recounted the story yet again, Jon wondered if the fascination Lee had with the day Sarah died was healthy. Dr. Kamarti said Lee's desire to hear the story over and over had more to do with his reawakening than the loss of his mother, likened it to being born again, said the story helped Lee understand his past. Jon wasn't so sure.

They were about a mile south of where the car accident had happened, only feet from where rescue workers had found Sarah's battered body pinned in the crotch of a twisted beech tree the day after she died. Harvey Aiello's body had washed up miles downstream a week later, after the floodwaters had receded.

During the weeks and months after Sarah's death, Jon had wandered the banks of the Accotink whenever he could find the time, and more often than not, he ended up by that twisted beech. There was something about the way the creek looked through the maples, the way the light filtered down through the leaves above, that drew him time after time, to sit and attempt to understand. Perhaps it was the same search that led Lee to ask about that day again and again.

Jon glanced at Lee as he spoke. His Nats hat was perched on his head. He had on his favorite player's jersey. On his left hand was a glove, in his right hand a ball. He wasn't back to normal yet, but Dr. Kamarti and the staff at Rainbow Pines were astounded by how fast he was recovering.

The first year and a half had been slow and excruciating, months and months of painful work to find the words to express himself, to feed himself with a fork and spoon, to toss a ball in the air, to walk smoothly—he'd had to relearn all the skills he'd mastered years ago, but was forced to do it with a body that wasn't as strong and a mind that wasn't as agile. But in the last six months, everything had started to fall into line, gaining more and more speed, until a flabbergasted Dr. Kamarti had admitted that Lee probably wouldn't need therapy much longer. Lee had laughed at that and said he wouldn't stop working until he'd signed with the Nats.

And so Jon recounted the story. Not everything of course—Lee knew nothing of Elle. There'd been questions because she'd been seen with Jon at Rainbow Pines, but the police seemed to accept his story that she'd come to him when she'd realized what Harvey Aiello planned. When they couldn't find her the questions had stopped. Jon had gotten a short letter from her six months later, no return address but the envelope postmarked from Vegas, the brief note an incoherent scrawl of excuses and apologies. But Jon told Lee the rest. It was a story the media had lapped up for weeks, spinning Lee's awakening in the swollen waters of the Accotink as a sacrifice-induced miracle.

Lee said little, but Jon suspected the deaths of Harvey and Sarah was a burden. Perhaps that was part of the reason he asked about that day so often. Sarah's sacrifice was painful, but at least understandable. Aiello's death was another matter. The media had lambasted him as a crooked cop who'd had a mental breakdown, but a lone interview with his grandmother painted him as a well-intentioned man, and so understanding why he'd tried to kill Lee only to help rescue him was confusing. Jon had tried to speak with the grandmother, but she'd politely refused.

Of course Lee wasn't the only one with burdens. Every day Jon thought he should've passed Lee to Sarah somehow, that he should've been the one to let go. All three of them probably would've drowned if he'd attempted it, but still he thought it. He thought it, he heard her last words as she was pulled away, and it ate him up inside—because he'd loved her, and because no matter the terrible things she'd done, she was Lee's mother and she'd done the best she'd known how for her son. No one could ask more of any parent.

When Jon finished the story, Lee was quiet for a long time, his hand caressing the baseball. "Sometimes I think I remember his face. That guy... Harvey."

Jon glanced at Lee, who stared at the creek below. "You've seen pictures of him."

"Yeah. But that's not what I mean. I can remember him carrying me into the water and sometimes I think I can remember his face above me."

"Maybe it's just your brain trying to make sense of it all."

"Maybe." Lee took his eyes off the creek and looked at Jon. "Dad, do you think he did it to wake me up?"

Jon stared at him in surprise. "I don't know, Lee. I never thought about it like that before. Do you think he did?"

Lee's fingers grew still on the baseball. "No. No, I guess I don't." He was silent for a moment, perched the ball on the back of his fingers and left it there. "It's like it was all a weird dream. And sometimes in the dream I was Arky Vaughan and sometimes I was me. But that doesn't make any sense either."

They were silent for a few minutes before Jon could think of what to say, his own mind turning back to the night Lee had appeared in his car. "I wish we had answers Lee, but we don't. And unfortunately we probably never will. All I know is that it happened, that your mother loved you more than anything else in the world, and that you woke up."

Lee looked at him for a moment and then returned his gaze to the Accotink. Jon put his arm around Lee's shoulders and gazed ahead as well, wondered and marveled at the absurdity of existence that one little creek had played such a large role in his life.

"Dad?"

"Yeah?" Jon answered, thinking Lee wanted to hear the story again.

"Do you think the Nats have a chance at the pennant this season?"

THE END

ACKNOWLEDGMENTS

The Butterfly Tattoo wouldn't exist in its current form without the superb editing of Melissa K. Starr and Clarissa Goenawan, as well as the input of Michael W. Farmer, Brett Starr, and Brooke B. Thomas—emergency physician extraordinaire and, as always, my indefatigable source of medical knowledge, who also happens to be my wife.

BONUS MATERIAL

LAST WISH

ONE

I assumed my life had already hit bottom on the day that Elizabeth Bauer's car was T-boned by an early morning drunk. That's melodramatic, and I was very, very wrong, but I don't think it's reaching to say my life could've been better.

The call came in at nearly six in the morning, close to the end of my twelve-hour shift, but not close enough that I could duck and run. Not when Dicky Smith was the only attending. He was obnoxious—and certainly deserved the name—but you didn't get to choose who you worked under. You just had to shut up and deal.

Three weeks before I'm out of here and now this... Residency graduation was close and most of the time I loved my job, but I could almost see myself walking down the street without looking back, leaving the approaching ambulances behind and giving up on the whole damn thing. Forget the new job in rural New Mexico, forget emergency medicine, forget it all. If I had known what was about to happen I would have.

The department had been quiet and calm for the past couple of hours. Nurses, techs, janitors, volunteers, everyone moved at the lackadaisical pace that meant the night had been blessedly slow, their shoulders relaxed, their fatigue softened by smiles as they waited to punch out and meet at the nearest pancake house before they went home, drew their blackout curtains, and crashed, another night in one of the craziest job atmospheres in the world survived.

But that call was the kick that knocked the top off the anthill.

I walked through a swirling mass of people toward the ambulance bay, hitting the switch on my way by that would keep the doors open. There was no need to check on the preparations behind me. I would only get in the way, and everyone knew their job.

The street behind the emergency department was deserted, and although the hum of morning rush hour traffic filled the air there was no sound of sirens yet. The sky was cloudless, and despite the early hour it was going to be another hot July day in Washington, the air so humid it made my throat feel tight.

"You take the kid, Davies," a grating voice said, my surname only as usual—perhaps Linh was too Asian for him. "You could use the practice."

Richard Smith stepped up beside me, already lighting a cigarette. He was a pack-a-day guy, a habit not as unusual in the medical profession as you might think. Anytime somebody called him out on it he would just say that you had to die from something, so why not something you loved? I disliked him, but after witnessing so many deaths over the years I could see the logic in that.

He was a tall man, and—I hate to say it—striking. Dressed only in scrubs, his wavy brown hair just covered the tops of his ears and the nape of his neck, framing a face that made me think of a Roman emperor, all noble brow and hatchet nose. His blue eyes were intimidating, and he never seemed to blink. His shoulders were wide, his waist as trim as a man half his age. It was a shame he could be such an ass.

"There's two?" I asked. That I needed the practice was likely only a provocation, but while I wasn't adverse to picking a fight with Dicky there wasn't enough time.

"Three," Dicky said as he exhaled acrid blue smoke through his nostrils like a snorting bull. He gestured with the hand that held the cigarette. "Kid, her father, and the douche who hit them. Said douche is pretty much fine of course. He won't need much. The other two sound like roadkill. EMS had to open the car up like a can of tuna."

Anyone who hasn't worked around the dead and the dying might be offended by his tone, much less his words, but I had lost that luxury years before. People get used to anything if they're around it long enough, even horrible things, and human nature compels many of us to joke about the horrors we can't control. I can't give you any statistics, but I'm pretty sure the kind of people that crack jokes in the face of death are over-represented among emergency department workers—either it's the personality type drawn to the profession or the ones who can't joke tend to get weeded out of the job before they take root. Either way, we all have to watch our tongues when we're around normal people.

"You wanna paper, rock, scissors for the dad?" I asked, aware it was futile, but unable to stop myself. "I'm sure the trauma surgeon will be down here any minute now to take the kid off your hands."

Dicky snorted and took a long drag on his cigarette. The sound of the ambulance sirens had grown irritating. "Too late, Davies. I know you wouldn't want to leave here feeling like you hadn't learned everything you could." He flicked the half-burnt cigarette down the sidewalk that stretched toward the street. The first ambulance rounded the corner just as the butt rolled to a stop, a thin curl of smoke rising from its tip.

Two ambulances roared into the bay, one in front of the other, sirens off already but their emergency lights still dancing across the roof and the walls. Rear doors swung open before they had even come to a complete stop and the medics jumped out, pulling the gurneys after them.

I stood there long enough to see which ambulance carried the kid, then started moving as Dicky stepped toward the other gurney. I can remember what it felt like the first time I was the only doc to meet a trauma. Sheer terror doesn't adequately describe it. There was sweat on my palms and the tight, dizzying feeling of the blood draining too rapidly from my head as I tried to recall what I was supposed to do first, second, third, at all. But as I met the gurney bearing Elizabeth Bauer training took over and deliberate thought faded.

"What do we have, DeSean?" I asked as I fell in beside

the gurney which the medic had started toward the doors at a rapid walk. A second medic I didn't know was using a bag valve mask to keep her oxygenated.

"Not good, doc," DeSean said. He was a veteran, one of my favorites. The man should have been a doctor but said he could never stand the thought of being cooped up in a hospital. "Some old rich guy Mercedes, no airbags. Right lateral head contusions. Right chest trauma. Abdomen distended and rigid. Right femur is snapped and her arm is like a jigsaw puzzle. We had to sedate the father on scene because even he could tell it was bad."

Part of me listened to DeSean as he began to rattle through the list of meds they had pushed, but the greater part of me took in the patient. New residents tend to focus on the numbers—blood pressure, pulse, Oxygen saturation —but over the years I had learned to really look at the whole patient first, then move on to the numbers and the treatments. What I saw didn't look good. The girl was thin and petite and at first glance could have passed for twelve or thirteen. But a closer look at her face and chest suggested she was probably fourteen or even fifteen. The broken arm and leg made her look like a worn rag doll, but weren't too worrisome by themselves. They could wait. What mattered was her distended abdomen, suggesting an internal bleed, and the way her head looked slightly flat on the right side, the symmetry of her face gone awry. Not good was an understatement.

This is bad, I thought. *Real bad...*

The girl went into trauma bay one while Dicky and the father went straight through to A pod, one of the four pods that made up the emergency department. If there was any chance the father might come to again they wouldn't want him anywhere near his daughter. That kind of drama would be good for no one.

Before I even started giving orders the girl was swarmed, nurses and a couple of techs flanking the sides of the gurney, where they started new IV's and prepped for a central line. I took my place at the head of the gurney and got ready to intubate her. The airway was always first. Our job wasn't to fix the girl but to stabilize her so that the trauma surgeons could take over. But getting an operating room ready always took time, even if it wasn't a lot. Until then I had to keep the girl alive.

One of the nurses handed me the laryngoscope and tracheal tube and before I could even bend over my muscles locked up and I felt like I might vomit. I wanted to touch that girl about as much as I wanted to touch a viper. Normally I don't hesitate to do my job, but my head was already full of voices that weren't my own. Not metaphorical voices. Not tumor-induced hallucinations. Not some psychobabble problems from my past that expensive hours of therapy couldn't banish. Real voices, not mine, but those of former patients who'd died while I was touching them. All of them with a last wish they wanted to lay on me, a wish I couldn't refuse if I wanted to get them out of my head.

"Is something wrong, Dr. Davies?" asked the nurse who had handed me the laryngoscope.

Because of the frenzy that surrounded the girl the only other person that noticed my hesitation was the nurse who had taken over the bag valve mask. That level of activity made me want to run. The staff never put work like that into the average druggy, or geriatric on their way out—most of us didn't invest much emotion in those patients. But it was always different with kids. The staff cared. You could tell. There was atmosphere in the room. They didn't want her to die.

"Just taking a breath," I said to the nurse, swallowing hot bile as I forced myself to bend near the girl. The other nurse removed the bag from the girl's face and I took her chin in my right hand, opened her mouth, and inserted the laryngoscope.

I was just about to slide past the vocal cords when the Surgeon's voice erupted in my head. *Don't tube the 'goose!'*

The laryngoscope blade slipped in my hand and I just barely avoided banging into the girl's teeth as the Surgeon chuckled with delight.

Do you really think you can help this one? he asked. *She's a lost cause...*

I ignored him as I inserted the laryngoscope again, getting it in place straight away. The tracheal tube in, I backed away so she could be hooked up to oxygen. I replaced the laryngoscope on its tray and went to the side of the gurney where the nurses shifted smoothly out of my way.

It won't matter, you know, the Surgeon said. *This one's a goner.*

The Surgeon was the worst of the three voices in my head, with all his advice and all his know-how. Always telling me how to treat my patients. Residents are an insecure bunch, so the last thing I needed was the most arrogant of specialists telling me how to manage my cases. I had learned how to tune him and the others out, but it required a focus that was difficult to maintain at the best of times, much less when I was treating a patient. It was far easier - though no small feat - to just ignore them.

"Pressure's tanking," the tech called out. "Eighty-five over fifty, doc."

"Damn," I said, suddenly afraid the Surgeon was right. *No way are you going to die on me, girl...*

That's right, Linh! chimed in Amanda. *God helps those who help themselves! You can do it!*

I had no idea whether I believed in God or not, but I figured even if I was wrong he sure as hell didn't have any interest in helping me out. But Amanda was right to a degree. The girl's life was in my hands and I wasn't going to let it slip away.

But if there was a God he was laughing at me right then because the kid started to drop. I knew what we could do— we could give her air, give her fluids, fill her up with someone else's blood. And when that failed? What then? Shock her heart when it crashed. Maybe, if the case called for it, crack her chest and pump her heart by hand. But really, what good would that do? What would that result in other than bloody hands and a butchered body? And if I kept my hands on her and she died then I was going to get another voice in my head and then what would I do? I couldn't forget what had happened the last time - the Surgeon. He'd been nothing but a disaster.

No, I thought. *No, that won't happen. I won't let it happen. She may die, but she won't die here with me. I can do this...*

"Mannitol," I said. "And two units uncrossed blood up, now. All we have to do is stabilize her long enough for the trauma surgeon to put her back together. I'll get the central line in."

Mannitol? Really? said the Surgeon. *I think that ship has sailed, honey.*

I could see the fear and the hope in the staff's eyes as

they complied with my orders. I started on the central line and said, "We can do this people. We're okay."

But we weren't okay, because a second later her pulses disappeared and her heart rhythm changed and of course my hands were on her, *touching* her. The blare of the heart monitor cut through the air. It didn't matter if the cause was a massive intra-abdominal injury or a traumatic aneurysm, either way she was toast.

"Shit," I muttered, fighting the urge to cry or hit myself on the head, the fantasy of saving the girl slipping away.

There was more after that of course. More pumping, more drugs, more everything, because it was a kid and we wanted to bring her back. All of it useless. None of it mattered.

I told you! said the Surgeon as he cackled with glee.

If you enjoyed this excerpt of *Last Wish* and would like to read more, visit:

www.theMDThomas.com

ABOUT THE AUTHOR

M. D. Thomas grew up in the middle of nowhere Louisiana, a locale that let him spend most of his free time reading. When that got old he left, eventually earning a Ph.D. in Microbiology at the University of Virginia. He ditched a career in science a few years later, became a stay-at-home dad, and settled in Tidewater Virginia, where he's been writing ever since. His works have won writers conference awards and were selected for the Pitch Wars mentoring program in both 2017 and 2018.

To join the mailing list for updates and a free eBook, visit:

www.theMDThomas.com

Made in the USA
Las Vegas, NV
21 November 2020